A MAGE IN SHADOW

Tracey Lander-Garrett

Glass Carousel Press

ISBN 978-1-7334545-5-1 (print) | ISBN 978-1-7334545-4-4 (ebook)

First printing, 2020

Glass Carousel Press
Pflugerville, TX 78660

Cover Design: Steven Novak, Novak Illustration

For Marcel
because sometimes you meet someone
and you get a feeling

Prologue

I'M IN DARKNESS AGAIN. DRAGGING MY FINGERS across the wall, hesitant footsteps stopping short. *Quiet. Stay quiet. Don't let him find me.* I hear his feet, heavy on the ground. I want to run but I don't want him to hear me.

Keep moving. Find a way out.

But there's no way out and the ground disappears beneath me and I stumble. That's when he hears me.

I stumble up and fall again. I turn into another wall. A dead end. The footfalls coming closer.

I have to risk it.

Fire erupts from my hand and it becomes a torch.

"STOP, THIEF!" the voice bellows, echoing off the walls.

I'm blind from the searing red glare.

I'm gone, running.

Ow—right into a wall—shoulder and cheekbone stinging.

I push away, running again.

Running, running to the next opening, the next corner, tripping, scrambling.

"COME BACK HERE!" The voice is his voice but isn't. Another corner, another dead end, double back.

I see him, the back of his head, the wide horns.

He's more than fifty feet away but facing the wrong direction.

"THIEF!" comes from the distance.

The minotaur snorts, creating clouds of vapor. His head pivots toward me and I see the grayed-over eyes of his blindness.

It's not with eyes that he seeks me.

There's a cubbyhole, an opening low in the wall, where I hope he cannot fit and will not find me.

It's my fire he's after.

I extinguish the flame.

I pant as quietly as my pounding heart will allow, my lungs and blood desperate for oxygen. I press myself into the wall, compressing myself into the corner, but there is no corner: the space goes on, forward. A tunnel.

My fingers once again finding the way, I creep towards what I hope is freedom.

The tunnel ends and opens into a larger area. The walls have an odd texture now, irregular, then regular, then irregular again. Something jagged, something smooth, like a huge block of stone, then again the irregular bumpy, odd texture.

I listen for the heavy steps of the minotaur, for the sound of his snort.

Nothing.

My thumb traces the edge of what feels like a small niche, then another of similar size. A space, then another. Another. Small niches, closely packed together, my fingers fitting just into the openings. Are these statues I'm feeling? Have I been putting my fingers into the mouths of stone babes?

I chance the light of a single flame on one finger, a candle in the darkness.

Breath exits my lungs as if I've been punched in the solar plexus.

Skulls. Skulls upon skulls stacked to the ceiling, separated by stone sarcophagi and niches with full skeletons.

My hand trembles as I realize I have been putting my fingers in their eye sockets. My gorge rises.

And that's when the skulls begin to fall, to roll towards me, when the skeletons clamber up from their stone niches and stagger toward me, their bony hands reaching for me, the cold skulls laughing with their rictus grins as they bury me alive.

CHAPTER ONE

I WOKE WITH HALF A SCREAM IN MY THROAT.

Dream. Fading.

My eyes fluttered open.

Bright. Ow.

Bare bulb.

Bare brain?

Cold, clammy air. Small room.

Where . . .?

Door. No windows.

A cot?

Dressed. Boots on.

I sat up.

Lightheaded. Thoughts slogging.

Slogging? Is that a word? Mud. My name is Mudison.

I steadied myself with my hands on my thighs.

What I'd thought was a cot was a table. A plastic table with a split in the center.

I swung my legs over the side. Boots onto the concrete floor.

Tingling numbness.

I wiggled my toes in my boots to wake them. I looked around.

An inset drain beneath the table was speckled with brownish stains on the metal.

I hoped it was just rust.

Think, Maddy. Think.

Coat pockets. No smartphone.

New backpack nowhere in the room either.

I sat there, just blinking.

The corners of my eyes felt oily and itchy with sleep sand and I rubbed at them, trying to clear it.

Where the hell was I?

I lurched over to the door and tried the knob. It was locked.

I wrenched the knob. Nothing.

Thunk went my booted foot against the very solid door. *Ow.* If I could kick the knob off, would that help me get the door open? Maybe I could use the table. I went back to it, looking for ways to take it apart.

Then a noise at the door. The jingle of keys.

I whirled and watched the knob turn.

Then the door opened inward with a creak.

"I see you've awakened," the old man said, his voice familiar. "Well, girl? Speak up. Don't you have anything to say for yourself?"

I stared at him.

He had a receding hairline, but what hair was left was wispy and white. A smattering of liver spots framed his forehead. His rheumy eyes had two sets of deep bags beneath them, and the jowls of his cheeks created deep, slanted lines along the sides of his mouth.

There was nothing familiar about his face. But the voice. It reminded me of—

"Playing it cagey, are you?" he scoffed.

He wore a white collared shirt and a black ascot with a diamond stick pin beneath a burgundy jacket, just like—

"You pulled a pretty trick on me, Madison," he said, sneering at me. "That is what you're *called*, isn't it?"

—the memory vendor. The one from the Goblin Market.

I pressed my lips together in response.

"*Speak*," the old man commanded, and there was power in the word.

I tried to set my jaw closed but a feeling like an electric shock arced through it. Unable to keep my mouth from forming the words, I spat out "Who are you?"

"That's better," he said, and smiled a sinister smile. "You may call me Ammit."

Ammit? I didn't want to give him the satisfaction, but my aching jaw opened and more words spilled out.

"Like the Egyptian myth? The crocodile-monster?"

"Ooh, color me impressed," Ammit said. "Yes. Just like that. You seem much more knowledgeable . . . now."

Now?

"Do you know me?" came from my mouth though I tried to keep it shut. The pain in my jaw radiated through my gritted teeth, an unpleasant feeling like biting into tin foil.

"You know it's much more comfortable if you don't fight it," he said. "*Do* I know you. Do I *know* you? *How* do I know *you*?" His tone alternated from sarcastic to curious to simpering. Then, in a woman's voice with a British accent, he said, "Have we met? I beg your pardon, *sir*, but we haven't been properly introduced."

He batted his eyelashes at me.

"How did you do it?" he asked, returning to his regular voice.

"Do what?" I asked. He was right. It was more comfortable if I didn't try to fight it.

"It's been thirty years. One minute you were here, but when you were supposed to be, you weren't—you were supposed to go thirty *hours* forward, not thirty years—but here you are again. Is it a sign, do you think? Do you believe in signs, *Madison*?"

He began to pace, like a lawyer about to give his final summation.

"I'd gotten much closer than ever before—unfortunately, you *stole* the memories of that nice Jewish policeman. Such a *good* man, so hard to find these days. Like you, I took name and—with it—memory. But the heart was left behind . . . you see?"

"No. I don't see."

"Come now, my dear, don't be coy. *Tell me.* Where have you been for the past thirty years, hmm? How have you remained the same age? And where is my sundial?"

My mouth opened of its own accord and I said, "Nowhere. I don't know. I woke up a year ago and I have no idea about any sundial." I clamped my lips shut.

"Did you?" he asked, looking at me the way someone might look at a dog that could ride a tricycle. "Well, that *is* interesting. Let's see."

He moved toward me.

I recoiled, but he said, "*Stop. You can't move.*"

A headache like a spike of ice knifed through the crown of my head down my neck, torso, and out to my limbs. Frozen, from the inside. Paralyzed.

The old man caressed my cheek with tentative fingertips and looked into my eyes. I'd have shuddered in revulsion but I couldn't even change expression, much less shiver.

His fingers moved from my cheek and touched my forehead near the hairline as he stared into my eyes. I became overly aware of my eyelids, as they were the only part of me that could move, though they seemed to blink of their own accord, independent of me.

His fingers combed my hair back and then clamped onto the crown of my head. I felt a strange sensation, as if my memories were being shuffled like a stack of cards, back one year to my awakening on Madison Avenue, standing on the sidewalk without memory or any idea of who I was. The feeling stuck there and then, like a movie, fast-forwarded through the events of the past year, until I was there in the room with him again. I felt dizzy.

"*Sit,*" he said.

I sat.

"Very interesting. And you've tapped into your magical potential as well, *without* training? Very impressive! But it wasn't you, back then, was it? And you don't have my sundial, do you? Of course you don't. Well, that's a pity. It was quite useful.

"I must say, though. You seem quite different than you were. What a wonderful experiment you are!" He squinted, looking into my eyes again. "But you don't like this do you? Or me. Yes, I can see that. Now you may be wondering why you can't call power here and I can? Don't even bother. You'll just hurt yourself."

I hadn't been wondering about "calling power," whatever that meant, but now that he'd brought it up . . . yeah, nothing. The magical flames and other effects I'd been able to produce before seemed to be dormant.

"It would have been foolish indeed of me to allow you access. I had no idea when I took you all those years ago that you'd become so, so . . . fiery. *Death* I'd seen in you, but so much else was bound-up, closed, waiting to—you'll forgive me—blossom?" He lifted my chin and tilted his head, and his eyes roamed across my face as if he was trying to find one particular freckle that he'd somehow misplaced.

"Oh, fine, *speak*," he said at last.

"You took me?" I blurted. My voice came out as a croak and I swallowed painfully.

"Oh, yes. And I had to convince the police that they'd found your killer, without your body . . . very tricky stuff. But here you are again. I do think it's a sign."

"A sign of what?" I asked.

"What indeed? *Sleep*," he said, and everything went black again.

Chapter Two

When I woke again, he was gone.

I was still in the cell-like room and found that I was once again lying on the table. I blinked my eyes a few times and rolled onto my side, glad to find that I was able to move again. My hands and arms felt slow and heavy. My thoughts moved slowly, like my limbs. There were so many things to think I couldn't quite process it all. One thought was at the front of my mind.

I'm trapped. Trapped by a creepy old magic man. No way out.

I felt panicky.

Don't freak out. Don't freak out. Don't freak out!

A feeling of hysteria was building. My chest, my throat, tightening, making me hyperventilate. My eyes produced the beginning of tears.

No. No, you are not going to cry. Calm down. Breathe. Like smelling roses and blowing out candles.

The last time I felt helpless like this, my maybe-ex, maybe-boyfriend Kip had said that. Roses and candles. In. Out.

I breathed. Slowly. Deeply. In through the nose. Out through the mouth.

I wiped my eyes on my sleeve.

Perspective. Calm.

Right. So I was trapped in a little room by a magical psychopath who could paralyze me at will, make me go unconscious, and read my mind. Or if not read my mind, precisely, my memories.

But who is he? What does he want with me? How did he find me?

Breathe. Think.

I touched the spot on my forehead where he had before I'd felt my memories being shuffled through. It tingled and I closed my eyes. And then, like the spark of a match being lit in the dark, my own memories ignited. From his touch and backwards. Then forwards to my falling asleep at his command, then waking up.

The edges were dark, the center light. The colors weren't as vibrant. The voices echoed and went fast . . . I slowed them down.

Was I magically reading my own memories?

I was.

I went back through everything, from our meeting at the Market as well as our most recent encounter. All of the things he'd said. And one stood out.

Memories. Of course. *He* took my memories.

The doctors had thought I had what they referred to as a dissociative fugue: a psychological condition in which a person has an unconscious desire to erase her own past. Possibly to forget some trauma or situation. But no. It was magical. I had *magical* amnesia.

I hadn't *wanted* to forget my past, my identity. They had been *stolen* from me. Ammit was responsible for my amnesia.

What had he said about the nice Jewish policeman?

"Such a good *man, so hard to find these days. Like you, I took name and—with it—memory. But the heart was left behind . . . you see?"*

The nice Jewish policeman's name was Hank. Hank had been dead. But walking-around, filled-with-sawdust dead, not dead-dead.

It had been such a weird year.

But I had no idea what Ammit was talking about with hearts, though.

The old man had been disguised, vending memories in the form of feathers—including Hank's—at the Goblin Market I'd gone to with Kip. I'd been able to return those memories to Hank using that feather.

So if other memories were in feathers, maybe mine were too?

Or should I say Christina's memories? It was strange to try to think of myself as Christina. I thought of myself as Madison.

Frankly, I don't think I look like a Christina.

But am I a Madison? Madison is just an invention. A name suggested by an intern at Bellevue when I was diagnosed with amnesia.

There hadn't been a single clue to my existence. I had no ID and no one came forward to say they knew me. The first lead I'd found was a yellowed newspaper clipping with a photograph of a missing eighteen-year-old girl named Christina Marie Taylor. She looked exactly like me.

A flyer with additional details of what Christina had been wearing when she disappeared exactly matched the outfit I'd been found in.

There was only one problem. Both the article and flyer were dated October 1987.

And I'd been found in 2016.

The doctors estimated my age to be late teens or early twenties.

So if I *was* Christina . . . I'd been missing almost thirty years without a single sign of aging. That was just too crazy, I'd thought at the time.

Then again, most people thought the amnesia was the crazy part.

Having amnesia—magical or not—and no form of ID makes a lot of things very, very difficult. Talk about a search for identity. Until you don't have one, you have no idea what it's like to wake up and not know who you are, or where, or why.

You don't know what you like, where you're from, your favorite color, or food. Everything is new. Everything is strange and yet familiar too.

I'd spent the past year learning to be Madison.

Now it seemed I might learn more about who I used to be, and what happened to her.

"It's been thirty years. One minute you were here, but when you were supposed to be, you weren't—you were supposed to go thirty hours forward, not thirty years—but here you are again."

Why was I *supposed* to go forward in time? And why thirty *hours*? I'd briefly wondered if I'd been his apprentice or something, but apparently not.

"Death *I'd seen in you . . .*"

He'd "seen" death in me. Well, that would at least kind of explain why ghosts were more powerful around me. I had some kind of death power in addition to being able to magically produce fire and manipulate small objects with my mind.

Which should be impossible, my brain reminded me.

My thoughts began to spin out of control with fears that I'd gone insane or maybe I was dreaming or under the influence of drugs or . . .

Don't freak out.

My face hurt. Especially my jaw. I inhaled deeply through my nose and blew it out slowly from my lips. More roses and candles. It calmed me. I would have to thank Kip for that phrase and image. If I ever saw him again.

I realized I'd had my eyes closed for a while and opened them. The light seemed painfully bright and I blinked a few times, once again viewing the brown brick room with the bare bulb in the ceiling and a drain in the floor. Well, at least I had somewhere to pee if I needed to, as gross and humiliating as that would be.

I massaged my jaw and temples and cheeks and shaded my eyes from the bulb. The only exit from the room was the door.

I swung my legs off the table to the floor, putting my feet down as quietly as I could.

Creeping to the door, I put my ear against it, listening. Nothing.

I tried the knob again, but it didn't turn this time either.

Listening at the crack between the door and the door jamb, I could hear something, but I couldn't tell what. Noise, repetitive. High pitched.

There was a wider space beneath the door at the jamb, so I got down onto my hands and knees and put my head to the floor. It was classical music. "Night on Bald Mountain" by Mussorgsky, if I wasn't mistaken.

Seriously? This guy listens to evil soundtrack music in his spare time?

I stretched my body out and put my left ear on the floor and my eye level with the crack. The crack between the door and floor was wide enough that I could see concrete floor beyond it. A distant light source left most of the room beyond in shadow, but there seemed to be a utility shelf of some sort. I could just see the bottoms of two cardboard boxes on it. Nothing else.

I shifted and listened again. The music paused and a murmuring female voice mentioned something about Mussorgsky and "New York's classical station." Of course. He was listening to a radio. Or a radio was *on*, in any case. Maybe he was there listening to it. Maybe not.

I listened and the female voice introduced Bach's "Moonlight Sonata." It was one of the songs I was pretty sure I knew how to play on piano, though I hadn't tried. I could feel the notes at the end of my fingers and began silently tapping them out on my jeans, then stopped myself.

Don't get distracted, Maddy. How are you going to get yourself out of here?

I got to my knees and peered at the doorknob. There was no locking mechanism or keyhole from this side. There were two screws on either side of the knob on the baseplate, but I didn't have a screwdriver. The bolt was visible in the crack between the door and the doorframe, so it was obviously locked, but I couldn't manipulate the bolt with my fingers.

There was that folding table in the room though. Maybe it would have a part I could use as a screwdriver or a wedge? I looked, but none of the pieces seemed thin or small enough to get into the spaces I'd seen. I'd also make a hell of a racket trying to get them off, having no tools.

I could fold the table, but what use would that be? It would be a little too unwieldy to use as a weapon. Maybe I could trip him with it if the light was off. Where was the light switch?

There wasn't one, not in the room, anyway.

But the bulb *was* bare.

I pushed the folding table to get it into position beneath the bulb. The dragging of the legs on the concrete floor made a thumping, vibrating noise, and I stopped, wide-eyed, listening intently. When nothing happened, I went over to the door and listened at the crack again.

Still Bach on the radio. No other sounds.

This time, I picked the table up and moved it, setting it down beneath the light bulb as quietly as I could. As I set it down, a sticky residue clung to two fingers of my left hand. A partial sticker remained on the table, torn in half. It was a white sticker with a blue drawing. From what I could tell, it seemed to be a family having a picnic.

I was most certainly not having a picnic.

I climbed up onto the table and stood, then reached for the bulb.

Ow. Lit bulbs are hot.

I could just break it, but then I'd be in the dark.

I shrugged off my navy peacoat and spent a minute or so figuring out how to hold the coat on my shoulder while using the sleeve to protect my skin while I unscrewed the bulb. That worked. But then it was dark and I was standing in the middle of the dark room on a folding table with a hot lightbulb wrapped in a wool coat.

I felt a slight wave of vertigo and put my hand on the ceiling. It was no good standing there in the dark. A sliver of light shone beneath the door, allowing me to orient myself.

I carefully eased myself back to sitting on the table.

If I broke the bulb, I could use the jagged glass as a weapon.

I didn't think Ammit was much taller or heavier than me. And he was old, so he probably wouldn't be stronger. But if he had one second, just one second to say "Sleep," it would ruin everything.

Maybe I could pull my jacket over his head and stuff the sleeve in his mouth to shut him up. Or maybe I could figure out some way to whack him over the head with the table until he passed out.

The bulb had cooled off enough for me to handle with my fingers. I carefully stood on the table again and felt around the ceiling blindly until I found the socket and screwed it in. The white light seared my eyeballs that had grown accustomed to the dark. I squeezed them shut in response and sat down hard.

My stomach growled. I suddenly noticed I was both hungry and thirsty. How long had I been there? I didn't usually wear a watch, having begun to rely on cell phones to tell the time.

The time. *God.* I was supposed to meet Michael Adderly that evening!

The evening of the day I was captured. Whenever that was.

I thought that Michael Adderly was the person who had sent me the yellowed clipping about Christina Marie Taylor.

Michael Adderly, who was a vampire.

Like I said, it had been a weird year. A super-duper deluxe weird year with an extra dollop of weird on top.

But even in the middle of a very weird year, I was having a strange day, to say the least.

Was it even still the same day? Or had it been longer?

I put my face in my hands and rubbed my eyes.

I heard a distant metallic creak and then a thud, as of a distant door closing. Was it him? Someone else? Was he coming or going?

I got down on the floor in front of the door and listened. Footsteps. Coming closer.

I scrambled up and took two large, silent steps across the room to the table and sat down. Then I remembered that I'd moved it and was about to jump up again to put it back in its original place when the bolt clicked and the door opened.

Chapter Three

"Awake again, I see," Ammit said. "Here, I brought you food." He proffered a brown bag.

Inside was a deli sandwich, a bag of potato chips, and a bottle of water. I opened the water—it was sealed, so I was reasonably sure he didn't drug it—and took a drink. It rolled down my throat like a cool river. I took a second drink and recapped the bottle. My mouth watered as I reached for the sandwich. I was starving, but could the food be poisoned?

"Why are you feeding me?" I asked.

"I don't want you to die," he said.

"Do you need to fatten me up before you eat me?"

A partial smirk-grimace twitched at the corner of his mouth.

"Oh, I won't be eating you, my dear."

"But isn't that what you do? Eat souls?" His namesake, the crocodile-monster from Egyptian myth, consumed the souls of those judged unworthy to enter the afterworld.

Once again, he seemed amused. "Eat now," he said. "Questions later."

I tore into the white paper the sandwich was wrapped in. Tuna with lettuce and tomato on a deli roll, cut down the middle.

"Are you just going to stand there and watch me eat?"

He laughed. "Fine. I'll be back."

The door closed behind him.

I took an enormous bite of the sandwich. It was delicious. I took two more bites, then opened the chips and alternated the salty crisps with the savory squish of the sandwich, then washed it down with more water.

I finished the first half of the sandwich and was about to take a bite of the second when I wondered if I should ration it in case he didn't feed me again for a while. Then I thought of rancid mayo and food poisoning and finished the sandwich. I did leave myself about a third of the bottle of water, careful not to backwash into it. There were two napkins at the bottom of the paper sack and I used one to clean my mouth and fingers, then dampened the other and wiped the oily feeling of sleep from my eyes and the rest of my face.

Now what?

Take stock.

Of what?

Your assets.

Who's talking?

You are.

I am?

Yep. To yourself. Calm down. You'll find a way out of this.

I will?

Yes. You will. So what have you got going for you?

Well, Ammit wants to keep me alive for some reason. Which can't be good.

Don't worry about whether it's good or bad. Staying alive and keeping up your energy is your first priority. Concentrate on that. What else?

Um, a table? And a lightbulb?

The table's not bad. As you noted, though, unwieldy. The lightbulb, that's an interesting idea, making it a weapon. You'd have to hide against the wall in the dark and then stab him in the neck the second he opened the door.

I don't think I can do that.

What else do you have? What are you wearing?

Jeans, shirt, boots.

And under that?

Bra, socks, undies.

Underwire?

What, you think I can pick a lock with that? There's no lock on this side of the door.

Good to keep in mind though. You could use strips of your clothing or your bra to create a rope of sorts, maybe a loop you could throw around his neck and tighten. Or you could use your socks to cover your hands while handling the lightbulb so you don't have to use your coat.

True.

The door opened inward again. I'd been so busy talking to myself that I hadn't heard him coming.

"Finished? Good." Ammit plucked the paper bag from the table.

"How long do you plan on keeping me?"

"As long as I need to."

"Are you always going to talk to me in riddles?"

"I suppose that depends."

"On?"

"Whether you behave."

This guy.

I sighed. Maybe if I just asked him a bunch of questions, he'd answer one or two.

"How long have I been here? Are you going to kill me? Did you take my memories when I was Christina? Is there a way to get them back, like with a feather or something?"

"I am not going to kill you," he said. "And yes, I took Christina's memories. No, there isn't a way to get them back; I sold them long ago."

"You sold them? To who?"

"How should I know? It was so long ago."

"So how long are you going to keep me?"

"As long as needed. Why? Are you bored already?"

"Am I bored? I'm going out of my mind wondering why I'm being kept prisoner."

"All answers will come in time," he murmured. "Do you want the television?"

"No." More than an hour or so of TV gave me headaches.

He took on a look of interest. "Your former self was very glad to have a television to watch."

"You mean Christina?"

"Indeed."

"Well, I'm not her." I stared at the bulb on the ceiling until its afterimage was once again burned into my retina. When I looked at him again, half of his face was a dark, lightbulb-shaped shadow, blanked out by the reverse image. But he continued to stand there, watching me.

"What do you want?" I asked. "Did you think we were going to play Parcheesi?"

"You have the same spirit as your former self. I wondered about that. Perhaps it would be better to . . . hmm." He tapped his fingers against his chin. "No, it might be too risky. Damn."

"So you kidnapped Christina the same way you kidnapped me?"

"Of course," he said.

"Didn't anyone look for her?"

"Oh, I was worried for a time, but then the headlines and news reports gave way to a helpless babe trapped in a well, and the teenage runaway was forgotten." The babe in a well. Baby Jessica. He was talking about the little girl who'd been trapped in a well in Texas the day after Christina disappeared. I'd wondered how I'd known about it. Apparently, I'd watched it all on TV in Ammit's dungeon.

"How long did you keep her?"

"A few days."

"And then?"

His eyes locked with mine and he gave a small grunt. "Enough. I will return later."

As he turned on his heel and pulled the door closed after him, I yelled, "But what about a bathroom?"

"I suggest you wait until I come back," he said, his voice muffled by the door. Then the lock slid home.

I screamed inwardly. Then outwardly.

There was no response.

Time went by; I couldn't tell how long. At some point, I realized I should have asked for the TV so I could brain him with it. Or strangle him with the cord. Or electrocute him somehow.

Maybe I could still ask for it.

I thought and fretted for a while. Maybe an hour. Maybe more. My bladder felt like it was going to burst, and I was giving the drain in the center of the room serious consideration when he opened the door and stood outside it with one hand beckoning me to come forward.

I got up from the table and walk-waddled towards the doorway.

"It's the first door on the right," Ammit said, gesturing down the hallway.

The area opposite the door was packed with metal utility shelves, those stacked with glass jars, boxes, trays, and random sundries. A tall jar filled with clear, brownish liquid caught my eye—there seemed to be a white creature of some kind suspended in it. Was that an organ I saw in another jar? I wanted to take in every detail; this was my chance to look around and try to figure out an escape plan. But I *really*, really had to pee.

The first door on the right was a slapped-together bathroom if ever I'd seen one. There was a large utility sink with one faucet, a toilet, and a shower stall. No windows. The water in the sink was freezing cold. The high-end French hand soap and soft towel I used to wash and dry my hands seemed out of place. There was no mirror over the sink. I wondered what I looked like. Probably tired. My hands felt cold from the freezing water and I stuck them into my armpits to warm them.

I listened at the door. Classical music still threaded itself through the air, definitely coming from the right. There were more rooms further down the hallway but I'd only had eyes for the one that would give me relief. Now I'd get a better chance to look around. He wouldn't like that though. Maybe if I tripped and fell, I'd buy myself more time.

I cleared my throat. "Are you still there?"

"Waiting," said Ammit's voice.

I opened the door and emerged from the bathroom.

His white eyebrows were drawn together as he surveyed me with . . . was it suspicion? Dismay? Some negative emotion.

We seemed to be in a basement. The floors were unfinished concrete, the ceilings low, with beams exposed, and from where I stood, there were no windows. A hall went on to my right. The door of the room I'd been in was diagonal to the bathroom. Across from that were the shelves of weird stuff. I could see a stuffed and mounted skunk posed next to a large jar filled with shriveled human ears.

Total creeptown.

Ammit grunted and raised his eyebrows, looking at me expectantly as I crossed the hall to my "cell." I wracked my brain for any excuse not to go back in there. What if I pleaded for tampons? I mean, luckily, I didn't need tampons right then, but would he know that?

Instead, I walked right in. The door closed behind me and I turned in time to hear the lock click loudly again.

God, why hadn't I run when I had the chance? But run where? I didn't even know where I was, much less how to escape.

I growled and whirled angrily. I wanted to kick something. I wanted to break something. I wanted fire to come out of my hands and blow the hinges off the door . . .

Wait . . .

The hinges.

The hinges were on the *inside* of the room. On the side with me. And if there was anything I had learned about locked doors from my favorite hardware store worker's daughter, Zoe, it was that screwdriver + hinges = open sesame.

Too bad I didn't have a screwdriver. Maybe I could get Ammit to give me a pen? But a pen would be too flimsy, and probably too thick. A pencil? Even worse.

Goosepimples broke out along my arms and I realized I was cold. I pulled on my navy peacoat and sat down on the plastic table. I scanned the ceiling and the corners to make sure there weren't cameras. If there were, they were miniscule and well hidden.

My hands were still cold from the freezing water in the bathroom. I rubbed them together and blew on them for warmth. *Ugh. Tuna breath.* I wondered if he'd give me a toothbrush and toothpaste.

What the hell did Ammit use this place for? Why was I here? Why did he have jars and jars of weird stuff? A stuffed skunk? Ears? I hated to think what might be in the boxes. More weird dead stuff.

Dead stuff.

A stuffed skunk.

Ears!

I needed to get the hell out and fast.

But how?

How?

I put my cold hands in my coat pockets and rubbed the fabric against my jeans. And that was when I realized I had one small secret weapon.

CHAPTER FOUR

TIME PASSED. I PLOTTED.

I discovered that while Ammit wouldn't check on me if I called to him or yelled or even screamed, I could get him to come running after a few minutes of singing "*It's a small world after all, it's a small world after all . . .*" at the top of my lungs. My former roommate Kara had once described it as the most annoying song in the world.

She wasn't wrong.

"Stop that this instant!" Ammit screeched, slamming the door open.

Startled, I stopped abruptly.

"Uh, sorry?"

Ammit glowered at me. "It's no matter to me to put you back to sleep. Shall I?" He took a menacing step forward and I hopped backward.

"Nope, no. I'm good. I'll stop singing."

He turned to go and paused in the doorway. "Are you hungry again?"

"I'm kind of always hungry."

"Any requests?"

"Um, would you please let me go?"

He turned fully to face me with a look of amusement on his face. "Food requests."

"Oh, um, not that I can think of. Thank you for the sandwich earlier, though. It was good."

He gave me a glance, seemed about to say something, then frowned and went out the door, locking it behind him.

More time passed.

The next time he came into the room with another bottle of water, I was sitting under the table with my coat beneath me. This seemed to confuse him.

"Why are you . . . what are you doing down there?"

"The light was bothering my eyes."

"Shall I turn it off?"

"Oh, no, thank you. Then it would be weird dark."

"Weird dark. I see."

"Well, that's why it would be weird. Not being able to see, that is."

He shook his head. I couldn't tell if he was annoyed or amused. He had a hell of a poker face. "You have realized by now that no one can hear you where we are, yes?"

"Uh, yes?"

"Good."

"Why?"

"You'll wear yourself out, screaming. Possibly damage your vocal cords. I don't recommend it."

"So what are you going to do with me, Ammit? Put me on stage? Take me to karaoke?"

"Pardon me?"

"Why do you care what I do to my voice?"

"All answers—"

"*—will come in time.* Yeah, you said that. When?"

"Are you in such a hurry to meet your fate?"

"It's better than all this waiting around."

He shook his head again. He seemed reluctantly amused. "You will know more tomorrow. For now, I must depart."

"Depart?" He was leaving? He was leaving! I knew shouldn't let my excitement show and kept my face carefully neutral. In fact, I'd probably better seem worried. "For how long?"

"Not long, so don't get any ideas." He took a step toward me and I shuffled back several inches. "Come now, no more foolishness."

"Are you going to put me to sleep again?"

"You would prefer otherwise?"

"Well, yeah, obviously. Are you not used to kidnapping young girls? I kind of thought that was your thing."

"I am not accustomed to it, no. Fine. If you wish to stay conscious, I will allow it. Enjoy it, if you can." He set the bottle of water on the floor by the door and went out, locking the door behind him. His footsteps receded down the hallway. Then, minutes later, the distant sound of hinges and a heavy slam.

I was alone.

I *hoped* I was alone, anyway.

I listened. Maybe he was trying to trick me.

Or maybe he would only be gone a few minutes.

I reached into my coat pockets and removed my secret weapon. A nail. An antique iron nail, about four inches long and skinny and sturdy as a screwdriver.

Kip, my ex or whatever he was, had told me that carrying an iron nail in my clothing could help me spot faery glamours. I'd sewn one into the lining of my peacoat a few days later. I never dreamed that I might use it for some other purpose.

I knelt in front of the door and tried to wedge the pointy end of the nail beneath the pin of the middle hinge. Then I tried the flat edge of the nail. Nothing.

The hole at the bottom of the hinge wasn't capped—I could see the outline of the pin inside it from beneath. I tried pushing with the sharp end of the nail, but it didn't budge.

How to get the nail inside there with any sort of force?

It took trial and error, a bruised palm, scraped knuckles, a pinched bit of skin on one finger, and several frustrating minutes until I got the bright idea to use my boot heel to drive the nail into the hinge to pop the pin out of the top.

I'd given it a couple of good whacks and hit the door a few times, but the next one dislodged the pin with a pop and a high-pitched tinkle-tumble to the floor. "Yes!" I stage-whispered happily. *One down, two to go.*

And then in the distance, I heard that familiar shriek and slam of the outer door once more. All the blood drained from my face.

The footsteps were coming.

I scooped up the pin, grabbed my boot and scooted back beneath the table. The footsteps stopped and I could hear rummaging of some sort going on—a kind of plastic sound.

I finished zipping up my boot just as the door opened.

It was Ammit, carrying a plastic shopping bag in one hand and a paper sack in the other. "Another sandwich. And not a word," he said with a warning glance.

I had been about to thank him but instead pressed my lips together and smiled cheerfully.

He grunted at me and left, leaving the bags on the floor. The footsteps receded once more and the familiar screech and slam sounded again.

I let out the biggest sigh of relief that has ever been uttered and collapsed on the floor on top of my coat.

The third hinge was the most difficult, being so close to the floor. It was hard to get the right angle and momentum going, but now the door was on the floor of the room and I was in the hallway with the skunk and the ears. The white thing in the jar appeared to be a fetal sheep or calf. It had tiny hooves.

I walked past the bathroom in the direction I'd heard the classical music coming from. I passed doors on either side, and the hall turned to the right up ahead. I ignored the doors and continued. As I came around the corner, I almost screamed but managed to swallow it. I came face to face with a huge owl, only to realize it was a stuffed bird in a room full of them—a peacock, a duck, a swan, a rooster . . . was that a pheasant? And a hawk of some sort, posed as if swooping down on prey. What. The. Fuck.

The birds were arranged somewhat artfully on the walls and shelves in what appeared to be a storage room. A doorway with the door ajar stood to my right, and the hall continued straight ahead.

Bare light bulbs were interspersed throughout the hallway, distant enough to leave deep shadows between them, but light enough to see my way.

My need to escape had been vying with the hope that I might find my phone and backpack. I peeked into the room with the door.

The room was enormous. Much larger than I was expecting, anyway. An antiseptic smell hung over the place, sort of a hospital scent that reminded me of my stay in Bellevue. Two metal tables on wheels took center stage, while strange machines with various tubes and hoses stood sentinel nearby, flanked by two large square pillars. A large steel sink. More drains in the floor. A desk in the far corner. Ventilation ducts in the ceiling. A tank with murky water. Was that an aquarium?

I stepped into the room and heard a strange fluttering sound coming from somewhere behind my right shoulder.

I gasped. Butterflies. Over a hundred of them, pinned on cork boards and hung on the wall in glass frames. And several of them were fluttering, flapping, trying to take off. I thought it was sort of beautiful at first, a neat trick, fake—motorized maybe? I looked closer and then the horror set in. Their bodies had been tacked to the backing. Some had gotten loose and were flying around inside their frames, bouncing against the glass. A few had ripped themselves to pieces.

It was cruel, beyond cruel. *What kind of a monster skewers live butterflies?* Then I noticed something. A feeling. A sort of unknown vibration in my hand. Somehow I knew that the butterflies weren't *alive.* Not technically. They were animated: Zombie butterflies. I dropped the hand that had been touching the glass to my side and took a shuddering step back.

I explored the room further. I found the radio he must have been listening to. Next to the wheeled tables stood other metal trays with instruments on them, all made of stainless steel that shone like chrome. The fish tank was closer to the desk. The murky water was dark, but I could make out a shape of some sort. Probably just another weird specimen.

As I came around the side of the tank, I could see the silhouette of a creature, and then more of it from the front. It looked like a mummified monkey from the head to the waist, but with a fish's tail. I sank down onto my haunches to get a better look at it.

Splash, thump.

It moved.

Sweet Mary Mother of God, it moved. I flung myself away and began shaking my head frantically. This was not happening. This could not be happening. I was clearly having a nightmare. I pinched myself. *Ow.* I didn't wake up.

Fuck.

I swallowed and steeled myself for more horrors. My stuff had to be here somewhere. Then as I came around the desk, I noticed another door, like the one to this room. And yet another door, a wider, metal one. The desk seemed to have a calendar on it, a couple of notebooks with handwriting, a lamp, a magnifying glass attached to a metal arm. I paged through a notebook. Were those hieroglyphics? And a spidery handwriting in . . . maybe Latin?

Who the hell takes notes in Latin?

A transparent plastic case contained rows upon rows of different shapes and colors of glass eyes. A thick, curved needle had been stabbed into the desk calendar, a piece of suture still hanging from it.

On the other side of the first pillar stood a wooden sarcophagus. It had been painted in the Egyptian style with the features of a black-haired man with dramatically lined eyes. The image of the body was represented in wrappings. Was there a mummy inside? I didn't want to know.

I moved to the far side of the second pillar. Here, encased in a glass box, was a super creepy skinned and preserved corpse, the kind I saw advertised on subway trains: BODIES: THE EXHIBITION. The shellacked muscle fibers looked like red clay that someone had raked with a fine-toothed comb. The blue eyes bulged from their sockets. Had it once been male? Female? Without flesh, I couldn't quite tell.

I stood staring at it for a moment, willing it not to move. Willing it to be just a body, to just be what it looked like and nothing more.

Nothing happened. It was completely still. I let out the breath I suddenly realized I'd been holding.

And that was when it blinked.

I shrieked and ran for the closest door, the normal-looking one, yanking it open, only to find myself being battered by a pile of objects falling from it in disarray: mops, brooms . . . and arms.

Arms. *Human* arms. Five or six or them, detached, falling from the closet onto me.

I shrieked at the top of my lungs and ran out of the room the way I'd come. What the hell? What the *hell?*

I caught my breath and calmed myself in the hallway. *No more sightseeing. You have to get out of here. He could come back any time.*

I came around a corner to a set of ascending stairs. Across from those stairs was an iron gate and a rough-hewn tunnel beyond. Which way could I expect Ammit to come from?

The stairs. It would be why I'd hear the footsteps.

So I should go the other way.

But what if there's no way out that way?

I have . . . a feeling. Like this is the way to go. My hands feel . . . almost warm in that direction. Drawn that way.

The latch on the metal gate was simple and I was able to relatch it from the other side.

Then I began my journey down the rough-hewn tunnel, toward whatever it was my hands were telling me to follow.

Within twenty-five feet, the shadows began to close in as I moved farther from the lights. Soon, I was in complete darkness, hands out, one on the wall to my right, the other ahead, moving slowly so I didn't trip and fall. The sound of my footsteps seemed impossibly loud in the darkness.

The odd sensation in my hands—almost a tingle—increased gradually. I didn't know what could be causing it.

There was a fresher smell to the air as I continued.

I am going the right way. I must be.

I must have walked hundreds of feet in that darkness when I—*ouch*—bumped up against what felt like another metal gate. I oriented myself in the dark, figuring out where the hinges and bars were, reached through, and felt the same sort of latch. I undid it, and the door squeaked on its hinges. I took halting steps and pitched forward as the floor disappeared beneath my foot and I turned my ankle.

Argh. Stupid ankle!

Steps. There were steps leading downward. I checked my ankle out by feel and thought it wasn't too bad. I was lucky I'd been wearing boots or it would have been much worse.

The fresh air was definitely coming from this direction. I could hear a whistling sound, like wind through a drafty window.

I picked myself up and limped my way down the last few stairs. I continued forward, feeling the sides of the tunnel with my hands, where the tingle grew steadily stronger. Then I tripped again. I felt around. Stairs again, only going up this time. I climbed several and continued down the tunnel for some time.

Now the tunnel narrowed and jutted off to the right. Where it ended.

That's it? Just a dead end? After all of that?

You'll have a dead end if you don't find a way out of this.

It doesn't make any sense! Why have a tunnel that just ends in nothing?

The warm feeling in my hands was definitely coming from this direction. It had gotten stronger and stronger as I came towards the last wall. There had to be something there. I felt around on the walls, hoping to find a door knob, something, anything.

There had to be!

Light. I need light. Flames?

I concentrated on . . . what had Ammit called it? Calling power. I slowed my breathing. I thought about two flames igniting at my thumb and index finger on my right hand. Two small orange flames burst there, temporarily blinding me as my eyes had become accustomed to the darkness.

When my sight returned, I saw a small niche in the wall at about head height. Inside that niche was a lever. I pulled it.

A stone slab in the wall in front of me made a scraping sound as it rose to about five feet, leaving a small entry way into a dim room beyond. Ducking my head, I stepped forward and saw a brilliant flash of ruby red and sapphire blue. I realized it was a gorgeous stained-glass window depicting three white lilies with a red and blue border. The window was on the opposite wall. For a moment, I wondered if I was in a church, but no. The stone sarcophagus and stone urns set into recesses in the wall gave me the clue I needed.

I appeared to be in a crypt or mausoleum. It was a large room, with a double door. From the light shining through the stained glass, I guessed it was morning or afternoon.

The warm feeling in my hands led me toward the double door, which was slightly ajar. The chain and padlock on the outside wasn't locked.

The chain fell to the ground as I pushed the door open and shaded my eyes against the brightness of the cloudy day. The sun peeked out for a second before fading again in a patchy white haze above.

Everywhere I looked I could see a massive spread of tombstones. Mausoleums. Angels, saints, and cross statues. Headstones both big and small, light and dark, with different shapes. Flowers on some. Flags on others . . . and this going on as far as I could see until the raised expressway in the distance one direction and Manhattan's familiar skyline in the other. I was in a garden of death—all that was grown here were stones of tribute.

This was where the feeling had been coming from. It had been the feeling of death on a massive scale. Death everywhere. I'd thought Washington Cemetery in Brooklyn was big. This cemetery was easily three times the size, probably more.

More clouds seemed to gather above, and the brightness dimmed.

And then from behind me, from somewhere inside the mausoleum I'd just emerged from, I heard an odd, skittering noise, followed by a kind of *kerflumpf, kerflumpf* sound.

The creature that trundled into view dragged itself on what had once been hands, but were now skeletal spindles festooned with shreds of decayed flesh. Three hands in all, attached to . . . was that a small dog?

A sound of revulsion escaped me as my eyes widened in horror. The creature scuttled towards me as more stealthy sounds came from the darkness within the crypt.

I did the only thing I could do: I ran.

CHAPTER FIVE

I RAN AS FAST AS I COULD, GIVEN THAT MY INJURED ankle and boots were most definitely not made for running. I glanced behind me: the thing you are not supposed to do, but I did it anyway. The tripod zombie dog scrambled along the row, following me. Other small white things were also clambering over various headstones, but I couldn't quite . . . Were those rat skeletons? *Don't need to know, don't* need *to know.*

I was breathing hard and fast and my heart was beating like crazy. I fled down a row of tombstones, then another. I was approaching a road of some kind. *Which way?* I couldn't just get to Manhattan from here—wherever here was. I'd have to find a subway. These thoughts raced through my mind and I decided—going toward the expressway would probably help me find a subway station faster so I chose that direction.

My lungs were burning and my mouth was a vacuum. My ankle didn't seem to hurt as much anymore, but if those skeleton things were still behind me, I needed to keep going. But were they?

I glanced behind me once again (I know, I know) and saw that the tripod dog was still bearing down in my direction, running on two hands with the other held upright, as if awaiting a high five.

I put on extra speed, only to hear the clattering sounds of the skeletal rats as they somehow caught up with me.

I changed directions again, veering away from sharp yellow teeth. I could now see a fence at the perimeter of the cemetery, a stone wall topped with chain link fence, and above that, round rolls of razor wire. There was no way I was getting over that.

The perimeter was no good. I needed a road. A road would lead to an exit.

Now as I came around a mausoleum on a hillside, I could see a road down below. A road inside the cemetery, with a car and a person, not close, but certainly closer than the cemetery's perimeter and Manhattan in the distance.

"Hey!" I yelled, running. "Hey!"

The person got into the car. An elderly woman. A late model sedan.

I kept running, hoarsely yelling, "Stop! Wait!"

I got close enough for the bright red brake lights to sear my eyeballs and to catch a cough full of exhaust.

I stopped, coughing, gagging.

Something landed in my hair.

Something else grabbed my injured ankle. I shrieked hysterically, whipping my head around and smacking at it in a vain attempt to dislodge whatever it was, while kicking my leg to do the same. The thing on my head held fast. I screamed and gripped it and felt sharp poky bits bite into the flesh of my hand. I flung whatever it was and a chunk of hair away over an ornate brown tombstone. The thing on my ankle was a skeletal hand. I slammed it against the tombstone. When it fell off, I ran.

I wanted to cry. I needed more air. I wanted water and I needed to stop running. Mostly, I wanted to wake up, but that wasn't happening. The clicking of the small creatures' skeletal digits on stone seemed to echo from all around me. The wind picked up, and the sky darkened.

I reached a crossroad with a wider road, and from there I could see a gatehouse and exit in the distance.

I wondered if I could hide somewhere, behind a huge statue maybe or behind a mausoleum—inside one, even. But then I'd be trapped if they found me.

My only choice was to run.

Run fast, and far.

Now I was feeling lightheaded and sick. My hand was bleeding from a puncture wound from whatever sharp thing I'd grabbed.

Something landed on the back of my coat, between my shoulder blades where I couldn't reach. *Stop, drop, and roll,* said my brain, so I did.

That dislodged it. It was another—or the same—rat skeleton with sharp yellow teeth. It lay on the ground for a moment then jerked up and ran towards me once more.

A cold drop fell onto my forehead. And then one on my hand. A drop left a dark spot on a light gray tombstone. It was starting to rain.

There was no way I was going to make it to the entrance. It looked like the perimeter wall went under the expressway, so I changed directions abruptly and ran that way, putting on a final burst of speed that I thought might kill me.

Maybe I could flag down a car?

There was no razor wire on this side for some reason. I clambered over the stone wall and stood there hunched over as I tried to catch my breath.

I attempted to wave down a car. I got honked at. Beeped at. One driver pressed his horn for at least five full seconds, possibly longer.

No one would stop. Maybe it was against the law. No standing. No parking. Not even to help.

I watched the wall where I'd come over, awaiting the horrors that had chased me across the cemetery. Nothing. My breathing slowed, though my dry throat caused me to cough several times.

Then the skies opened up and poured a deluge upon the city streets. I was dry underneath the expressway, but I couldn't stay there forever.

Where were the creatures? Were they afraid of the rain?

I took a tentative step toward the wall and looked over it cautiously.

A hand shot up from nowhere and grabbed my cheek, digging bone into my skin as it held tight. I shrieked and flung it into the street, where it was promptly run over by a box truck, then a BMW, then a taxi. It didn't get up again.

A taxi! I could wave down a taxi, couldn't I?

But what would I pay with?

My money was in my wallet. My wallet was in my backpack, wherever that was. God, and the phone. The $700 smart phone I'd just gotten a few days before.

I felt sick.

I didn't know where I was, and I wasn't really sure where I should go, but I had no interest in sticking around and seeing if I could get more creepy crawlies to come over the wall. I began walking beneath the expressway to see if I could get somewhere, anywhere I might recognize.

Chapter Six

I WANDERED AWHILE, FEELING SWEATY AND exhausted, coming down from my frantic run. By the time I'd gotten away from the overhead protection of the expressway against the rain, it was just sprinkling.

A sign told me I was walking along 58th Street. Lots of cars were parked on both sides. One side of the street was the cemetery wall. The other side was all two-story homes. Some were made of brick, others covered in white siding. They were packed together side-by-side with fenced-in yards and driveways.

Which borough was I in? All I could tell was that I wasn't in Manhattan. It was a residential neighborhood. The next corner I got to said 52nd Ave. The one after that, 52nd Rd. Then 53rd Ave. What the hell kind of numbering and naming system was *that*?

A guy rode past me on a bike. He was already more than half a block away at a stop sign by the time I realized I should try to flag him down, and then he was off again.

The back of my head hurt. So did my ankle. And my hand.

While there was plenty of traffic on the streets, there weren't too many pedestrians. After a couple of blocks of houses with concrete driveways instead of front yards, I overtook a white-haired woman with thick glasses plodding alongside a little white dog.

"Excuse me, could you tell me how to get to the subway from here?"

"Sorry, *no habla Ingles*," she said with a heavy accent.

"Ah. Subway?" I asked, pointing to the left or right.

She pointed left, back the way I'd come.

"*Gracias*," I said, heading back that way.

The cityscape got a little more interesting as I approached the next major intersection. A couple of tall brick buildings stood near the corner of Laurel Hill Blvd and a little side street named 58th Place. After that? 48th Ave. There was no logic to these street names.

Perhaps I was in hell.

The neighborhood transitioned from small houses to mostly deserted commercial warehouses and, after another few blocks, back to two-story homes and apartment buildings. A huge jet roared overhead, flying too low. It seemed to be landing, which meant I was either near JFK or LaGuardia . . . or possibly even in New Jersey. Could you see Manhattan from the Newark Airport?

I walked several blocks more with even more confusing numbering. I asked a guy leaning on a car and smoking a cigarette for directions to the subway. "Yeah, sure, you go up and make a left on Queens Boulevard—"

"So I'm in Queens?"

"Uh, yeah?" said the guy, giving me a funny look.

Right. It's not normal to not know where you are. "Got trashed with my friends last night," I said. "Please don't ask."

He chuckled appreciatively. "So yeah, you go up to the boulevard. Cross the street, like, go straight, and then turn left. And then it's like, three blocks. Make a right. You should hear it by then and see it. The El." For a second I thought he meant the L train, but then realized he meant an elevated subway.

I thanked him and turned to go.

"Yo, did you know you're bleeding?" he asked.

"What?"

"From your head." He pointed.

I felt around the back of my head and came to a damp spot in my hair. My fingers came back red. Further exploration of my scalp indicated a very small but freely bleeding wound.

"I don't suppose there are any napkins in your car?" I asked.

"Huh? Oh, naw, that's not my car."

I thanked him again and went on my way.

Queens Boulevard was an eight-lane monstrosity of fast-moving vehicles. There were two single-lane side-streets that went parallel to the main boulevard, but there were still six lanes of speeding cars, trucks, and cabs. Here there were tall brick apartment buildings and other signs of urban civilization: a hotel, a bodega, a dentist's office, a hardware store.

The distant *click-clack* of a subway train on an elevated trestle reached my ears. It reminded me of Washington Cemetery again, which was very close to the elevated F train tracks in Brooklyn.

Man, I was sore. Exhausted.

Groups of teenagers wearing school uniforms were meandering down the sidewalk, some laughing, some with their heads down and their headphones turned up. Most carried backpacks of one kind or another. Several of them went up the steps to the 52nd and Lincoln subway station, and I followed.

I wasn't sure what I was going to do. Maybe ask someone if I could borrow a swipe.

At the top of the stairs stood a MetroCard machine and three turnstiles to the platform, which was labeled *Downtown and Manhattan*. Several of the students swiped MetroCards and went through the turnstiles, but one boy who had been waiting for the others to go now quickly vaulted over the center stile.

So I, in my broke and ultimate wisdom, decided to do exactly what he had done.

Which was how—only some hour or so after I'd escaped Ammit's lair—I got myself arrested.

The handcuffs were much heavier and more uncomfortable than the costume pair my roommate

Julie had let me try. They also didn't have a safety release like those had.

Being packed into the floor of a van that went from one subway stop to another to pick up "other delinquents" was also not fun.

I was bustled upstairs immediately on arrival. After having my fingerprints scanned and my photo taken, I filled out some paperwork and was then escorted to a small elevator that smelled like sweat and desperation. Back to the ground floor, where a female officer showed me into a large room and pointed at a chair next to a desk. "Wait here for a detective."

There were eight desks, with three detectives working. One doing something on a computer, one interviewing an elderly man, and the other one talking on a desk phone.

The room seemed to be adjacent to the entry hall, sort of around the corner.

I waited. At least they'd moved my handcuffs to in front of me instead of behind my back.

My head hurt. My shoulders were stiff. My wrists, swollen.

I closed my eyes with weariness. And waited.

Down the hallway, the elevator went *ding*. The doors opened and a janitor wearing a blue jumpsuit got out with a garbage can on squeaky wheels. The doors closed.

I let my eyes close again. A trickling sound caught my attention. Water cooler.

Ding. Doors. Squeaky wheels. *Trickle*.

"Jane Doe, huh?"

I opened my eyes. He wore a dark tie and a blue and white striped dress shirt with the sleeves rolled up and pushed back. A gun nestled beneath his left armpit in a shoulder holster.

"Sorry?"

"Your case file," he said, brandishing a thick manila folder and tossing it onto the desk I was sitting next to. He plopped into the chair behind it and regarded me expectantly.

"Ah," I said. "Did you talk to Detective Mitchell at the 13th Precinct?"

Mitchell had been the one who'd helped me the most in trying to get a lead on my identity.

"No, that's why they rushed me this file. He's not around."

There was another detective I'd met, but I couldn't remember his name. The one who'd been nice to me when cops came to our old apartment because a ghost stabbed a knife into my roommate's pillow. The other cop had thought I'd done it. Which, honestly, was a more believable explanation.

"What about Linda Lopes at Bellevue?" Linda was the social worker who had been assigned my case while I underwent testing at the hospital.

"Voicemail."

"Mac Goodman at Chris Street Comics?"

"Just left for the day."

"What about the managers?"

The detective sighed heavily then nodded at someone entering the room.

A uniformed officer and an elderly man in handcuffs came into the room from the entry hall. The elderly man was skinny with wispy gray hair and wore a Hawaiian shirt. He walked sideways in halting fashion, the uniformed officer coaxing him along.

The detective turned his attention back to me.

"You know, you seem well spoken enough and fairly smart, so I have to ask why you would run from police officers."

All I had heard was a man's voice yell "Stop!" and I'd panicked. I thought it was Ammit coming after me.

"I was scared."

"Scared they would find your stash?" the detective asked.

The uniform and the old man passed by me, headed toward the elevator.

"Never let 'em find your stash, girlie," the elderly man muttered.

"C'mon, Frank," the uniformed officer said, leading him away from us.

I sat up in the chair and looked into the detective's eyes. "I'm telling you like I told them, I didn't throw any drugs anywhere. I didn't *take* any drugs, I'm not *on* anything."

Why did the police always assume I was on drugs? That was what the first cop who met me thought, what the female detective at my apartment thought, and those guys who had arrested me thought so too. They might have let me go if I'd had ID. Instead they treated me like I was a junkie.

"Uh, huh. Listen, we can't help you unless you tell us the truth."

"Don't tell them anything!" the old man shouted from down the hall. "You have a right to remain silent!"

"Shut up, Frank!" yelled my detective.

I had already decided it would be useless to tell them I'd been kidnapped. If they wouldn't believe I wasn't on drugs, why would they believe that? It wasn't like I could tell them where I'd been held. I could lead them to the cemetery, but it was so huge, I'd never be able to find the crypt I'd escaped from.

"And you have a right to an attorney!" yelled Frank.

Ding went the elevator.

"And if you can't afford one—fine, fine, I'm going!" Frank complained as the uniformed cop gave him a little shove. "I know my ri—"

The doors chopped his last word in half.

I sat back and sighed. "If you would just talk to the managers at Chris Street. Ask for Erica or Jackson. They'll vouch for me."

"Oh, I already spoke with Jackson," he said.

"So why are you still asking me these questions?"

"Something just doesn't add up about you, *Jane.* What were you even doing in Queens?"

I almost told him to call me Madison but I thought better of it.

Don't antagonize the nice policeman.

He's not nice!

Shh!

Whatever I said I'd been doing, he'd check up on it. And ask me more questions.

"Look, officer . . . officer . . . what's your name, even?"

"Detective. It's Detective Carboni."

"Detective Carboni. Will you take the handcuffs off if I answer you?" My wrists ached.

"Sure. *If* you tell me the truth."

"I'm telling you what I told the other officers. I fell asleep on the subway. A guy hit me in the back of the head and grabbed my backpack. I chased him out of the station, but I lost him."

"Uh huh. And I suppose you don't want to press charges?"

"Against who? The guy? I barely saw him. He got away hours ago, thanks to your officers."

"Where were you before that?"

"My, um, sort-of boyfriend and I broke up. I was upset, so I walked around for a long time and then I got on the subway and you know the rest."

"Sort-of boyfriend or drug dealer?"

I gave him a look.

His tongue seemed to search his cheek for an answer. "What's the boyfriend's name?"

"Kipling Jack Donovan."

He wrote this down. "What's his phone number?"

"I don't know. It was in my phone which was in my backpack."

"Where's he work?"

"He drives a carriage at Central Park."

He wrote this down as well, stared at me for several seconds, then shrugged and took a set of keys out of his pocket.

I outstretched my hands onto the desk with a metallic clink, offering him the handcuffs.

He looked through the keys for a moment, chose one, then brought it to the cuffs' keyhole, but didn't insert it. "I'm not going to charge you with anything. To be honest, I don't want to deal with the paperwork. When I look at you," he said, tapping the thick folder, "What I see is a pain in the ass. Not worth it."

A shout came from the entry hall. "Check this guy outside!"

"No way! Halloween's not 'til Tuesday!"

Detective Carboni looked down the row of desks toward the front of the room then back at me. "So I'm going to release you on a desk appearance, but if I see you—"

Boom, thud.

The building shuddered.

"Sir, back away from the building!" a distant voice shouted.

"What the hell?" said Detective Carboni.

Boom, thud.

The building shuddered again.

The two detectives without interviewees jumped to their feet and rushed from the room toward the sounds.

Crasssssshhhhhh. Breaking glass. Shouting.

Screams.

BANG!

Detective Carboni ducked reflexively. "Get down!" he yelled, pulling me to the floor.

BANG BANG!

Gunshots. So loud.

A horrible bellow . . . It hardly sounded human.

Then I felt it. That weird tingly feeling in my hands like I'd experienced in Ammit's lab. The feeling of death . . . or death *magic*. And if I could feel death magic in the police station, something was very, very wrong.

"Stay here," Detective Carboni said, pulling his gun and edging toward the front of the room.

"Fuck that," I muttered.

"Holy shit," came Detective Carboni's voice. He aimed.

BANG BANG went Detective Carboni's gun.

And there went Detective Carboni's limp form, flying across the room into the wall, hard. He slid down it like a rag doll and didn't get back up.

I hunkered down behind the desk.

The thud of heavy boots came across the wooden floor, sending tremors through the boards.

It entered at the front of the room. A huge figure, eight feet tall or so, wearing a studded leather jerkin, carrying a spear. From the neck down, he appeared to be a huge man. But the horns that stood out from the sides of his head, matted fur . . .

This was no man. This was the minotaur.

The minotaur had been security at the Goblin Market. When I'd stolen Hank's feather from Ammit, he'd come after me. The only thing that saved me was the unexpected intrusion of two undead creatures from stage left. When I'd escaped, his eyes promised payback and I wondered if he'd come to collect.

Or maybe there was more to it. The tingle in my hand told me death magic was afoot. Maybe he wasn't after me. Maybe he was hunting the undead.

A series of shots as a uniformed officer appeared from behind the hulking creature. The minotaur paused just long enough to stab him in the chest with the long spear.

Then the minotaur turned in my direction.

The fierce brown eyes I remembered were no more. Now two orbs of gray stared sightlessly. He wasn't hunting undead. He *was* undead.

His face and neck were stitched up like a baseball. The leather armor was riddled with gun shots, but there was no blood. A golden ring hung from his nostrils and flapped slightly as he expelled and inhaled air with a series of snorts. *Why is he snorting if he's dead?*

Then his head turned my way, and the zombie minotaur began to lurch sightlessly toward me, knocking a desk out of the way as it picked up speed.

There was no question now.

It was after me.

I pushed a chair over, and then the water cooler, a bubbling splashing mess, hoping it would slow him down, even just for a second.

I ran the only direction I could.

CHAPTER SEVEN

I RAN STRAIGHT FOR THE ELEVATOR. THE LONG hall was deserted. The various posters and flyers tacked to a bulletin board fluttered in my wake.

I raced through the archway into the short vestibule and pushed the button frantically.

BANG BANG BANG

God, were guns always this loud?

A desk went flying past the end of the hall.

The big heavy feet. I could hear them, steps reverberating through the building.

Where was the elevator? I pressed the button again, smacking at it.

Behind me, the loud snort as it caught my scent. I pounded at the elevator doors, slapping the button, crying out as the loud steps pounded toward me.

I turned to meet my fate as the minotaur bore down, but lost my nerve and cringed, squeezing my eyes shut at the last second.

A horrible *crunch* shook the vestibule.

My eyes popped wide to see enormous skull-crushing hands grabbing within an inch of my face.

The minotaur bellowed with a scent like bad meat. Its horns were embedded into the archway outside the vestibule, trapping it.

I tried to meld into the doors behind me, pressing my spine and shoulders into the cool metal. I slid downward, whimpering as the beast clawed in my direction, unable to reach me.

The minotaur grabbed for its spear.

Ding.

I fell backwards into the elevator as the doors opened and the spear thrust missed me. I shoved myself against the back wall.

A roar of frustration and a loud *thud* and reverberation as the doors closed.

Fuck.

The elevator doors opened on the second floor and I ran. Multiple doors, and hallelujah, two EXIT signs, one over the stairs continuing down, and another down the hall. The crashing and smashing noises and shots and screaming continued from the first floor

I ran down the hall to the emergency door. ALARM WILL SOUND IF . . . I pushed it open, heard the high-pitched wail of the alarm, and stepped outside onto a square platform with a rusted railing. Flaking metal stairs clung to the side of the building.

Evening air. Cooler. Clanking down the stairs in a side-waddle with my handcuffed hands in front of me. I couldn't quite get a grip on the railing, so I took them one at a time, sidle step, sidle step.

Down to the ground. More gunshots coming from the building.

I was maybe a hundred feet from the building when I sensed the minotaur again, barreling through the emergency door and busting the railing with a bellow.

I full-out ran.

CHAPTER EIGHT

PANIC.

Sidewalks, streets.

WALK / DON'T WALK signs.

Buildings. People. Screams behind me.

Run.

Don't look back.

Just run.

Garbage bags. Flattened boxes. Recycling. Stacked in neat rows.

Like an obstacle course.

More garbage bags. A mountain of them.

Stumble over garbage and slip.

Something wet.

A roar from behind.

Back to my feet, hindered by handcuffs. Ankle hurting again. Limping.

DON'T WALK

Run.

Behind: The squeal of brakes. Angry honking. Yelling. Shattering glass.

Ahead: in the intersection, a silver sportscar. The door open.

"GET IN!" yells the driver—he looks familiar—I can't—another roar behind me—

Behind: The minotaur hurls his spear. I fling myself backward and it skims my shoulder, missing my skin by millimeters, leaving a rent in my wool navy peacoat.

Ahead: Off-balance stumble.

Vertigo and a rush of air.

Somehow I am in the passenger seat of the silver sports car.

The male driver reaches across me, pulls the door shut, and the car speeds off.

"Yeah, the 95th in Queens. A fucking zombie minotaur, Quinn! Awesome, but *fuck*, what a mess," he said. "The clean-up crew's going to be there all night."

I sat up, dazed, still panting from my run. *Seatbelt.* I found the strap and tried to buckle myself in, but couldn't reach, still awkward with handcuffs.

"Yeah, I have her," he said, looking over at me. "God only knows what she thinks." He offered a hand and buckled the seatbelt for me, glancing back and forth at the road.

Then I recognized him. The excessively good-looking detective from the freaky investigation at my apartment in the spring. In his mid-thirties, with dark hair and a square chin. Nice lips. Intense brows. What was his name? Williams? Wilson? "Detective . . . Wilson?"

His eyebrows raised in surprise and he winked at me. "Yeah, gotcha. Later," he said into a headset.

"Hey, sorry about that. You okay?" he asked.

"What the . . . how the . . . *why*?"

"I got a notification when your prints were run," he said, a look of concern on his face.

"You got . . . a notification? About me? Why?"

"Does the name Rowan mean anything to you?"

"I've heard it. A powerful magus who wants to protect me . . . though I have no idea *why*!" That last bit came out louder than I'd intended. *Kidnapping, minotaurs, maguses.* It was too much. I bit my tongue, but the hot tears came to my eyes anyway. Too damn *much*.

"Why is all of this happening to me?" I wailed.

My feet stomped up and down on the floor and my fists beat my knees. I let out the scream I'd been holding and

. . . I am no longer in the car. The car takes off below me as a silver thread spools out from my navel after it, a gossamer filament of light.

I am translucent, floating, me, but more, and less, too. More mind. Less feeling.

I am outside my own body. Disembodied, the literal interpretation of the word. This is magic. I am not my shadow self but rather my personality, intelligence, but without emotion to clutter my judgement.

I want to be back at the car, and as I have the desire, so I am there. A beam of light, a heartbeat. My body is slumped against the window. The window is cracked. All of the glass in the vehicle is cracked.

I did that, I realize.

The moment replays in my memory, untinged with the frustration and fear of my meltdown, or its magic.

As I scream, a ball of force emanates and detonates from my body in shock waves. A blue glow briefly illuminates Wilson as the waves flow—and don't touch him.

My head lolls in the seatbelt. Wilson puts two fingers to my jugular, checking my pulse while driving with the other hand. He breathes out and lets go of my neck, then puts that hand back on the wheel and keeps driving.

I want to—

. . . before I even finished the thought, I was back in my body.

I was aware I was in the sportscar. The vibration of the tires on the road rumbled beneath my body as the leather bucket seat cradled me.

Everything hurt. My ears, my neck, arms, chest, everything. I felt weak, nauseous.

A taste of blood in my mouth.

No sound. Almost like my ears were plugged.

I inhaled slowly. New car and leather smell. Sweat. A little aftershave. A garbage smell too, and over that, the smell of fresh blood. A droplet fell from my nose.

I rolled my head away from the window and opened my eyes.

The handcuffs were in pieces on my lap, my wrists sore and red. The pieces were smoking.

The streetlights and the brake lights of other cars seemed to glow much brighter than I was used to. The silence giving way to a high-pitched whine that became mixed with muffled highway sounds. At an intersection, the red light seemed to shoot a laser into my brain. I squeezed my eyes shut and immediately started to lose consciousness.

As though coming from a great distance, I heard a voice say, "We're almost there."

Chapter Nine

I DREAM THAT I AM FLOATING UNDERWATER, surrounded by glowing blue. I try to swim but never seem to make any progress. The surface of the water is a mirror, the bottom an underwater carousel, far far away.

Next, I dream I'm flying, over and through a winter landscape dominated by pines blanketed in thick white snow. In the clouds above, ribbons of iridescent color dance green, pink, lavender, pale aqua, rippling like flames from one side of the horizon to the other. The night sky emerges from beneath a wispy cloud bank and the stars are more numerous than I have ever seen, like thousands of tiny diamonds on midnight blue velvet. The Milky Way stretches like a silver-veined mountain range viewed from above. Like piles of glittering sand.

I float on my back. Nothing to worry about. Lighter than air. No pain. No sadness. Just existing and acknowledging the power of nature to transform and transcend.

The sky lightens and becomes empty azure blue.

The sound of birdsong, a trilling melody, catches my interest.

I fly toward the sound and land. I stand in a square courtyard, surrounded by columns and archways, an empty fountain or pool in the center. All stone, with the ground tiled in a checkerboard pattern. There are eight archways per side, thirty-two in all. Whatever lies beyond the archways is wreathed in shadow.

There is no bird in sight.

And then behind me, a polite cough.

I turn to face an extraordinary woman. She is nearly six feet tall, with long dark hair that falls past her shoulders. She wears a simple white gown, Grecian in style. But the most remarkable thing about her is her presence, a manifestation of joy and confidence and curves. Her body type is similar to that of a woman I once heard Jackson describe admiringly as "thick." This woman is no waif. She radiates strength, well-being, and energy.

"I'm Vita," she says. "Do you think you're dreaming?"

"Well, yeah. I mean, I can't fly. Time can't go that fast. So yes, definitely a dream."

"And if I told you that this courtyard is a space in your higher consciousness that you created—"

As she speaks, puffy white clouds float into view in the sky behind her, and I smile.

Her face takes on a quizzical look and she looks over her shoulder. "What is it?"

"Clouds. I was thinking that the sky was missing clouds, and then there were some. So, okay, maybe this is a dream, maybe it's the thing you said. So *what if* that? How would I feel or what would I say?"

"What's the last thing you remember?"

"The minotaur. No, the car. I blew up the car."

"Yes, and yourself as well."

My eyes widen in panic. "Wait, are you saying I'm dead?!"

"No—no, you are *not* dead. Not yet, anyway."

"So I'm . . . I'm dying?"

"Well, they say technically we're all dying from the moment we're born—"

"So I'm *not* dying?"

"There was . . . a moment where we thought we were going to lose you, but here you are. And as long as you are here, you are not dying. You're healing. Magically."

"So I'm healing in a magical dream with . . . who are you, exactly?"

"I told you. I'm Vita."

"Are you friends with Detective Wilson?"

Her lip twitches impishly. "Sometimes."

"Did Rowan send you?"

"He did."

"Are you a . . . magus?"

She nods. "I am."

The courtyard needs a bench. I'm tired of standing. As I try to picture a bench . . .

. . . everything goes dark

a searing pain

through my right eye

sobbing

forearm to my forehead

an unfamiliar bed, white sheets

"Hold her!" a voice, distant

faces fading

in

the
dark

The courtyard again. Calm. But I feel weak.

"Easy," Vita says. "Slow down. You need to rest and recharge. Expending energy here will divert your healing process. You will sleep deeply, allowing your body to repair the damage you did to it. Do you understand?"

I nod. Weariness is setting in. I wish my arms would just fall off so that I wouldn't have to carry them around with me anymore. I briefly picture myself as an armless knight and smile as everything fades away.

I'm in a cellar. Somewhere dark. I climb steps, my feet going *thump-thump* on the stairs. A rectangle of light above, darkness below. *Thump-thump*, I hear; something is calling me upwards, some forgotten notion—a sound, both regular and familiar, a *thump-thump, thump-thump* sound.

I snap back to a room I don't recognize, antique furniture, an antique bed, and a girl lying there. In a chair nearby sits a white-haired and white-bearded man wearing a plaid shirt with a book in his lap.

It's Roland, the librarian and bookstore owner. The one my friend Zoe called Hipster Santa. He has a concerned look on his face as he regards the girl. The girl in the bed . . . is me.

A pull, the air in my lungs gone, the old man jumping up in alarm and calling for—

I dream of sinking.

Then, nothing.

I dream of the courtyard.

I dream of the cellar. The darkness and stairs. The sound. *Thump-thump. Thump-thump.* It's even louder now. *THUMP-THUMP, THUMP-THUMP.*

Like a heartbeat.

My heartbeat.

A sense of rushing and movement and heaviness.

I was thirsty.

I opened my eyes and blinked a few times.

"Roland?" I said, and my voice cracked. His beard looked a bit bedraggled and the blue shirt he wore was wrinkled at the elbows.

"Ah, you're awake!" He stood and brought the chair close to my bedside.

I raised myself on to my elbows, clearing my throat.

"Let me pour you some water." He filled a glass from a crystal pitcher and handed it to me. It was two-thirds full and I drank slowly, thirstily, until I needed to breathe.

"What are you doing here? What am I doing here? Where is here?"

I glanced around the room, seeing dark wood furniture with intricate carvings on the arms and feet. I was in a big bed with white cotton sheets.

"Er, well, this is my apartment. So I expect I'm here because I live here. You're here . . . well, for several reasons. But mainly you are here now because you seriously injured yourself. You're lucky you were with Zero. He saved your life."

"Who the hell is—? Oh, you mean Detective Wilson," I said. "Wait, how do you know . . .?"

Slowly, the tumblers fell together.

"You're Rowan," I said.

"Yes. Although . . . have we met? Otherwise?"

"Do you not remember me or something? Did someone mess with your memory too?"

"Ah, no. You see, though you may have met me before, this is *my* first time meeting *you.* In fact, in all likelihood, it is this meeting that causes me to go back in time to meet you and provide you whatever assistance I can."

Wait, what?

"You're . . . a time traveler?" I asked.

"Well, not exactly. I can't help it. I'm less a traveler and more a . . . well, a servant of Time, I suppose you could say."

"Like Time's butler?" I asked.

"If you like," he said with a smile.

"So when I met you at the library the first time . . . that hasn't happened to you yet?"

"No, and please don't say another word about it. Not one!" His eyes were wide.

"Why not?"

"It's best not to. Things might change. Possibly for the worse. We wouldn't want that."

"But why didn't you tell me about magic and being Rowan when I was at the bookstore asking about my fake essay on zombies?"

"I can't say for certain as it hasn't happened to me yet. Because it is at *this* meeting that I first meet you and you learn my identity."

"Let me get this straight. You're meeting me for the first time, even though I've already met you, so now you have to go back in time to pretend to meet me so that I'll know who you are when you meet me now."

"Exactly. Simple, no?"

"So how long have you . . . has Zero . . . been watching me?" I looked down for a moment and realized I was wearing a long-sleeved men's pajama top. It was big on me, striped, with a wide collar, a breast pocket, and buttons down the front. I peeked beneath the sheet. Matching pants too. "Wait, are these *your* pajamas?"

"They are. Your clothes were damaged."

I inhaled through my nose, taking a surreptitious smell of myself. Soap. I could smell soap. Not sweat or blood or body odor or garbage.

"Did you bathe me?"

"Hmm? Oh, no. I had a nurse come and take care of you. She bathed you and dealt with your injuries and other needs."

A nurse. I was in a strange apartment with a not-exactly stranger (but *not* not-exactly either), had required a nurse, and didn't remember how I got there or being bathed or clothed. But I had had that weird dream. "Vita?"

"Yes."

Not a dream then. Too weird. I shook my head. "How long have I been here?"

"Six days, fifteen hours, and twenty-seven minutes, give or take."

He didn't glance at a wristwatch, and his eyes didn't leave my face. I looked around the room for a clock but didn't see one.

"Is that a time butler perk?"

He smiled. "One of many."

"*Six* days? I was asleep all of that time? Why didn't you take me to a hospital?"

"You sustained a rather serious injury. You've been healing, magically."

"Can I use your bathroom?" I asked. The feeling of pressure had been growing slowly.

"Of course. It's through that door, on the right." He gestured at one of two doorways in the room, the one with the open door.

I climbed out of the bed and stood up carefully. I could feel the blood leaving my head and going to the rest of my limbs.

"Where's that one go?" I asked, pointing at the closed door.

"Just a closet," he said.

"It's not full of arms, is it?"

"I beg your pardon?"

"I'll tell you when I get back."

I walked down a hall with a small table, an old black landline telephone, and a small antique lamp casting light beneath a stained-glass shade.

The bathroom was stomach medicine pink. Pink tiles, pink sink, pink tub. White shower curtain. A window with white curtains cast a glow in the room. A fuzzy green bathrobe hung on a hook behind the door. Men's toiletries lined the shelves.

I took a look in the mirror over the sink as I washed my hands. I looked a little pale and had circles under my eyes. My hair wasn't nearly as messy as it usually was when I woke up, but I made some attempt to smooth it with a little water. Then I rubbed some toothpaste on my teeth and rinsed my mouth.

I finished up and went back to the bedroom.

Roland was reading and looked up when I came in.

"Would you prefer to sit elsewhere?"

"No, this is fine," I said, climbing back into the bed. I stopped in the middle of making myself comfortable. "Oh, I mean, unless you want your bed back?"

"No, no. That's alright. If I want to sleep in it, I can always go back a few days before your arrival. You use it as long as you like. I suspect you've been through a lot more than any of us know . . . and all alone. I would like to help you, if you'd allow it."

"You mean, like, in the past?"

"No, I mean going forward. I will explain, to the best of my ability, what I'm able to glean of your powers, and guide you so that you are better able to control them, direct them, hone them."

"You're going to help me do magic?"

"Well, yes." He shrugged. "Unless you'd prefer to start with someone else. Zero, perhaps?"

"Uh, no thanks," I said quickly.

"Something I need to know?" he asked.

"Oh, no. I just don't want to take a chance of blowing up his car again. I think the once was enough."

He nodded, seeming amused. "Are you feeling rested enough to tell me—leaving out the parts that involve me—about what you have experienced of the magical world?"

"I don't know. Maybe. I can try. If I get tired, we can take a break and talk more about it later."

For the next hour, I talked. I drank water. I ate a banana.

At one point, his eyes seemed to bulge slightly. "*Two* vampires? This was in 1991, you said?"

"Yes."

He nodded slowly. "Go on."

"And I—or that is, Christina—went missing in 1987!"

"Yes, your timeline has . . . most definitely been *tampered* with," Roland said with an air of confusion. "I saw that at once—and yet . . ." His eyes lost focus for a moment and he seemed to be looking for a gnat as his eyes darted around. "No, it's quite strange. It's as though your timeline *was* disturbed, but now it's . . ." He frowned.

"Now it's what?"

"It's been, well, braided, I suppose. Repaired." He shook his head in what might have been wonderment, but he didn't seem happy about it.

"Is that weird?"

"Er, well, yes. I've never seen the like. Being ripped from one's own timeline is also . . . weird."

"I know more about that now. But it isn't what happened next."

"Alright. Tell me what happened next."

"Well, I met a dryad, I guess."

"Yes, I was aware of that." At my look of surprise, he said, "I asked Sylvie to watch over you."

"Oh, right. But I don't understand how if you hadn't already met me why you would put anyone—much less a former dryad—in my apartment. I mean, listen to me! Did you hear how easily I was able to say 'former dryad in my apartment' like it was just a regular thing? That's not a regular thing!"

"Yes, the order of events can get rather confusing. My future self told me to do so several months ago. He didn't tell me why, but he didn't have to. I always trust myself. Do you happen to know what became of Sylvie? I haven't heard from her in over a week."

"Oh, she's a dryad again. She's got a tree in the Brooklyn Botanical Garden."

His eyes widened. "How ever did she manage that?"

Roland's mouth fell open when I explained, but when I mentioned who I'd gotten the acorn from, he seemed even more alarmed.

"*The Baba Yaga*? Are you certain?"

". . . a bunch of memories for sale. One sounded so familiar I thought it had to be more than a coincidence. I was handed a magical memory feather, but then I accidentally stole it . . . and a minotaur came after us . . . but then a killer zombie thing chased us and I had to kill him with a platter dripping with holy water—"

"So the minotaur at the police station came from the *Goblin Market*?" At some point Roland's mouth had dropped open again and he hadn't closed it yet.

I nodded. "Yeah, I haven't even gotten to that part yet. See, the memory vendor—"

He held up his hand to stop me.

"And how did you know to use holy water? Whose idea was that?"

"It was yours," I said.

His eyebrows were nearly at his hairline. His mouth opened and moved but no words came out. Then he blinked a few times, cleared his throat, and spoke. "There's nothing for it then." He stood. "I have to go."

"Wait, where are you going?"

"You mean *when.* I'm going to go to our first few meetings. I'll be back as soon as I can." He moved to the closet and began sliding hangers of shirts and suits around.

"But you . . . I . . . why right now?"

He turned back to me. "To prevent any further knowledge of your past polluting my future timestream. I can sense those threads that might lead to an unraveling of space-time. Causal loops are one thing, but we must avoid any manifestations of paradox."

"What are you talking about? Could you try talking like a regular person?"

He pulled two suits from the closet. "I don't suppose you happen to recall what I was wearing?"

"Huh?"

"When you saw me previously. Did you notice—was I wearing either of these jackets?" One was blue and the other was red and blue plaid.

Of course. The Hipster Santa jacket.

"Um. Yes. The one on the left. With the shirt and pants you're wearing, come to think of it."

He pulled the suit jacket on and tied his bow tie. "Isn't that . . . lucky?"

"I don't understand how you can go to when I met you the first time. I mean, I don't even know what day it *is*, much less what day that *was*."

He checked a golden pocket watch and snapped it shut, tucking it away in a vest pocket.

"That's alright. I can see it just fine." His eyes unfocused once more as he looked me over. Then he did something complex with his hands—and goosebumps raised on my skin. There was a subtle pressure in the room that hadn't been there before.

Then he faded from view. I don't know what I'd been expecting, maybe a *bampf* like a comic book sound effect, or the *pop* of a vacuum, but there was no sound at all. He was there, he became translucent, and then he was gone.

I laid back and stared at the ceiling for a while. It was made of tin tiles, pressed with repeating fleur-de-lis patterns, painted white. I drifted off and woke abruptly when a noise in the room nearly gave me a heart attack. I sat upright and saw it was Rowan, hanging up his red jacket. I sighed with relief.

He turned and saw me and froze. "Everything alright?" he asked.

There was something different about him. The shirt was a different color, I thought, and his beard had been trimmed. He looked well rested.

"Yeah. I just didn't realize you'd be back so soon."

"*Soon* is a matter of relativity."

"What do you mean?"

He loosened his tie from around his neck and began to unknot it. "It's an amorphous concept, dependent on the perception of those who consider it. If you tell a three-year-old that he can have his birthday cake 'soon,' when his birthday is a month away, he will ask every day for the next thirty if today is his birthday and where his cake is. He has no concept of *month* or *day* or *soon*. It's relative. Had you asked if you'd see me soon before I left, I would have said no. To you, it's been two hours. For me, it's been . . . two weeks." He hung the tie in his closet. "So you see? It's relative."

At the thought of food, my stomach growled.

He heated minestrone soup and served it with sliced Italian bread and butter. We sat in a small kitchen at a round half-table with two chairs.

The soup was savory and salty and filled with vegetables. I raised a second spoonful when out of nowhere, I had a sudden realization. "Oh, no!" I said, abruptly clanking my spoon as I dropped it in the bowl.

"What is it? Is the soup too hot?" Roland asked anxiously.

"No, no, the soup is great. I just realized Julie is probably super worried about me and I am probably fired from my job."

"Julie is your roommate, correct?" I agreed she was. "I'll have Zero stop by in his official capacity. He can offer her an explanation and relieve any concern she has."

"Thank you. I don't know what I'll do about work. God only knows what Jackson thinks after talking to the police. Jackson's one of the managers at my job," I explained.

"Let's not worry about that for now. You should really eat. It will help keep your strength up. You need it."

I'd felt queasy for a moment, but the savory scent of the soup wafted up and my mouth watered. I began eating again.

After we ate, with the soup sitting warm in my stomach like a hot water bottle, I felt relaxed and sleepy. My eyelids grew heavy and I yawned.

Roland suggested we wait to finish our discussion.

As I settled back into bed, I asked, "Roland, do you have any kids?"

"Why?"

"I don't know. I guess I was just thinking you'd probably be a pretty good dad."

"Why, thank you, Madison." He seemed pleased by my comment. He paused in the doorway, hand on the light switch. "Sleep well."

"Thank you. You too. Oh, hey, can you ask, uh, Zero to get some clothes from my roommate for me? I appreciate the pajamas, but I'd like to wear my own stuff."

"Of course. Goodnight."

" 'Night."

Chapter Ten

"Because it's your fault," Billy says. Then he jumps.

"Billy, don't!" I shout, reaching for him as he falls from the Empire State Building. But I am too slow. Pain erupts in my chest as I watch my friend disappear from view.

"Noooo!" I scream.

Opening my eyes, I focused on the odd patterns on the tin ceiling in Roland's bedroom. In the daylight, they looked like strange faces.

Right. Dreaming. Or nightmaring. Whatever.

I sighed. It wasn't bad enough that I had to live through this stuff, now I had to have nightmares about it too?

Poor Billy. Poor me. I scrubbed my hand over my face to wipe away the vestiges of the dream.

There was a scent in the air.

Cinnamon. I rolled over slowly and inhaled the aroma. Was Roland cooking?

I climbed out of the bed and stretched. On the chair next to the bed sat a burgundy suede duffel bag that I recognized as Julie's. Inside I found two pairs of jeans, two tops, two of the oversize t-shirts I liked to sleep in, a few pairs of underwear, several socks, a bra, and my black Converse sneakers wrapped in a plastic bag on the bottom. There was a comb and a toothbrush with a mini travel toothpaste in a plastic bag as well.

I could smell the cinnamon more strongly now and . . . was that bacon? My mouth watered.

"Hello?" I called. "Roland?"

No answer.

I stuck my head around the doorway and saw that the kitchen table had been set with one plate. On the stovetop, a skillet with a clear lid held pancakes and small stack of bacon. But where was Roland?

My bladder signaled its unhappiness that I'd not yet emptied it, so I padded through the kitchen and down the hall to the bathroom. The door was closed, which had not been the case the day before. I raised my hand to knock and stopped my knuckles just short of the wood when I heard a muffled voice coming through.

It was Detective Wilson—Zero. Who was he talking to? Was he on the phone? I turned to go back to the kitchen, not wanting to eavesdrop when he said, "You should have seen the Alfa. Every window. Shattered. You know how much is cost to import that much custom glass? From *Italy*?"

Oh, crap. His car. I stood, listening.

The other person must have been speaking because he was quiet for several seconds. Then he said, "Yeeeah. She put herself into a *coma*."

Was he talking about me? I was in a coma?

Then after another pause, "Yeah. Vita accelerated her healing."

"Of course I was shielded."

"No, dude. I'm telling you, she's too fricken powerful for her own good."

"Then we'll have to keep her here."

Keep me? I didn't like the sound of that. I wished I could hear the other side of the conversation.

"If we have to. I mean, I think it would be safer."

"Yes, including her."

"You're right. I don't know."

"Yeah, I should probably check on her. I'll catch you later."

Shit. I scurried down the hall and into the kitchen and heard the bathroom door open. *Should I go back to the bedroom?*

I turned in the bedroom doorway and said, "Hello?" just as Detective Wilson walked into the room.

"Finally up, huh?" He wore khakis and a blue dress shirt and was immaculately shaved. He was shorter than me. Exceptionally good looking—almost *too* good looking. How old was he? Thirty-five? Older? Younger?

"Oh, yeah," I said and yawned. "I slept really well. Where's, uh, where's Roland?"

"Rowan? He had to go out."

"Oh," I said. "Why do you call him that?"

"That's his magus name. Mine is—"

"Zero?"

He nodded.

"How'd you get stuck with that?"

"Oh, I chose Zero," he said. "Zero to sixty in 5.1 seconds. Zero-G. Zero as a construct—both an abstract and yet the mathematical foundation for all imaginary numbers, like negatives. Half of binary, the foundation of digital electronics. But if you think about it, a one—the numeral 1 is just a line. It's finite. Whereas a zero is a circle—both finite *and* infinite. Circles themselves are magical—"

Ugh. My bladder signaled to me once again that it needed attention. "Sorry to interrupt, but I need to use the bathroom."

"Sure," he said, taking a mug out of the cabinet. "You want coffee? OJ?"

"Any chance there's tea?"

"I'll check."

Fuck, I thought. What was I going to do? There was no way I was going to be made prisoner again, not after escaping Ammit. Who knew what Detective Zero wanted to do with me? I sat down to let my body do what it needed to and once again noticed the white curtains. Behind them was a small window that overlooked an overgrown courtyard from the second floor.

Unfortunately, there was no fire escape. I wondered if there was one in Roland's room.

Back in the kitchen, my would-be warden was carefully plating my breakfast.

He set one plate with pancakes and bacon on the table. A bottle of maple syrup and a steaming mug sat next to it. A white string attached to a paper tag hung from the lip.

I stood in the doorway. "Need any help?"

"No, thanks though. Have a seat."

I sat.

"You should do the syrup yourself. I didn't want them to get soggy."

"Aren't you going to eat?" I asked, drizzling the syrup over my pancakes.

"Already did," he said, sitting down at the table with me.

My mouth watered at the smell of the cinnamon, bacon, and maple syrup, and I set to devouring it at once.

"So, what's your school?" he asked. He seemed much more casual than his "just the facts, ma'am" attitude the previous spring in my apartment.

"I don't go to school. I work at a comics shop," I said around a bite of pancake. It was thin and buttery and delicious.

"What school of magic do you take inspiration from?"

"There are magic schools? Like from those movies? My friend Nidhi from work is obsessed with them."

He grimaced. "No, I mean, what techniques do you use for your conjuring? The doctrines of Hermannstadt? The methods of ancient Egypt? Who trained you? What did you study?"

"Uh, I didn't? I haven't been trained. Didn't study anything."

I checked the tea to see if it had steeped long enough. It hadn't.

Zero's blue eyes regarded me impassively. "No training. None?"

"Not that I know of." I continued eating. I was going to get food in me while Detective Zero did his interrogation.

"Do you know what aptitudes you have?" Blue eyes staring.

"What do you mean?"

"You really don't have any idea what I'm talking about, do you?" I swear, the man needed to blink more often.

"Nope." I looked at him and he looked at me. He was so serious. I tried to stay as serious as he was but was mostly mystified. I checked the tea again to keep myself from giggling.

The tea was done. I removed the bag with a spoon and wrapped the string around both, squeezing out the last drops of yummy tea-flavoring.

"Okay, try this on for size: there are twelve types of magic. Six of them are abstract concepts. Three pairs, each with its opposite: Life/Death, Time/Space, Mind/Matter. Those are the cosmic spheres. Got it?"

I nodded, chewing.

"There are also six elemental spheres."

I swallowed. "Six?"

"Fire/Water, Earth/Air, and Light/Sound."

"How is light an element? Or sound?"

"Ask Melodia about it some time. She makes a persuasive argument."

"Who's Melodia?"

"A magus."

"Is that her magus name?"

He nodded.

"When do I get a magus name?"

"We'll figure something out for you. It's why I was asking about your aptitudes—what spheres of magic you have. Many magi choose names based on their unique talents."

"What are your talents?" Thinking of the brief blue glow I'd seen surrounding him when I did whatever I did in his car, I asked, "Forcefields?" and then, in a much smaller voice, "Also, I'm really sorry about your car."

He chuckled, then shook his head ruefully. "I am lucky to have as an associate a Time mage who returned my car to its former glory. You are also lucky because I might have had to kill you otherwise," he said with a feral smile.

I stopped mid-chew. "Do you threaten a lot of people while they're eating pancakes?"

He guffawed. "No. How are they?"

"Yummy. How'd you learn to make pancakes?"

"What, a man can't cook? So you *really* don't know what kind of magic you can do, huh?"

"Well, I made fire."

"*Made* fire? As in there was no fire and then suddenly it was there in your palm?" There was a sudden tension to him that I was picking up on, but I couldn't tell why.

"My fingertips, actually. It's kinda weird. Then there was another time where I maybe made light?" I stuffed a big bite of pancake in my mouth.

"Very mysterious." He seemed both distant and amused. Like he was taking my measure.

I finished chewing and sighed. "It's hard to explain. I shot a light at a faerie portal and it disappeared. You kinda had to be there."

"You shot a light at a what now?"

"A faerie portal. Like a diamond of darkness that comes from fog? Super creepy."

He blinked a few times but didn't say a word. So that was what it took to make him blink.

"Um, oh, and I guess I can detect ghosts? I can sort of see shadows where they are. Which is also creepy, but maybe not as creepy as knowing there are ghosts around you can't see. I don't know. I'm of two minds on the subject."

He stood and started pacing. Something I said had vexed him. "Death magic, that makes sense. And Fire? A potent combination. Probably Sound too, given your demonstration in the car. I can't imagine you'd have a fourth aptitude at your age, especially in Light. It's even more unusual for a mage to develop opposed pairings. The leader of the New York magisterium, Janus, is gifted in both Space and Time. And that's why he's the leader of the New York magisterium, because that combo is exceedingly rare and extremely formidable. You only see such someone able to channel such power every few centuries."

I could almost hear him using capital letters as he talked about the kinds of magic.

"What's a magisterium, exactly?"

"A magisterium is ruling body of magi."

"So like, what about life and death? Can you bring someone back from the dead?"

He looked at me sharply. "True resurrection happens very rarely. It's incredibly draining on the magus. Reanimation on the other hand . . ."

I shuddered. "Don't remind me." The memories of the creatures in Ammit's lair were still just a bit too fresh—even if the creatures themselves hadn't been.

He sat back down. "The things you can do, considering you have no training—or no *memory* of training anyway . . . I've never heard that. It usually takes years of practice to manifest flame." He paused, seeming ready to launch into some kind of lecture.

"Question," I said.

"Shoot."

"Did you know that my apartment really *was* haunted?" I said, stabbing my fork into the last slice of bacon.

"Yeah, sorry about that."

"Is that what you do? Go around to weird supernatural situations and tell people to leave and pretend that it will just go away?"

"I didn't know that you were novitiate-ready when I met you."

"Novishi-what?"

"Novitiate. Ready for training. I *did* refer Anubis to the apartment."

"Who's Anubis? Another magus?"

"He was out of town at the time, and by the time he returned, your ghost was gone."

Anubis, Anubis, where did I know the name Anubis—of course! The Egyptian god of the dead—oh, no. What if . . .

"Yeah. What's wrong? You look—"

I coughed, pretending to choke on a sip of tea. If Anubis was Ammit, then it was possible that Zero was working with him. Or maybe that was who he'd been talking to on the phone earlier.

"You talk to him much? Anubis? He can see ghosts and stuff?"

Zero shrugged. "He travels a lot. He's in New Orleans right now." Okay, so probably not Ammit.

Unless he can teleport.

Oh God, what if he can teleport?

"So. How many people can do magic?" I asked.

"How many people are there now? Seven to eight billion?"

"Wait . . . *everyone* can do magic?"

He leaned back and began gesturing with his hands. "Everyone has the *potential* to develop an aptitude in one sphere, sometimes even two. Think of a renowned artist like Van Gogh. He developed his affinity with the sphere of Light and created masterpieces. The same goes for any world-class musician, or athlete, or computer genius, with talents in Sound or Life or Mind. Some who are gifted work in groups to create works of art, like an orchestra or even a visual effects studio."

"But that's not *magic* magic."

"They may be everyday miracles, but they are miracles, nonetheless. There's a reason that they call it 'movie magic', call conductors 'maestro'. Because their creations take you on a journey outside of yourself so that you hear or see or understand exactly what was in their mind, to feel what they felt, to see what they saw. How is that *not* magic?"

It *was* pretty magical when I thought about it.

He continued, "Then you get people with minor powers or influence, like psychics or witches. And while an entire coven of witches is a bag of rabid weasels you don't want to mess with—the *scope* of their power is still limited: clairvoyance, curses, enchantments."

"How is that different from a magus?"

"The difference is that over time, a single magus will develop mastery in multiple spheres on a much grander scale: from transformation and creation to command over the fabric of reality itself."

"So maguses are basically superheroes is what you're saying?"

"Magi. *Mage* or *magus* singular, *magi* plural."

"How many *magi* are there?"

"Total? In the world? Thousands, I'd guess. The New York magisterium has twenty-eight members. It's one of the larger ones."

"Are there magisteriums in every city?"

"Most of the major ones. And Boston."

I drank the last of my tea. It was cold. "Do you mind if I take a quick shower?"

"Be Rowan's guest."

"Huh?"

"It's not my apartment." Still with the straight face.

So weird. I grabbed the duffel bag and went into the Pepto-pink bathroom and shut the door.

Ten minutes later, I was clean, damp-haired, and wearing my own clothes. I folded Roland's pajamas neatly to bring back to the bedroom.

In the kitchen, Zero was doodling geometric shapes on a small wire-bound notepad. The dishes had been washed and were on a drainboard next to the sink.

"Feel better?" he asked.

Feel better?

"Yes. Much." I went into the bedroom with Rowan's folded pajamas and the duffel.

I pushed the curtain aside and checked. No fire escape outside the bedroom window. What little piece of sky I could see between buildings was gray and overcast.

"Thinking of going somewhere?"

Thinking of going somewhere?

Why was he asking me that? Did he think I was planning on jumping out? I wasn't. Not really. He stood in the doorway, on the other side of the unmade bed, still doodling away on his notepad.

"Yeah, I don't know. Seeing what kind of a day it is. What day is it, by the way? Oh, and thank you for my stuff. What did you tell Julie? What did she say?"

"It's Thursday," he said in much the same tone as he'd used while we talked over breakfast. But then his voice changed when he spoke next. "I told Miss Moon that I wasn't at liberty to discuss details in an ongoing investigation, then assured her you were fine." His voice was stiffer, somehow. More monotone. It was his official voice again.

Thursday. Thursday? "Wait, what is the date today?"

"It's November 2nd."

I'd missed weeks of my life. Weeks. Being kidnapped, arrested, in a coma apparently. I realized how lucky I was to be alive.

I'd been staring at the unmade bed long enough that it was starting to bug me. I picked up a sheet corner and began straightening.

"How do you do that, by the way?" I asked.

"Do what?"

"I don't know, like, be all 'official investigation' stiff policeman one minute and then you're just a guy talking about stuff over pancakes the next? It's like you're two different people."

"Ah, I just compartmentalize. Everyone does that."

"They do?" I walked around the bed to the other side and pulled the sheet straight.

"Are you the same at work as you are with your roommate?"

"Pretty much, yeah," I said as I fluffed the pillows.

"I suppose it's different in retail," he said.

"I guess I swear less? Mac doesn't like us swearing in the store." I pulled the blanket up over the sheets and smoothed it out.

"Yes, it's kind of like that. You isolate the swearing version of yourself so you don't get in trouble. But once in a while you might . . . lose control, right? Get a papercut or something and drop an f-bomb or two."

"Probably." The blanket was uneven, too long on one side, so I tried straightening it more equally.

"Besides what happened in my car, have you ever lost control of your magic?" He was doodling again.

Have you ever lost control of your magic?

What was this echo I was hearing? "Uh, no, I don't think so." I stood back and surveyed the bed. Now it was too long on the other side. I tugged on the blanket just a little and decided it was good enough.

"Never?" Standing in the doorway, doodling. Who does that?

Never?

Is he reading my mind? Magically?

"Well, I guess my hands caught fire when I was about to die because someone was strangling me?"

That seemed to take him aback. He stopped doodling and looked right at me. "Someone tried to strangle you?"

"Yeah. I mean, he did strangle me. He just didn't kill me. I had bruises around my neck for days. Rol—I mean, Rowan didn't tell you?"

"He didn't tell me anything. Time mages are squirrely."

"Do you know when he's going to be back? I didn't even get to finish telling him everything."

"He didn't say."

"Can't you text him?"

"How? He could be in the Middle Ages for all we know."

"Oh."

"Also, he thinks cell phones are intrusive."

"Well, they are."

He shrugged noncommittedly.

I put my hands on my hips. "So now what? If Rowan isn't coming back soon, I should probably get going."

"Get going where?" he asked, carefully drawing something on his notepad.

"I'd like to check in with work. You know, see if I still have a job." I bent over Julie's burgundy duffel and zipped it up.

"What are you going to tell them?"

"Uh, that I was arrested?" I picked up the duffel bag and slung it over my shoulder.

"What for?"

"Huh?"

"They'll ask."

"Oh, for jumping the turnstile."

"We don't arrest people for that."

"Tell that to Officer What's-His-Name in Queens."

"He didn't arrest you. He *detained* you for not having ID."

"What's the difference?"

"A shitload of paperwork," he said.

I'd been *detained* in that precinct for hours. Until hell broke loose. "What happened with the monster? I forgot to ask."

"The minotaur? One of our teams captured it. It's been put on ice for the time being."

"Literally?"

"Literally."

"And what about that officer? Did he make it? What about all the witnesses? Like, what happens when something crazy and magical happens in public? Why don't more people know about it? Do you erase their memories like they do in . . . what's that movie? With the blinky thingy?"

"Good questions. You want to come sit in the living room? It's a little more comfortable in there."

I shrugged. "Sure." It wasn't like another ten minutes or however long it would take him to explain would make a big difference.

I followed him down the other end of the hall to a small living room with built-in bookcases on one side with a fireplace and mantle on the other. The centerpiece of the room was a tall wing-backed chair next to a round table with an antique wooden radio. It was about two feet tall and arched like a church door with pillars on either side of the front. There was also a loveseat with a swooped back and striped cushions in front of a window. Zero didn't hesitate to sit in the power chair, so I sat on the loveseat, placing the duffel bag on the multicolored rug at my feet.

Zero put his notepad on his knee. "You don't mind if I doodle? Helps me think."

Sure it does. Or helps him eavesdrop on your brain.

"Yeah, no problem."

"So, you wanted to know what happened after."

"Uh huh."

"What do you think happened?"

"Uh . . . I don't know. That's why I'm asking you."

"Well, it was a hell of a distraction."

"A distraction? I mean, sure, I guess. An undead eight-foot-tall mythological creature *could be* pretty distracting."

"Where does such a creature come from, I wonder."

"Didn't Rowan tell you? Oh, right—you said he didn't tell you anything."

"I'm just trying to figure out why."

"Why what?"

Zero drew on his notepad. "Why use a creature like that? To get attention?"

To get attention?

There it was again. The echo.

It's not a bad question. Why use the minotaur?

"I really don't know why. It seemed like several people got hurt."

"Did you want them to get hurt?"

Did you want them to get hurt?

Oh, no. He thinks—

"Wait, you think *I* did this?"

He shrugged. "It's not like there's anyone else, aside from Anubis, who is not only out of town, but also knows better."

"Sure there is! A creepy old magus dude named Ammit."

He rolled his eyes. "Uh huh. A creepy old magus dude *we've never heard of* who starts making undead creatures all of a sudden, who gets involved with a young runaway who claims to have amnesia. Why don't you just admit that you made that thing so that we can help you figure out how to control your magic?"

"You think I made the minotaur? That I set it on myself?"

"Could be. An accident, right?"

An accident, right?

"Get out of my head," I snapped.

His head jerked up as he looked at me in shock. "What? How did—?"

I held up a hand. "Don't bother denying it. I could *hear* you."

He was very still. His head didn't move. He didn't draw anything. He just looked at me like he didn't like what he saw.

Fuck it. "I'm going. I'll find Rowan later." I picked up the duffel and stood, slinging it over my shoulder.

I was partway out the living room entry when he said, "It's safer here. Stay."

Stay.

For a second I thought I should stay, and then I realized what was happening. "I said get out of my head!"

I suddenly found myself physically unable to move forward. My body could still move; I could breathe, move my arms, pick up my feet, but I made no progress toward the exit.

He'd drawn a sigil of some sort on the notepad and he looked very, very tense. Very still. Was that what was keeping me here?

"You know what? I *do* mind your doodling," I said.

"That's too bad," he said.

"It is." I wanted to punch him right in his smug face but, while I could still move all of my limbs, I couldn't get closer to him. It was like I was inside an invisible box.

I stared at the piece of paper, willing it to burn. Nothing happened.

"What's with you? I thought you were here to help me," I said.

"This is for your own good. I can't let you leave."

"Why not?" *Burn. C'mon, burn!* I thought at the paper. Still nothing.

Maybe I needed to be closer. But he was doing magic from across the room.

If he could do it, so could I.

"Because you're dangerous," he said.

"If I'm dangerous, maybe you shouldn't antagonize me." I remembered how I'd gotten my finger to produce a flame in the dark cemetery tunnel. I'd thought through the sensation of my fingers catching fire before. But now I didn't want my finger to ignite. I wanted the paper across the room on fire. "Did you make this invisible box? How long do you plan to keep me in here? What are you going to do with me?" I asked. "Do your cop colleagues know you like to *detain* young girls in your spare time?"

Zero just shook his head at me.

I remembered Julie lighting a candle in our apartment, using a book of matches. I pictured a book of matches, how a match snaps against the strike pad on the book and ignites. So I thought of the page as a strike pad and snapped my fingers. The snap was off. It barely made a noise. I tried again. This time the snap was slightly better.

I felt a spark, a jolt, in my fingers, but nothing happened. I needed something. Some emotion to set it off. Maybe if I poked the bear . . .

"Is this a sex thing?" I asked. "Kinky Kidnappers 'R' Us?"

Zero looked at me wearily. "For fuck's sake, you're just a kid," he said.

Just a kid, huh? That was what did it. I snapped again and the paper ignited.

Zero's eyes went wide as he yelped and dropped the notebook, then began stomping it out on the rug.

Suddenly I could move again. The invisible box was gone. I ran down the hallway to the front door, unlocked it, and fled.

Chapter Eleven

The outside air was much colder than I'd expected and it was raining. I wished I'd thought to look for my coat before I'd left.

The sidewalk was busy with foot traffic and people carrying umbrellas, which made navigating a bit tricky. I didn't want to run down the sidewalk like a crazy person, but I *really* wanted to run down the sidewalk like a crazy person. *A magus is after me!* I would yell, and people would give me a wide berth.

Or maybe not. This was New York City after all.

I got to a street corner. I knew this intersection. I was near 13 Books and Chris Street Comics. When I'd last checked, 13 Books was closed. If I went to Chris Street, there was nothing keeping Zero the Mage Cop from finding me there. Same with my apartment.

So what was the point of running if there was nowhere to run to?

I didn't know. I just didn't like being kept. Too many shades of Ammit.

The rain began to fall harder. I held the duffel bag over my head and ran across the street to stand beneath an awning, where I was 80% protected from the pelting drops.

I had nowhere to go.

I wished I could call someone, anyone who would believe me.

Zoe? Kip? But their numbers were in my phone, and my phone was in my backpack, which I presumed was somewhere in Ammit's lair. In Queens.

No, there wasn't any way I could get in touch with Zoe easily. I guessed I could go to a library and use their computers to send an email, but how long would that take? And for her to come from her place into Manhattan . . . and in the meantime, I'd what? Loiter at the library? I didn't think the librarians would be cool with that.

Kip though . . . I could go to Central Park. A sixty-block walk from here. In the rain.

I shivered, wrapping my arms around myself.

The shop door opened and a snooty-looking lady dressed in all black looked at me like I was a cockroach on a coffee cake. "You can't stand here," she said.

"It's raining," I said.

"You want me to call the cops?"

"For what, just standing here?"

She made a face like she'd just tasted something disgusting and pulled a phone out of her pocket. "Have it your way," she said. She held one finger over the touchscreen and frowned at me.

"Fine, fine! I'm going. Have a *nice* day," I said, heading back into the rain.

I walked to the corner with the suede duffel bag on my head and I realized I'd probably just ruined it. I'd have to buy Julie a new one.

On the corner, a broken umbrella protruded from a trash can. One of the spokes was broken but the rest of it worked okay. It was wonky on the one side but it was better than nothing.

After walking with it for several blocks I realized that, while it was better than nothing, it wasn't *much* better. My jeans and my sneakers were soaked. So was one of my shoulders and sleeves, and I was freezing. It reminded me of the time that Kip and I had gotten caught in the rain and we'd gone to his friend's apartment. Dave's.

Wait a minute . . . where was that place?

On the corner of 7th and 20th, wasn't it? That was only ten blocks away.

Granted, Kip and I *had* broken up, but he had told me that Dave was out of the country until December, and I knew where the spare key was hidden. I could change clothes and wait out the rain there.

I picked up my pace with renewed purpose.

Just then I felt a weird jolt of energy in my right arm, a spiky sensation somewhere between pain and an electric current. If it had been my left arm and I was prone to eating cheeseburgers, I'd have worried I was having a heart attack. But this feeling was familiar. It was reminiscent of the tingles I'd experienced in Ammit's lab and at the precinct.

I scanned the block, but there was no cemetery. There was a sketchy-looking homeless guy with a shopping cart beneath a construction overhang across the street, but he seemed to be busy picking through his stuff. He wore a clear trash bag over his clothes like a poncho. Smart.

The spiky feeling came again and I looked over my shoulder.

Umbrellas. Lots of people holding umbrellas.

The feeling faded. I continued on.

At the next corner, a taxi drove through a huge puddle just in time to shower me with a wave of dirty street water. I cried out in disgust. What parts of me had been protected by the wonky umbrella were now sodden. Just me, though. All of the other pedestrians had been savvy enough to stand a few feet back.

I had already regretted my decision to leave the warmth of Rowan's apartment and now felt even more stupid. I wondered who Zero was talking to on his cell phone that morning. I wondered who he was talking to now and what he was saying about me. Why hadn't he come after me? Because I was dangerous? Could he be working with Ammit? Was it really possible that Ammit and Anubis were the same person?

I felt bad about destroying more of Zero's stuff. But he shouldn't have used magic on me. I didn't like it.

I didn't like rain much either. Though the time that Kip and I had ended up kissing in the rain and we'd ended up at Dave's . . . that had been my first sexual encounter. Well, that I remembered.

I felt my cheeks go warm as I remembered being in bed with Kip. Too bad he'd proven himself to be completely unreliable immediately afterward.

Granted, someone was trying to kill him at the time, but still. You don't sleep with a girl for the first time and then not call her for six days. Or maybe my priorities are a little messed up, I don't know. *Ow.*

This time the nagging spiky feeling tugged at my left elbow. Someone, or something, was following me.

I looked over my left shoulder and caught a glimpse of a too-pale face beneath a black umbrella. The sight settled in my stomach like a stone fist. Shit, shit, shit. *Merde, merde, merde.*

What was I going to do? What or who was it? Was it a zombie? Another golem? What the hell was Ammit's problem? Why did he want me so badly?

Couldn't he find another blond girl to kidnap?

I crossed the street and wondered if I should double back. I didn't want to lead whoever (or whatever) it was to Dave's. I'd have to lose them. But how? And how were they tracking me?

I could catch a taxi, but I had no money. And none were available anyway. Of the numbers and letters on the roof of every cab I could see, not a single one was lit. Julie always said the second the first raindrop fell, you could count the number of available yellow cabs on one hand. One minute later, she said, there'd be none. She wasn't wrong.

What was I going to do? I was at the corner of 13th and 7th. Only seven blocks from Dave's. On the corner, there was a church with a construction scaffolding out front. There were subway stairs next to it, but they were exit-only.

But where there was a subway exit, there'd be an entrance nearby. I knew that 14th Street was a major hub for most of the lines. On 7th Ave, that'd be the 1, 2, and 3.

I glanced behind me but couldn't tell one umbrella from another. There was a yellow one being held by a girl in a blue slicker, and a blue-sky-with-clouds umbrella in someone else's hand, but the majority of them were black.

One block later, my eyes were thankful to see the green painted ironwork outside the subway stairs. I quickly tromped down into the station, closing my pathetic excuse for an umbrella on the way.

Now what?

I moved against the wall with a pillar blocking me from view on the stairs and waited, watching.

CHAPTER TWELVE

THE STATION WAS CROWDED WITH PEOPLE WHO didn't want to be outside in the cold rain. It was damp, the air weirdly somewhere between clammy and steamy. I didn't see whatever it was that had been following me. Maybe I'd imagined it? But there was that feeling I'd had, and I was learning to trust my feelings.

Some fifty feet away, at the turnstiles for the downtown trains, a gaunt man in a baseball cap repeated variations on the same question over and over to every person exiting the turnstile. "Anybody got a swipe?" "You got a swipe?" "Hey, swipe me?" Finally, an exiting guy in a leather jacket pulled out his MetroCard, and swiped it for the skinny guy.

"Thanks, man."

"You bet."

That's about as friendly at New York gets.

I'd read an article in the *Metro AM* newspaper about how while *selling* swipes was illegal, it was legal to give them away. You just had to wait like fifteen or twenty minutes after the card was last swiped, which was probably the minimum time of most commutes.

The train status countdown clock indicated the next uptown train would be arriving in four minutes. The next one two minutes after that.

What did I have to lose?

"Excuse me, anyone have a swipe?" I asked as commuters pushed through the turnstiles, hurrying through the puddles, readying their umbrellas as they climbed the stairs. "Do you have a swipe?" "Anyone have a swipe?" Most people averted their eyes and brushed past me. One man looked at me like I'd insulted him personally, and a middle-aged lady made a sad face at me before she pushed past.

There was a lag in people until the next train showed up. "Can anyone give me a swipe?" More people avoided looking at me. As their numbers dwindled, I thought I'd have to wait for the next train.

"Here," said a kid. I say a kid, but he was probably only a couple of years younger than me. Maybe fourteen. Wearing a guitar-shaped backpack. He was on my side of the turnstiles.

"Thank you so much! But don't you need it?" I asked.

"Nah, just got off the downtown train." He pulled the yellow plastic card from a pocket and slid it through the reader. "Good luck," he said.

"You too."

The next uptown local train would arrive in three minutes.

I felt a little silly, knowing I was just going to take the train for four blocks, but getting a respite from the onslaught of sky-water felt very necessary.

I was soaked through and my shirt and jeans stuck to me uncomfortably

While I waited on the platform, I tried to remember where Kip had dried our clothes when we'd been at Dave's. A laundry room . . . in the basement of the building? Well, at least I had another set in Julie's duffel, if it hadn't sprung a leak.

I checked. It hadn't.

The train pulled in. I almost got a seat but a woman closer to it sat down before I could get there. I grabbed onto the overhead bar and hung on.

Four blocks later, I was exiting the station. I emerged in front of a dingy pub and oriented myself. I was just a block away from my destination. I brandished my sad umbrella and wasn't terribly surprised when a gust of wind turned it inside out, whipping it out of my hand and blowing it down the sidewalk like an urban tumbleweed.

As if on cue, the rain came down even harder. I put the duffel over my head and ran the rest of the way, feeling relieved as I entered the revolving brass door to the lobby.

Here was the tricky part. What would I say to the security guard? Kip had just told him his name and the apartment number and the guy had told him to go up after checking a clipboard.

A balding man with glasses wearing a blue suit jacket sat behind the desk, thumb-scrolling through his phone. His name tag read PETROV.

"Hi, uh, Jack Donovan?" I said. "6C?" Jack was Kip's middle name, the one that most of his fey friends seemed to know him by, though he went by both. He'd said it to the doorman the last time we were here.

"Go 'head," Petrov said in a thick Russian accent, barely glancing at me.

The brass doors of the elevator were shiny and I turned around inside and watched the doors close. They were mirrored on the inside and I discovered that I looked like a shipwreck victim. My lips were almost blue. I was pale and bedraggled, my sodden clothes pasted to me, my wet hair tangled and sticking to my face.

Ding went the elevator, signifying the first floor. I remembered Kip and I making out and giggling while in it the last time. *Ding* for the second floor and so on. The ride to the sixth floor seemed much longer this time.

Finally, the car jerked to a stop and the doors opened. Apartment 6C was a few doors down. I reached above the jamb and found the metal box that contained Dave's spare key.

I wondered briefly if I should knock, but then I remembered Kip telling me that Dave was out of town for six months.

I shrugged and let myself in.

Ugh! I set down the duffel in the foyer. It was so good to be indoors, I thought, and immediately began tugging off my wet shirt as I made my way down the hall.

It came off my shoulders with a squelching noise. I pulled it up over my face and made my way into the sunken living room, where I was about to pull it off entirely when I heard a sigh.

It was a breathy sigh. A sexual sigh.

A *female* sigh.

And then I heard a male groan.

A familiar male groan.

Even in the dim lighting, I could see the bed from the living room and the two nude figures engaged in sexual congress. One was Kip. The other, a lithe, beautiful girl with fair skin and long turquoise hair, had her eyes closed. She was on top.

"Oh my God," I said. Or maybe I gasped, and then said it. Or maybe I didn't say anything. I made a noise of some sort, that's for sure.

Her eyes popped open. She didn't seem upset or embarrassed at all. Just curious.

"Oh! Who are you?" she asked.

"Huh? What?!" came Kip's voice from beneath her and there was a confusion of sounds and movement. I turned and fled, pulling my soaked shirt back on as I blindly ran out the door to the elevator. It hadn't left the floor yet, so it *dinged* immediately. I got on and hit the ground floor button several times, tears blurring my vision.

Wow, Kip sure hadn't wasted time getting over me, had he? I thought, as I struggled with the sleeves of my shirt, which were wet and tangled, knotted and half inside-out. God, what an idiot I had been. I'd been lost in a stupid reverie, remembering being with him, kind of missing him, and . . . wow. Just wow. That hurt. A lot.

I got my shirt on just as the elevator touched down on the ground floor.

I stumbled out past the desk through the lobby and out through the revolving doors back into the rain. The hot tears coming from my eyes and the burning feeling in my chest created an odd counterpoint to the cold rain.

I could barely see where I was going.

Stupid. Stupid! I had walked in on my ex sleeping with someone else. And we'd been broken up, what, two weeks or something? God. Men.

Not knowing what else to do with myself in the pouring rain, I went back down the stairs to the 18th Street subway station to think, only to find a gate barring my way at the end of the passage. The stairs were exit-only.

I turned back and found the stairs blocked by a figure in a trench coat.

I rubbed my eyes and my elbow went cold with spiky pain when I pointed it at the stranger like a dowsing rod.

He didn't look like a zombie, but there was something wrong with him, something off—and I could feel it.

Beneath the trench coat I could see a white collar and striped tie. "Uh, it's exit-only," I said, for some reason. Like I was trying to tell myself that there was not anything wrong with the guy and that maybe he like me had made a mistake in coming down here. Just a normal guy.

Riiiiight.

Except he didn't talk.

He just stood there. Blocking my way.

The sounds of cars splashing through puddles, brakes chirping, engines revving, a blaring horn all came from the street above.

"Excuse me," I said.

He took a step toward me.

"Um, back off, buddy."

Another step.

The passageway was too tight; there was no way for me to get around him.

Another ominous step in my direction.

I thought quickly. I needed to make fire in my hands. I tried to remember the hot feeling. The tingle in my fingertips.

I could do this. I had just done it that morning to Zero.

I could do it again, couldn't I?

But nothing was happening. No heat.

No flames. No tingle.

Trench-coat Man was five feet away.

Another step.

His eyes were yellow and he smelled of . . . garbage. Spoiled garbage. My gorge rose.

I pushed my back against the security gate.

C'mon fingers. Fire! Please? Please!

Nothing happened.

He reached for me with a gloved hand, closing the gap between us.

All I could think was that I didn't want him to touch me.

My flight reaction had kicked in but there was nowhere to go.

Where was my fight reaction? What was wrong with me?

He was too close.

And then . . .

. . . he wasn't. A flash of movement, faster than my eyes could follow, and the figure was flat out on the ground, a second figure standing over him, holding something in both hands. This figure wore combat boots, black cargo pants, and a black leather jacket with three orange stripes on the sleeves around the biceps. He was pale, with long dark hair and a large, beak-like nose.

"Billy?" I squeaked in disbelief.

Chapter Thirteen

"Billy?" I squeaked again. "Is it really you?"

That was when I noticed the head.

The head he held in his hands.

Trench-coat Man's head.

I think I screamed, or laughed, or cried. Possibly all three. I went a little hysterical for a bit.

My eyes were wide with horror and disbelief.

"Hey Maddy," came the voice I knew so well.

That snapped me out of it. Now all I felt was anger.

"*Hey*? You say *hey* to me after disappearing for half a year and not returning any of my phone calls? *Hey*? What the fuck. What the fucking fuck?"

"To be fair, you never left a message until like a week ago."

"To be fair? To be *fair*? The last time I saw *you*, you jumped off the goddamn Empire State Building. Where have you been? How did you do . . . *that*?" I gestured at the corpse.

The last time I'd seen Michael Adderly, I'd asked about Billy. "He's fine," was all Michael would say. "Alive?" I'd asked. "I said he's fine," Michael had said.

He hadn't answered my question. Just distracted me.

Who could be fine after jumping from such a height?

Who could rip a head from a body without breaking a sweat?

And then I just knew.

"You're a *vampire*?"

I supposed a limited definition of "fine" applied.

"Can't talk about it," he said through gritted teeth. "Why the hell was this thing following you? That head was way easy to take off." Then he tossed the head on top of the body.

"What do you mean you can't talk about it?"

He gave me a look of distaste. "Jesus, Mads, stop asking questions." He surveyed the body on the ground and shook his head.

The sound of the traffic and trickling water made everything seem especially loud, and then the passageway lightened, as though the sun had come out upstairs.

"Fuck me running," Billy said. "You mind?" He gestured that he intended to go around me. His eyes seemed very dark in the dim lighting. Were they fully black? Michael Adderly's eyes had changed to full black on one of our prior encounters.

"It's exit-only," I said stupidly.

"Yeah, about that," Billy sneered, pushing past me and grabbing ahold of the exit gate. He gave it a hard quarter-pivot. *Kachunk*. Some part of the mechanism broke and the door swung loose.

I just stared. I noticed my mouth was hanging open and closed it.

"I gotta split," he said. "But I have to give you this first." He pulled out a dark blue business card embossed with silver numbers and handed it to me. He seemed tired somehow. Weary.

"Wait, you can't just show up and go away again and leave me your phone number!" I said. "I don't even have a phone right now!" While I wrung my hands at him, he made his way to the corpse and hoisted it by the back of its collar, dragging it over to the exit gate and pulling it through with some effort. A trail of sawdust was left behind.

"It's not my number. It's *his*. You know who I mean."

"Why are you being like this?"

"Why don't you call your ex-boyfriend and ask him."

"Kip?"

Billy rolled his eyes so hard I could almost hear it.

Fast and light footsteps entered the passageway and before I could whisper a word to Billy, Kip—as if I had summoned him—came into view. His dark hair was mussed but at least he was dressed. Even though he'd clearly just thrown on dark jeans and a dark sweater, he still looked amazing. The bastard.

"There you are!" he said on seeing me. Then his green eyes shifted to Billy. "Okay, so you really weren't making up a vampire ex-boyfriend just to scare me off."

Right. Vampire ex-boyfriend. Billy had meant Michael. I was feeling particularly slow, but I hadn't exactly just had the best day.

Billy inhaled deeply through his nose and let out a shaky sigh. "What . . . *are* you?" he asked, staring at Kip. His lips were parted and I could see small fangs extended in his smile. He looked like he'd just smelled the best apple pie ever. "You smell like cotton candy."

"I'm fey," Kip said lightly. There was something in his tone. Was he flirting with Billy?

"He's not my ex-boyfriend," I said to Kip, referring to Billy.

"Coulda fooled me," Billy said, thinking I was referring to Kip, or possibly to Michael. It was all very confusing.

The quality of light outside changed as a beam of sunlight illuminated the passage. Billy moved quickly through the barred gate, dragging the corpse with him.

"Oy, careful with that thing," Kip called. "There's some magic in its hand."

Billy paused at the top of the steps that led to the subway platform. "Magic? I'm not supposed to fuck with magic."

"Here, let me," Kip said. He pulled out a handkerchief and used it to grasp the small item from Trench-coat Man's gloved hand.

Billy seemed to be having an odd reaction to Kip's proximity: breathing very shallowly, some contained tension in his posture. With an effort, he turned once again to leave.

I clutched at his sleeve. "Don't go! Tell me what happened to you."

"Call the number on the card," Billy said, shrugging off my touch.

"Billy, no. I am not going to just let you—"

"Look, Mads, I appreciate your concern and all but there's sunlight and—" His mouth tightened into a pucker. His jaws worked but his mouth wouldn't open. He shook his head angrily, finally letting out a frustrated scream. "Arghhhh! See? I can't fucking talk about it, *okay*?"

I heard the sound of the body *thump-thumping* down the steps into the subway, and then he and it were gone.

"Madison." Kip said. "I'm sor—"

"Save it, *Kipling*," I said. Maybe if I used his full first name, I could stay angry at him. I mean, what did I expect was going to happen? Kip would moon around Manhattan sighing and spray-painting my name on billboards?

"Why are ye here? Why did ye come?" he asked.

"Just . . . why don't you go back to your . . . your whoever she was? I obviously didn't mean to interrupt you."

"Why haven't ye returned any of my texts?" he asked.

"Because I—" What was I going to say? I was kidnapped? Lost my phone? Was in a coma? *Ugh.* I suddenly felt incredibly weary. "Why do you care?"

He looked a little hurt when I asked that. "Because I care about ye, ye daft woman. And right now, ye look like ye need a haven, and I've got one upstairs. So come on then, eh?"

CHAPTER FOURTEEN

"AND THEN BILLY SHOWED UP AND RIPPED ITS head off," I said, in between sips of the tea Kip had made for me.

I had just finished recounting all that had happened to me in the past week.

It was a good thing that Kip had come after me; I had left Julie's duffel bag in the apartment in my haste to get out. After we'd gone back inside, I'd gone to the bathroom to dry off and change.

The girl with the turquoise hair was gone when we got there, and I didn't ask about her. What was there to say, anyway? Wow, your new girlfriend is gorgeous? Is she human or . . . ?

The sheets on the bed were conspicuously tangled.

I did my best to ignore them.

"So your friend Billy—the one who went missing, right? He's a vampire now?"

"I guess that explains why he went missing."

"Jaysus."

"So I don't know what to do. Ammit must have sent that guy in the trench coat after me, I have no idea how or why Billy showed up, and Zero is probably looking for me too, since I'm so dangerous or whatever."

"And you didn't want to go home since that's where you were taken in the first place."

"And because Zero—Detective Wilson—knows where I live. Yeah."

"Well, first of all, put this on," Kip said, pulling his moonstone amulet off his neck.

"Wait, isn't that what keeps *you* safe? From the high faeries or whatever? I can't take that from you, not after the last time."

The last time Kip had loaned me his necklace, it had been to hide my magical aura from the faeries at the Goblin Market, who wouldn't welcome . . . whatever I was. Unfortunately, the reason that Kip had been wearing the necklace in the first place was to hide his own aura, from the high fey who had once enslaved him. Once he had taken it off, they'd found him.

"Word on the street is, they called off the hounds on me after you closed their portal."

"Good for you. Then why are you still wearing it?"

"Never hurts to have a little insurance, does it?"

"I can't give you anything for it."

"No, just my life. That's all."

"I didn't give you—"

"Ye saved me, fer fuck's sake, Madison. Take the fooking necklace, alright? Jaysus." He scrubbed at his face with one hand and watched me put the amulet on. "Now, it's only at full power through the last crescent of the moon, which is . . . about a week from now. Then it will start losing power. In the meantime, it will hide you from anyone seeking you magically."

"Speaking of magic, what was that thing the Trench-coat Dude had?"

"Oh, this?" he asked, pulling the handkerchief out of his pocket and unwrapping it to show a stone beetle that was a bit larger than a bottle cap. "Can't tell. But I might know someone who can."

At that moment, my stomach gurgled loudly. I hadn't eaten since Zero's cinnamon pancakes and I'd expended a lot of energy since then.

"Come on, let's get you something to eat, yeah? Place downstairs has great pizza."

"Are you paying?" I asked.

"Probably not, but neither are you, and that's a promise." I smiled despite myself, remembering one of the perks of dating Kip. Various charges and checks just seemed to get waived around Kip. Before I'd figured that out, I'd tried paying for a couple of our dates. But something always interfered. I didn't know if it was a fey thing or something particular to him.

He snapped his fingers. "And I know just the place we should go afterward."

"Where?"

He winked a gorgeous green eye.

"Can't reveal all me secrets, can I?"

Chapter Fifteen

THE PIZZA PLACE KIP BROUGHT ME TO WAS TINY. We ate hot slices of cheese pizza at the counter. He entertained me with amusing stories about tourists and I tried not to be charmed by him and failed. It was very annoying. Afterward, he insisted on grabbing us a cab. During the ride he sent and received text messages while I stared out the window at the roadway and other cars.

Off the highway in Long Island City, we passed by two gas stations, then several trash-blown blocks of warehouses and boarded-up businesses. We turned onto a side street, driving past a few scrapyards and auto body shops that seemed to be closing. Then a deserted commercial block, several nondescript buildings with corrugated tin fences. At last Kip asked the cabbie to stop.

It was late afternoon, and the shadows cast by the warehouse we'd pulled up in front of made it seem ominous. The windows were dirty and few. Everything was cold and gray. I got an odd feeling in my stomach. A sense of foreboding.

"Uh, Kip? Are you sure about this place?"

He was paying the cabbie, standing at the driver's side window, using cash. He looked over his shoulder at me, and somehow sounded even more Irish than usual as he said, "I thought you said you were going to carry a nail from now on?"

"Huh?"

He finished paying the cabbie who rolled up the window and pulled away.

"To see through glamours?"

"It was in my coat." Kip had loaned me one of Dave's hoodies.

"Don't worry about it. It's an aversion spell."

"What's a what?"

"An aversion spell. To make people not want to go in. Like the opposite of a glamour."

"Well, I'd say it's doing a great job," I said. "This place gives me the creeps."

"I promise ye safety and no harm from anyone inside."

Up several steps to industrial double doors. Above them was an inscription in three-inch tall lettering. THE COLLECTIVE COLLECTIVE. Beneath that phrase, in smaller lettering: *Cross this threshold and give ye no lie.*

"Um," I said, pointing. "What's that mean?"

"What it says. Don't lie inside."

Great. There had been a rule about lying at the Goblin Market too.

Kip pressed a buzzer. Seconds later, the door swung open and a tall, imposing man in a fedora was revealed inside. "Jack," said the man, nodding at Kip who walked past him into the building. The large, bearded man frowned as he looked me over. "Who's the straight?"

"She saved my life and I owe her a debt," Kip said.

The doorman moved aside and let me walk in, holding his hat over his heart. The interior of the building was just as boring and non-descript as the outside, if less creepy-feeling. There was a small lobby area with black tile and a long hallway with unadorned doors.

Joining Kip, I softly said, "You don't owe me anything."

"A lifedebt is a serious thing among the fey," he said. "C'mon, this way." He strode down the long hallway and I kept up with him. "Not to mention that ye saved my life twice, Madison, if not three times."

"What are you talking about? I smacked a zombie with a serving platter. So what?" My still-damp sneakers squeaked slightly on the tile floor.

"And ye woke . . . Hank, was it? So he stopped trying to kill me, and then you blasted the blazes out of the shadow portal. Ye saved my life, woman. Don't deny it. Do ye have any idea what would've happened to me had I gone through that portal?"

"Uh, nothing good." I was pretty sure of that at least.

"No, nothing good. First, I'd have been tortured. Then shackled and starved. Then probably killed and made an example of, unless I somehow managed to make it seem like I could be useful, which is doubtful. If I had, though, then I'd be a slave for the remainder of my days until I died a most ignominious death."

He stopped in front of a door marked 133. A larger number seven had been stuck next to the standard door plate. He then knocked a series of knocks in a pattern I couldn't quite follow.

The door was opened by a hippy. I say a hippy because I didn't know what else to call him. He wore baggy, multi-colored striped pantaloons, sandals with socks, and a tie-dyed t-shirt. His brown hair was long and scraggly and he had a goatee and other facial hair that indicated he hadn't shaved in a while. He could have been twenty-something or thirty-something. It was hard to tell.

"Hey Lenny," Kip said.

"Jack, my man!" Lenny said, giving Kip an elbow bump and handshake. "Come on in. Introduce me to your friend."

Past Lenny, the area around the door was surrounded by shelves stacked with books that practically went to the 10-foot tall ceiling. The air smelled of musky incense. Beyond the bookshelves, a comfortable den of mismatched couches and chairs on a thick orange rug.

"This is Madison," Kip said as Lenny shut the door behind us.

"That's *her*?" Lenny said, turning and looking at me with surprise. "I thought you'd be older. And less pretty."

I blushed slightly, though I was a little bewildered. "Well, that's honest," I said with a laugh. "Why did . . ." and then it dawned on me.

"Kip—I mean, Jack—he told you about what happened?"

"He didn't have to. Between the hags and the goblinkind all talking about it, you're pretty famous. Among us, I mean."

"Is H here?" Kip asked.

"Yeah, Sketchy's downstairs. I'll let him know you're here. Sit down, have a drink. It may be a few minutes." He left us, going through a door I hadn't noticed.

Kip knelt in front of a mini fridge and began rummaging around in it. "Coke?" he asked. "Apple juice?"

"Coke," I said, taking a seat on a plaid couch. "You know, it's kind of difficult keeping track of all of these names. You're Kip but you're also Jack. Your friend's name starts with H, which is what you call him, but his buddy calls him Sketchy? What's so sketchy about him?"

"His name's Etch-a-Sketch. Not something that begins with H. Or if it is, I don't know it."

"Etch-a-Sketch?" I pictured a small postcard-sized gray screen, framed in red with two stubby round knobs beneath it. "You mean like the drawing game thing?"

"I guess," Kip said, sitting next to me and handing me a cold can. "Oh, and they aren't buddies. They're a couple."

I popped the top and took a swig. "Okay."

"You know, just in case you had your eye on Lenny there."

"Uh, he's not really my type. And now that I know he has a boyfriend, I'm really not *his* type."

"Satyrs aren't that picky," he said.

"He's a satyr?"

"Oh, yeah. And you know what they say about satyrs. They've got huuuge—"

The door opened and Lenny bounced back into the room. "Sketchy's cool, come on down."

We both got up to follow him through the doorway. I could see stairs going down and Lenny had already descended a couple of steps.

I whispered to Kip, "So satyrs have got huuuge what?"

"Cocks, sweetie," Lenny said from the stairwell. "And great hearing."

I felt my cheeks go hot with embarrassment. "I'm sorry—"

Lenny brayed a laugh. It was loud and nasal, and well, goatish. "Don't be. Please. Jack, sweetheart, tell her not to worry."

Kip was shaking his head and chuckling a bit. "Don't worry, Madison. He's very . . . forthright."

"I'm an oversharer," Lenny said with a grin. "TMI all day, all night. This way." He jerked his head toward the bottom of the stairs.

Kip walked confidently down the steps but after one of my feet almost slipped off a step, I held onto the handrail. There was something untrustworthy about stairs, I decided.

Lenny had already disappeared through the doorway at the bottom. After reaching the doorway, Kip and I emerged into a hallway that was painted dark blue. There was a series of small track lights on the ceiling in an S-shape, each burning dimly with a yellow-tinged light. A door in the right wall was open, and from it came sounds of electronic music: synthesizers, drum machines, a catchy and light melody over a rhythmic thumping.

From the hall, the room seemed dark but also lit with a flickering white-blue light. I gave Kip a look of doubt and he nodded pleasantly at me before ushering me into the room.

For a second, I was reminded of a sports bar I'd once walked into by accident. It was the bank of TV screens mounted on the wall directly opposite the doorway. Large flat screens and desktop monitors from floor to about eight feet off the ground, covering an entire ten-to-twelve-foot section of wall. But what was playing on these screens was not several different sports channels like the bar, but instead a grab-bag of retro television, cable news stations, and a music channel. All were muted except the music channel. *KAITO – Trust*, it proclaimed.

The room opened up to the left. At a desk in three-quarter profile to us sat a guy with dark hair, a beard, and squarish glasses with thick black frames. Three monitors were on the desk in front of him. He was typing. Fast.

Along the rest of the right wall was a long table with printers, scanners, maybe a fax machine? Farther down, I could see a camera, a laptop, and a tablet. Plenty of gadgets. A black leather couch took up most of the wall on the left. In front of it, on a glass coffee table, sat a red Etch-a-Sketch. The toy was just as I'd pictured.

"Hey, Etch," Kip said.

Etch continued typing like a maniac. His fingers were a blur over the keyboard with a soft tippety-tapping like a troupe of ants wearing dance shoes. The furious typing went on for several seconds. When he stopped, he surveyed the screen from top to bottom, his head scanning back and forth as he read over what he'd typed. I thought I read fast but this guy was the Flash of speedreading. When he got to the bottom, he put one finger over the enter key and hit it dramatically. "Ha! *Fini*," he said, his French accented perfectly. He then spun in his desk chair toward us and interlacing his fingers together, thrust both palms toward us and loudly cracked his knuckles.

A look of recognition came over him as he took in Kip, then curiosity for me.

"Full profile?" he asked, also with a French accent.

"I'm sorry?" I asked.

"Yes, the works," Kip said.

"*Méthode* of payment?"

"I'll owe you three favors of my service."

The braying laugh came again from Lenny. "Oh, to live to see the day that Kipling Jack Donovan would walk in our door and make such an offer! You should make it just two favors of service, though." He turned to me and explained, "Sylvie's a friend." Sylvie, a dryad, was friends with a satyr. This shouldn't have surprised me.

Etch seemed intrigued and nodded. "Terms?"

Kip took a deep breath and let it out slowly. "You tell me."

"Oooh, interesting," cooed Lenny.

Etch nodded. "*Bien.* I have one year to request my favors. If the time pass and I do not ask, my claim on you forfeits. If you do not discharge my two favors within twenty-four hours of the asking, *you* forfeit to me. The package will erase and you will serve me . . . a fortnight. What say you?"

"I say as long as such favors and servitudes cause no harm nor pain by my definition, you have a bargain."

"It is so," Etch nodded solemnly.

"Hot damn. You won't regret this, sugarbritches," Lenny said to Kip. He then picked up a small camera from the gadget table and looked at me expectantly. "Picture time!"

"Um, what?"

"We're going to need pictures of you, silly."

"What for?"

"Come on, my duckling," Lenny said, shooing me out the door. " 'What for.' What do you think? We can just make images of you out of thin air? Well, we could, given the proper incantations, but we're not going to."

I gave Kip a bewildered glance as I allowed Lenny to usher me into the hallway, past a vertical strip of black and white numbers attached to the door frame.

Well, Kip had promised nothing bad would happen to me.

I decided to go with it.

Lenny steered me across the hallway, then turned me by my shoulders so that I was facing the doorway. "Now just stand there." He stepped back to the doorway and touched something on the inside wall. Immediately the track lights brightened. "That's better." He looked at the floor and lined his feet up so that they were just touching the edge of the doorway, then held the camera in front of him. "Okay, shoulders back. Look right here." He pointed at the top of the camera. "Now, say 'Manchego.'"

"Manchego," I said.

Lenny brayed again. *Click*. "Now just smile." *Click*. "Pull your hair behind your ears? Yeah, that's good." *Click*. "And we'll need a resting bitch face. Perfect!" he said as I tried to approximate the face that Julie made on the rare occasions we took the subway together. *Click*. "Just three more. Look up?" I looked up. "Down?" I did that too. "Now over your shoulder, down the hall." *Click*. *Click*. *Click*.

"Birth date?" Etch was asking as I re-entered the room behind Lenny, who was already plugging a computer cable into the camera.

"Oh," Kip said. "I don't know. When is your birthday, Madison?"

I had thought that October 13th was my fake birthday—just the anniversary of the date I'd awakened on Madison Ave. But as I found out, it was also Christina Taylor's birthday, and the same day she had disappeared. "October 13th. Why?"

"Oh, hey! Happy belated birthday," Lenny said cheerily.

Kip's face went through the emotions of surprise, realization, disappointment, and self-recrimination. We'd been dating when my birthday had passed, but that was when he'd disappeared for several days. Sure, he'd had a good explanation (zombie attack), but he'd still missed my birthday, and I hadn't said anything.

From recrimination, Kip's face went to resolve. "How old do you want to be?"

"What do you mean?"

"On your ID, dear heart," Lenny said.

I stood there stupidly for a moment or ten, as the lightbulb finally went on over my head. "You guys are making me a fake ID?"

"Fake? Hardly! We're making you a New York State driver's license, Social Security card, birth certificate, passport, bank account, credit history, and a few other odds and ends. The works." Lenny smiled.

"Whoa, whoa, whoa. Look, I appreciate you trying to do this for me—"

"We're doing it for Jacque, not for you," Etch said, his fingers flying across the keys. "And Sylvie."

"But Kip, I—"

"I told you, a lifedebt is serious business."

"And you saved the life of a dryad. A dryad! Living in New York City. Never thought I'd see that day either. Sketchy, what else do you need from her?" Lenny asked.

"Year of birth, middle name, address, where she wants to have been born."

"How old should we make you?"

"I'm . . . well, I guess I'm eighteen?"

"So? Don't you want to be twenty-one?" Lenny asked. "Legal drinking age?"

"I don't drink," I said.

"What are you going to do with it? Vote?"

"Hey, that shit's important," Etch said in his French accent.

"Fair," Lenny said.

Lenny and Kip both looked at me, waiting.

Etch swung around and looked at me too, his hands hovering over the keyboard. "Year. Of. Birth."

"Oh, God. Okay, if I'm eighteen now then—"

"1999," Etch interrupted. He typed each number with a flourish.

"1999," sang Lenny, bopping his head.

"Middle name?"

Lenny belted out a few more lines of the Prince song.

"Lenobios!" Etch reprimanded.

Lenny blew him a kiss and turned back to me. "Prince didn't die, you know. He became a being of light. My cousin's friend's sister was there when he died."

Etch ignored him. "Middle name?"

"Um. I don't know. Edna?"

"*Ugh, non*," said Etch. "It does not flow. There is no *liaison*. You want a name that will tumble from your lips like . . . dice falling from a cup, not bricks falling down stairs. Hm. *Madison*. What do you think of *Naomi*?"

"Naomi is okay, I guess."

Etch did some more typing.

"David Bowie, too," Lenny said.

"David Bowie what?" I asked.

"Became a being of light. Not George Michael though. He's just dead. So sad." He frowned.

Etch continued to ignore his partner. "Jacque says that your *nom de famille*—your last name?—will be Roberts?"

"Madison Naomi Roberts," I practiced saying. "You're right, that is easier to say."

"Address?"

I told him.

"Email?"

I told him that too.

He quickly typed some more. "Place of birth?"

"New York?"

"What town or *cité* in New York?"

"New York, New York?"

"*Non.* Try again."

I wracked my brain, trying to think of other towns in New York. I had a feeling that Brooklyn would evoke the same response. Ah. "I know. What about Tarrytown, New York?"

He made a non-committal noise and typed it in. "Glasses?"

"Huh?"

"Do you wear glasses or contact lenses?"

"Oh, no."

"Lenobios, *cher*, will you get the signature samples?"

Lenny picked up a clipboard with a pen attached and brought it over to me. There was a blank piece of lined paper over some kind of form. "You should practice it at least ten times. Try different versions. With middle name, middle initial, just first and last. And try to write it really fast the last couple of times."

Madison Naomi Roberts

Madison N. Roberts

Madison Roberts

And so on. "Good," Lenny proclaimed. "Now again on the next page, on the lines and in the little boxes."

I carefully scribbled it another eight times and handed him back the clipboard. Lenny removed the paper and ran it through the scanner/printer, humming the same tune he'd been singing.

Etch continued typing. And typing, sometimes using the mouse for several seconds before typing more.

"Anything else?"

Etch shook his head, engrossed in his task.

Lenny picked up a remote control and pointed it at the bank of TV screens.

Seconds later, David Bowie's "Starman" began playing at the same time a printer began printing across the room.

"Okay, well, that's that." Lenny asked, walking to the printer and picking up a plastic card that had just printed. "Here you go," he said, handing it to me. It was a New York State Driver's License for one Roberts, Madison N., with my picture and address. Birthdate: 10/13/1999. Eyes: Blue. Height: 5'9".

"Oh my God. It looks—this looks official. It looks *real.*" I said. "How did you do this?"

"We can't give away all of our secrets, can we, my dove? Now, will you be wanting to pick up the others here, or shall we have them mailed directly to you?"

"Uh, I guess have them mailed? *Ugh*, I don't know. I mean, the bad guys know where I live so . . ."

"So a pick-up might be better. Of course! Here's our card," Lenny said, handing me a business card that said something about VistaPrint on it.

"VistaPrint?"

"No, no. Not that side. Flip it over."

It read: *The Collective Collective* with the address below it. Beneath that, *Ste. 133.*

"What's today? Thursday? If you come back . . . Monday? We'll have everything for you. Wait, even the passport?" Lenny asked Etch-a-Sketch.

"For a friend of Sylvie?" Etch said. "Yes."

"I just don't understand how you could have access to all of—"

Kip jumped in, cutting me off, "We should get going upstairs and let Etch work."

Etch was obviously engrossed, his eyes roaming across the screen and his fingers soaring over the keyboard.

"Oh-kay," I said, still marveling.

"I'll walk you out," Lenny said. We filed out of the crazy tech room and went upstairs. Back in the room with the orange rug, Lenny sat on a couch. "You're welcome to stay awhile if you need to."

"You are too kind," I said.

I was tempted to stay. But I had other things I needed to take care of.

"Oh, hey, Lenny, have you ever seen something like this?" Kip asked, fishing the handkerchief out of his pocket.

"Oh, hello, that's some magic you've got there, isn't it?" He leaned closer to Kip's hand. "Unwrap it for me, gorgeous?"

Kip unwrapped the kerchief, exposing the stone beetle.

The sound that came out of Lenny was something between a hiss and a gasp. "A scarab. That's so strange. A few magical ones like this turned up in the late 1980s. Then another one showed up last week." He scratched his head.

"You found another one?"

"No—someone else did. It was found at the site of your battle in the Botanic Garden."

"Oh wow," Kip said. "Maybe that's what Jonas was trying to put in my mouth!"

"Yikes," I said. "Can you tell what it's supposed to do? Someone—well, something—was trying to touch me with it."

"If you leave it here with me, I'll do what I can to figure it out. All I can tell right now is that it's a one-and-done. One use and then it'll crumble to pieces. Same as the other one."

"Lovely," I said. "Maybe it was supposed to make me crumble to pieces, too."

"Lenny, do you have a phone Madison can use for a while? Hers was stolen."

"Of course, dear one. I'll be right back."

Lenny galumphed down the stairs.

"Kip, this is really too generous."

"Is it? And when were ye going to tell me that I missed yer birthday entirely? What an arse I am."

"It's no big deal—"

"No big deal. If it hadn't been for you, I'd be a slave or dead by now and you—you say it's no big deal. Just let me do this for you, aye?"

"Fine."

"That's the spirit!" Lenny clomped up the stairs and presented me with a black flip phone, the exact same model that Kip had had when I met him.

"Is this . . . ?" I asked, looking doubtfully at Kip.

"No, no. I had to toss that one."

Lenny said, "It's prepaid. It should have at least four hours of use on it. Also, your Uber should be here in . . ." He tapped his phone screen a few times, then proclaimed, "Two minutes. So get your butts out there! I'll see you Monday." He nodded at me and blew Kip a kiss as we parted at the door.

CHAPTER SIXTEEN

THE UBER TOOK US TO THE MACY'S ON 34TH ST. I'd walked by it plenty of times, but having neither the money nor the desire to shop there, I'd never been inside.

As we stepped through the doors, I was immediately hit by an invisible wall of noxious perfumes—an olfactory kaleidoscope of more scents than anyone should ever have to endure. Vanilla, musk, citrus, jasmine, bergamot, *ugh*. Kip was leading the way past the glass counters of MAC, Elizabeth Arden, Clinique, and others.

"But why?" I didn't understand why Kip kept insisting we needed to stop at Macy's.

"We're stopping by the administrative offices."

"Because?"

"I told you, you'll see."

We took an escalator up. "Where are these offices?" I asked.

"Mezzanine."

"Couldn't we have taken an elevator?"

"And miss all of this charm?" Kip asked.

I hadn't noticed much charm between the mannequins, racks of clothing, glass cases of designer purses and sparkling jewelry. I just wanted to sit down.

In front of, and slightly above us, a woman said to a man, "When I was a little girl, my mom brought me here and we rode wooden escalators. It looks like they're all gone now. How sad."

"There's still one or two left upstairs. They renovated the rest," the man replied.

We reached the top of the escalator and the couple went in another direction.

Wooden escalators. Nice fire hazard. I could just imagine the steps catching fire, transferring it to the next floor, and so on. No wonder they'd renovated them.

And then it dawned on me: I could start a fire like that, if I wasn't careful. I could set a whole department store ablaze if I lost control of my magic, couldn't I?

Jesus. No wonder Zero wanted to lock me up.

We reached the Mezzanine level. "This way," Kip said.

We went past a visitor's center loaded with NYC pamphlets before arriving at the Coat Check room. Two elderly women stood behind the counter, both wearing matching red suit jackets.

"Hello, Annis," Kip said to one of them.

Annis was very short with a dowager's hump and white hair. She gave a girlish giggle and said, "Hello, Handsome Jack. How can we be helping ye today?"

"Always with his hand out, this one," said the other woman, slightly taller than Annis and a little pudgy around the middle. Her hair was dyed dark brown with white at the roots. Both women sounded vaguely British. I wondered what I'd see if I had a nail in my pocket.

"Aw, Nelly, you cut me to the quick," Kip said, clutching his chest.

"Don't listen to her, Jack. Ye've always done right by me," said Annis, smiling at him.

He leaned on the counter and put his hand over hers. "What do you need these days, Annis? What can Jack get you?"

"I could sure use a new pair of slippers," she said. "Against the cold, you know. The ones from L.L. Bean?"

"Done."

"And what can I be getting you?" she asked.

"How's your coat supply these days?"

"For you?"

"No, for my companion."

"Didn't even introduce us," sniffed Nelly.

"I'm sorry, I'm Madison . . . I mean, I'm *called* Madison," I said. The fey cared about names that way. If you weren't giving your actual name, you said so.

Both women perked up. "*The* Madison?" Annis asked.

Kip nodded, grinning.

"Oh, Jenny told us all about you! The revenant, the flesh golem, the platter!" Nelly said.

"Oh, and the magics!" Annis said.

"And the kimchi! Bring us some next time you visit, love."

"I don't understand. Who's Jenny?" I asked.

"Jenny Greenteeth, of course. She was there, wasn't she, love?" Annis asked.

"She was," Kip said. "That was our first meeting." They must have meant the wizened hag who'd witnessed the battle at the Brooklyn Botanical Garden, the one who traveled with cat-sized rats.

"A lucky day for you, my lad," Nelly said, crossing her arms.

"Lucky day indeed. So the young lady needs a coat, does she? Let's see what we have . . ." Annis said, plodding her way towards the back with a duck-footed walk.

"Oh, I don't want to take someone else's coat," I said.

"Fear not, Miss Madison. The cast-offs and left-behinds are donated after three months without claim. We just put a box together yesterday but it hasn't gone," said Nelly.

Annis came waddling forward with something red in her arms. "I think this one is perfect for her." She placed the bundle of material on the counter between us.

I unwrapped the soft red wool revealing a mid-length coat with a cowl neck, a thick belt, large silver buttons on the chest, and a wide hood. "It's beautiful," I said. "But why would someone leave this?"

Nelly shrugged. "Tourists, socialites, celebrities. Irresponsible children, the lot. Try it on, dearie."

"I really, this is so kind of you, but I—"

"*Won't take an offered gift?*" Annis said. Suddenly there seemed to be something dangerous about her.

Beneath that sweet old lady façade, something darker lurked. Something with sharp teeth.

"Now, now, Annis, this isn't a gift. It's a trade. I thought I was to be getting your slippers to keep your feet warm on a cold night," Kip said.

"Did I consent?" she said, still with a dangerous air. How could an elderly woman who was barely five feet tall seem so intimidating? I was reminded of the Baba Yaga, a fey-goddess-hag (no one seemed to know exactly what she was) with unlimited power. Hadn't Kip said she ate people?

Kip held his hands up in surrender. "No, no, you didn't."

"Is the gift binding?" I asked, hoping my terminology was right. I knew that in the Dark Market, and presumably the faerie lands—the Everlands, Kip called them—a gift was never just a gift; it was a binding contract between the giver and receiver.

Kip gave me an approving look.

"I give it freely with just one reserve," she said.

"And that is?"

She leaned towards me. "Take a selfie with me so I can post it on Facebook."

Nelly made a sound of disgust. "You and that Face-pook," she said. "Do you know what it said her stripper name is? 'Black Madeleine.' "

Annis cackled with glee. "Almost changed my name on the spot," she said.

"It didn't work for me," Nelly said, then conspiratorially whispered, "I go commando most days."

"What say you, Madison?" Annis asked.

"Commando Cheeseburger just didn't have a ring to it," Nelly sighed.

Kip raised a finger. "You are . . . being sought. Perhaps you should wear a mask of some kind before you broadcast your photo to the world?"

"A mask okay?" I asked.

Annis nodded eagerly. "Oh, yes, that's capital!"

"Done," I said.

I tried the coat on, buttoning it and pulling the belt through the buckle. It flared at my hips, creating an hourglass shape.

"Like it was made for her, wasn't it, Nelly?"

"Oh, indeed, Annis, indeed!"

I could get used to this, I thought, sitting on soft leather in the backseat of a black SUV, driving down 7th Avenue. Kip had arranged an Uber ride for us once more.

Annis had settled for a digital photo of the two of us, me wearing the red coat with the hood down over my eyes. She had two fingers out in a "peace" sign.

"So you'll sleep at Dave's tonight?" Kip asked.

"Um, I think that's kind of pushing it, don't you?" I'd said. "The sheets?"

"I could change them for you—"

"Just . . . no, Kip."

"What about my place in Crown Heights? No one will look for you there."

"Where will you stay?"

"I can stay at Dave's."

I thought about it. It wasn't like I specifically wanted to hang out with Kip more. But on the other hand, I didn't want to be alone.

The car door opened. I blinked, realizing that I had nodded off.

Kip handed me Julie's duffel bag and stuck his head inside. "Louis! You've got the new address, yeah?" he asked the driver.

"No problem, boss," Louis said.

"Wait, you're not coming with me?" I asked Kip.

"I have some unfinished business to deal with."

"Oh, yeah. I'm sure you do," I said, thinking of the turquoise-haired girl.

"I have an errand to run," he explained. "But I'll be there in . . . an hour or two."

"Sure you will," I said.

"I will. You have my word, that I will do everything in my power to arrive two hours from now."

I checked the time on the flip phone Lenny had given me. "Two hours. Don't be late, Kipling Jack Donovan. Call or text if anything goes wrong, okay?"

He'd already put its number in his contact list and made sure I had his.

"Okay," he said.

I hung my new red coat on the back of one of the chairs at the small kitchen table where I'd set Kip's keys, then came around it and dropped the duffel on the floor in front of the couch.

I dropped onto the couch seconds later. Except for a tiny bathroom, Kip's apartment was just one large room: kitchen, living room, bedroom, all in the same space, with tall ceilings and two tall, ivy bedecked windows. Opposite the couch was an old wood-framed TV roughly the size of a small dresser. Kip had said it didn't work.

I'd been there once before, a lifetime or maybe two, three weeks before? Kip and I had been unable to keep our hands off each other.

I searched around the room for an available outlet where I could plug in my new phone and found one next to the bed.

Also next to the bed was a small bookcase. I found a cloth-bound copy of *Alice in Wonderland* and curled up with it on the couch. Half a page later, I shivered, realizing the room was a bit chilly. I grabbed the quilt off his bed, and returned to the couch, wrapping it around me.

Within a few pages, I—much like Alice—nodded off.

I woke to the sound of a man's voice, yelling, "OPEN UP, YOU BITCH!" Followed by rapid pounding on a door.

Adrenaline raced through my body and I held completely still. Everything was quiet for a second, then the pounding resumed. "JASMINE! LET ME IN!"

I relaxed slightly when I realized the pounding was not at this door, not for me, not the door to Kip's apartment, but somewhere nearby, maybe a floor below.

I wondered if I should call the police. Then I remembered I was probably wanted by the police.

"Go away, Levon!" a woman yelled, presumably Jasmine. "I'm calling the cops!"

Oh, good.

"GO AHEAD!"

"Go away!"

"NO! YOU LET ME IN THERE!"

"I'm calling them!" came the woman's voice.

"FUCKING BITCH!" the man's voice yelled. A different loud noise—maybe he kicked the door? I heard footsteps. What would he do? Would he come up here next?

I wondered about using my . . . what did Zero call it? Aptitude? I could defend myself. *But what if I set the whole building on fire?*

After what sounded like another kick to the door, Levon, perhaps preferring to avoid the police, left. I heard his receding footsteps and a few other choice comments as he departed.

I checked the time. Kip had thirty-two minutes left. I also had a new text message.

On my way. -Kip

Yeah, sure, I sneered. Then I felt like a jerk.

So Kip didn't exactly have a great track record of showing up when he was expected or staying in touch. *He's trying, though. That's gotta be worth something. A benefit of the doubt, maybe?*

I wondered what errand he'd had to run.

More than likely he was "finishing his business" with Turquoise Girl.

I didn't like myself for thinking it.

The knock on the door made me feel like I could have jumped out of my skin and left it behind. As soon as I thought that, I remembered that horrible skinless display body in Ammit's basement and shuddered.

"Madison?" came Kip's voice. "It's me."

I went to the door and opened it. "Hi," I said.

"Are you alright?" he asked as he came in. "You look . . . upset." He closed the door behind him and locked the three deadbolts on the door.

"Some guy was yelling and pounding on your neighbor's door."

"No, was he? I thought Jasmine had him arrested after the last time. I'm sorry you had to hear that."

"Me too," I said in a small voice.

"Hey, now. Hey. I'm here." He held his arms open.

I went to him.

Just the feeling of his arms around me made me feel safer. My shoulders, which I hadn't realized were nearly up to my ears, relaxed. I melted into the hug.

He smelled good. Like shampoo. And like himself. Not quite the cotton candy that Billy had mentioned, but a hint of cloves combined with an intoxicating sharp and sweet scent that was unique to him.

And then, for some inexplicable reason, I started crying.

"It's alright. It's okay. I'm here now." He was speaking softly to me, his face inches from my face. He cupped my cheek and wiped a tear away with his other hand, then pulled me close again. "Come on, let's go sit on the couch, yeah?"

He grabbed a paper towel from the kitchen and sat next to me on the couch, lightly dabbing the tear tracks on my face. "Sorry about the paper towel. I ran out of tissues," he said.

I sniffled.

"That's a bit better now, isn't it? Do ye want to talk about it?"

I sniffled again and swallowed. "No. Not really."

I shivered. The cooler temperature of the room was getting to me again. Kip noticed and wrapped the quilt around my shoulders and then put his arm around me. "We'll just stay like this as long as you like."

I buried my face into his chest and breathed in. When I looked up at him, he was looking down at me and I was staring into those vivid green eyes of his and those full lips and the next thing I knew, we were kissing.

I wasn't thinking about what he had or hadn't done with Turquoise Girl. I wasn't wondering about whether we were getting back together or worrying about what it might mean for the future.

There was only him and me, and the feeling in my chest of something that was hurting, a vacant ache easing, feeling full once more.

And kissing. His mouth nibbling at mine. Mine at his. His hands in my hair, on my waist, my hands on his arms and then under his shirt.

My mouth needed to be on his mouth. Like his lips held a magnetic charge.

Everything was . . . right.

CHAPTER SEVENTEEN

EVERYTHING WAS WRONG.

I opened my eyes and the whole night came back to me. I was in Kip's bed, and he was still asleep. From his fair Irish skin and roguishly tousled dark hair to his full, rose-colored lips and chiseled torso, he looked like he should be in an ad for men's cologne.

And I had slept with him last night.

Oh, of course it had been wonderful and passionate and sensual and pleasurable and all of things that sex with your ex should be. I mean, not that I'd know from personal experience, having no memories of any other exes nor sex with them, but from things my roommate Julie had said, it seemed similar to what she'd described: Fun. Sexy. Hot. And sweet.

But then it was the morning after and I was lying there next to him, watching him sleep, and I didn't feel . . . anything.

Well, I felt a little ashamed of myself. What was wrong with me? *What kind of girl throws herself into the arms of a guy she caught having sex with someone else only hours earlier?* I asked myself. Did I want to be that kind of girl?

I didn't seem to have any feelings of romantic love for Kip. He was more than handsome—he was legitimately beautiful, with his dark lashes resting on the apples of his cheeks. As lovely and unknowable as a statue or painting that you could study for hours, filled with wonder. I did feel an affection for him, a gratitude for his help and kindness. But that was all.

I didn't feel like he was . . . well, mine.

And with a flood of relief, I realized that I didn't want him to be. He was like a jacket in a store that I tried on and decided not to buy.

That sounds unkind, but I didn't mean it to be.

Kip was—would always be—a wild card. A wild child. A creature of the wilderness that should be allowed to do as it preferred.

I didn't want to pin him like a butterfly. He'd always be most beautiful in flight.

He shifted and his eyes slowly opened, and he sighed and stretched like a cat. "Good morning, gorgeous," he said.

We were close in the full-size bed and I suddenly wondered if I had morning breath. "Hey," I replied, closing my mouth quickly.

He yawned. "What time is it?"

"No idea. I'll get my phone." I sat up in the sheets, then felt awkward, realizing I was still nude. Apparently, unlike the ingenues in the scandalous TV shows Julie enjoyed, I had not gotten up in the middle of the night to put my bra and underwear back on.

I leaned over the side of the bed and picked up the flip phone from the bookcase where I'd left it charging. "It's quarter after eight," I told him, sliding back under the sheets once more, wondering just where my shirt had been flung to the night before.

"Want some tea?" he asked, sitting up. In the morning light, I noticed something on his shoulder, a shiny patch of scarred skin about the size of a nickel.

"Tea sounds great. What's that scar on your shoulder? I never noticed it before."

He wiggled out of the sheets and climbed out of the bed, completely unself-conscious about his nudity, and then glanced at the scar. "Oh, that? I usually tell people it's a vaccine scar."

"But it isn't?"

"No, that's where my mistress branded me with her sigil."

"That's a brand?" I asked, horrified.

"No, that's where I cut it out so I could leave her lands." He plucked a pair of plaid boxers out of a drawer on the side of the bed and pulled them on.

I gaped at him. "Oh."

He shrugged. "It's the only way to rid yourself of that kind of magic. You cut it out, like a cancer."

"I'm sorry that happened to you."

"It's over now, thanks to you—"

"Please don't start thanking me again—"

"But you don't understand—"

"I do, I just, it's . . . I'm glad. I am. Really. But you know, look, Kip, I don't think this—"

He sat down on the bed and clasped my hands in his. "I know I have a lot to make up for. And explain. I know I do. Eileen, that's who ye found me with—"

"You don't owe me an expla—"

"She doesn't mean anything to me, alright? It was just sex. It's . . . it's different with you."

"Kip—"

"Look, I'm trying to tell you—"

Oh, God. What's he going to say? "Don't. Just don't." I pulled my hands gently from his. "Last night was . . . a mistake."

His eyes took on a confused expression. "Did I do something wrong? I thought you enjoyed yourself, I mean the sounds you were making—"

I quickly interrupted him. "No, I mean, yes, I enjoyed myself. You didn't do anything wrong. I'm just . . . I need some time to think."

"Oh," he said. "Well, that's alright then." He had an air of disappointment that he also seemed to be trying to hide. "I'll get to making that tea then." He went to the stove and picked up a kettle and began filling it with water at the sink.

While his back was turned, I scooted out of the bed, grabbed the duffel bag, and disappeared inside the bathroom. *Oh, no, that wasn't awkward at all.* I rolled my eyes at myself in the mirror.

Several minutes later, I had brushed my teeth, rinsed my face, combed my hair, and put clothes on. The whole time I was kicking myself for hurting Kip's feelings. But had I? I mean, what had he expected? Well, it seemed he'd expected that everything would be peachy.

I sighed. I couldn't stay in the bathroom forever.

When I came out, he was still in his boxers, making me feel overdressed. He didn't seem to mind. "Tea for thee," he stated, putting a mug on the small table in his kitchenette. I sat and took a sip.

"Earl Grey," I said. "Thank you." He'd already sweetened it and added a bit of milk, just like I liked it.

He sat opposite me with his own mug and looked at me frankly.

"So—" he began, just as I was saying, "I wanted to—"

"You go ahead," I said after an awkward pause.

"No, you."

"I insist." I took a drink of tea. The mug was warm beneath my fingertips.

"*I* insist." He took a drink of tea.

"Kip."

"Madison."

I glared at him and then looked down at the speckled pattern on the light green surface of the table and blew air out of my nose. "Fine. I . . . I don't even remember what I wanted to say. I just don't want you to think that you did something wrong."

"But I did."

"You don't owe me anything—"

"But I do—"

"Will you let me finish?!" I shouted. His eyes widened and he raised one hand palm up in a magnanimous *go-ahead* gesture. "You don't owe me an explanation of your . . . your . . . habits. You are *you*, okay? I get it. You're like this sexual carousel ride for anyone who lays eyes on you. And we were broken up and things happen. I mean, I was surprised, but I wasn't, you know? Like I should have known. What I'm trying to say is, Kip, I don't think you're cut out for monogamy. And I think maybe I am. I have a lot of gratitude for you, for what you've shown me, and made me feel. I do."

"But that's all," he said, flatly.

"But that's all," I echoed.

"What I've always liked about you is your honesty, Madison. Among other attributes, of course."

"I try not to lie in general, if I can avoid it. But my life is so weird . . ."

"Tell me about it."

"What is it with you guys and the whole lying thing? First in the Market and then at the Collective?"

"Between ourselves—the fey—it's considered the utmost insult for one of us to lie to the other. We do deal with other creatures, of course, and goblins are always trying to twist and deceive in some way. True fey cannot lie—at all. Whereas amongst the Wunderkinde, it's our tradition not to lie. At least not to each other."

"But it's okay to lie to other people . . . or creatures?"

He shrugged. "It's best not to make a habit of it, of course."

"Can you tell when someone is lying?"

"Often. Lenny is better at it than I am."

"Why?"

"Practice, I expect. He's a good two hundred years older than I am."

I took that news in, blinking. "Yeah, your life is pretty weird too."

Chapter Eighteen

I arrived at the Brooklyn Library a few minutes before it opened its doors for the day and spent that time studying the golden inlay of mythological figures and symbols that adorned the front entrance.

Kip and I had parted amicably, though he seemed somewhat less vibrant than usual. I felt bad about that but what was I supposed to do? I couldn't make myself feel something for him that I had maybe once felt and lost. Maybe he'd thought he could get it back. But I'd trusted him twice and gotten burned twice and I wasn't going to do it again.

I'd taken the duffel bag with me, as well as the phone. And though Kip insisted I could stay with him another night, he also gave me a MetroCard to use in case I decided to stay somewhere else. The last thing I needed was to trip all over myself falling for him again. That was what I told myself, anyway.

When the library opened, I went to the internet café and checked my email. There were emails from Nidhi, my co-worker from Chris Street Comics, from Zoe, my friend who could see ghosts, and one from my roommate, Julie. Each of them wondering where I'd been and what was going on. Julie also mentioned that rent was due.

I responded to each of them. I let Julie know I was okay and staying with friends and where to look in my room for my rent money. I said I was sorry I couldn't explain more right now, but I would when I could. I asked Nidhi if anyone had been by Chris Street looking for me. I told her not to tell anyone that she had heard from me. I left her my new number and hit send. While I was writing Zoe back, the flip phone began vibrating, so I picked up.

"Hello?"

"Maddy! Where have you been? We've all been worried sick!" came Nidhi's voice, high-pitched and frantic.

"I can't talk here," I said quietly. "Has anyone been looking for me?"

"Yeah, this detective came by and said you were a danger to yourself and others! What the hell is going on?"

"I can't talk here," I repeated. "I'm at a library."

"Can you meet me somewhere?"

"Where?"

At noon, I walked into a coffee shop on Union Square and found Nidhi sitting at a table in the corner. She jumped up and hugged me as soon as I got to her. "Girl, you are a sight for sore eyes!"

"It's good to see you too," I said. A half cup of coffee and a partially eaten croissant sat on the table in front of her.

Nidhi was probably my best work friend since Billy had disappeared. She'd started in the summer and was friendly and inquisitive and funny and we got along immediately. We were a study in contrasts: me tall and blond and lanky, her short and curvy and dark.

"So what happened to you?" she asked as I settled down at the table, draping my new red coat over my chair. "Alien abduction? That's what Trendon had in the pool."

"No, but what happened to me sounds equally insane. But I kind of sort of have proof."

She looked confused but nodded. "Okay . . . what is it?"

"You have an iPhone, right?"

She took out the phone she'd fitted with a panda-eared case. "Yep."

"I want you to look up, inside quotation marks, 'Christina Marie Taylor' and the word *missing*."

"OH MY GOD DID YOU FIND OUT—"

"SHHH!" I said.

"Sorry! Sorry! I just got excited for you!" She quickly typed out the search query and several hits came up.

"Oh my God, that's you," she whispered.

"Click on that one," I said, pointing at the newspaper article I'd read.

She began reading, her eyes flitting across the webpage quickly. "Wait, so they thought you were *dead*? That's nuts!"

"Shh! That's not what's nuts. It's worse than nuts. It's cuckoo-bananas."

"What do you mean?"

"Look at the date."

She scrolled upwards and her brown eyes darted around for a few moments and then widened. Her mouth opened and formed a shape like it might make a word-sound but didn't for several seconds. Then she simply said, "What? That's . . . that's not possible."

"And I slept with Kip again."

"You *WHAT*?"

"SHHHH!"

"Oh my God, we're getting out of here," she said, standing and taking me by the arm.

"Are you going to eat that?" I asked, pointing at the croissant.

"How can I even think about eating at a time like this? You're fifty years old and *you slept with Kip! Again!*"

I grabbed it and let her pull me out the door.

We sat on a bench in Union Square Park, beneath tall trees along the center path. Away from the chanting Hare Krishnas and the tourists playing Pokémon Go, the massage hawkers, and the artists selling their prints, we had relative privacy. Sure, there were lunchbreak employees sitting and walking nearby, listening to earbuds and involved in their phones or conversations, but none of them paid us any mind.

I ate the half croissant right after we sat.

Nidhi stared at me the whole time, her expression softening. "You're really hungry, huh?"

"Kip only had toast and tea."

"So what happened?"

I shook my head. "I have found out that my life is much much crazier than we ever suspected."

"So are you like, a time traveler? From the past?"

"You believe in time travel?"

"Sure. Nicolas Cage is a time traveler."

"Who?"

"The internet said so." She laughed. "I'm sorry, there are just all of these websites out there that make all of these crazy claims about old photos that supposedly show how certain celebrities are time travelers. So, you know, some people seem to believe that stuff. I didn't think I did, but now, I don't know. That was weird! And it wasn't the only article, was it?"

I shook my head. "No, there are several. I've read a few and couldn't do any more."

"Why not?"

"Why not? Because what does it mean if that's me?"

"But it can't be."

"Nidhi, the clothes I was wearing when I was found are the same clothes that Christina Marie Taylor went missing in. My *vintage* jeans, and *vintage* Chuck Taylors, too." A sneaker connoisseur on the subway had once admired them and asked where I'd gotten them. I'd said my aunt's closet.

"So maybe they weren't vintage at all. Because of time travel."

"Right. Except not with a DeLorean."

"Is this some kind of superpower you have? Are you an X-Man?"

"I don't think so. But um, well, it seems to be some kind of . . ." I couldn't even say it.

"Some kind of what?" She stuck her chin out at me. "Come on."

"Don't laugh."

"I won't laugh."

"People who are going to laugh always promise not to laugh."

"I'll try not to, okay? Just tell me!"

"It's . . . magic."

She raised an eyebrow at me. Then she tilted her head a little and squinted at me. "You're serious."

"Yes."

"Do you have a mystical amulet or something? Is that the necklace you're wearing?"

"No, no. It's not like that. It's something else." Just then my phone began buzzing. I opened it. "Hello?"

"WHAT THE HELL IS GOING ON WITH YOU MADISON?" came Zoe's voice loud from the tiny speaker. "I NEEDED YOU! YOU SAID—"

"I was kidnapped!" I said in a stage whisper.

Nidhi gave me a puzzled look.

"—YOU WOULD HELP ME WITH MY NEXT CASE!"

"Zoe!"

"WHY—wait, what?"

"I. Was. Kidnapped," I said between clenched teeth.

"Holy shit! Are you still kidnapped?"

"No, I got better."

"Where are you now?" she asked carefully.

"Union Square Park. Look for the girl in the red coat."

The battered yellow station wagon with wood paneling that Zoe drove pulled up alongside the park, and Nidhi and I climbed in.

"Where to?" I asked, sliding into the passenger seat while Nidhi sat in the back.

Zoe turned to look at Nidhi, who she was meeting for the first time. "You mind going to Queens?"

"I don't," said Nidhi. "I'm along for this ride. Just tell me one thing."

"What?"

"Are you a time traveler too?"

"No. I see ghosts."

Nidhi's eyes opened wider. "You're *all* X-Men."

"Let's go?" I asked, buckling my seatbelt.

"Let's," Zoe said, and pulled out into traffic.

We pulled onto a residential block, where Zoe took three tries before she was happy with her parallel parking job on the street across from her building.

While Zoe had driven, I'd explained how Ammit had kidnapped me, taunted me about stealing my memories, paralyzed me, and how I escaped. I left out the extra creepy details about the butterflies and other living dead creatures because the whole thing was implausible enough as it was. Then again, it was so implausible, maybe she'd *have*

exactly the same in size, dimensions, format, and finish. "This isn't a fake ID. See the hologram? This is *real.* Where did you *get* this?"

"I can't say. I mean, I don't know if I'm allowed, you know?"

"Okay, okay, so skip to the part where you kipped Kip," Nidhi said.

I glared at Nidhi and then Zoe said, "Ohhhh."

"Just joining us?" Nidhi asked in a friendly tone.

"Hey, you got to her first."

"You two mind?" I asked.

A warm feeling of happiness radiated through me as I watched my two friends interacting with one another and getting along. After all the fear and frustration and confusion and angst, this was uncomplicated. Finally.

"Oh my God, it is so good to be around you two right now. You have no idea. No idea!"

"You're kidding. *He* was sad?" Zoe asked.

"Seemed that way," I said.

"Maybe he's just not used to girls *not* falling in love with him," said Nidhi.

"Do you care?" Zoe asked me.

"*I* might," Nidhi said. "You know, if he needs comforting."

"Nidhi!"

"Maddy, you have got to admit he's ridiculously hot."

"You've seen him?" Zoe asked.

"He came into the store," I said.

"I still think he might be a druggie," Nidhi said. "But you know, tweaked or not, that boy *fine*."

"You're an adult," I said. "So's he. Have at him." And it was true. I didn't have an ounce of jealousy over him.

"Meh, we'll see. I don't know how I feel about all the horse stuff."

"Yeah, I thought that was kind of weird too," Zoe said. "Did you end up meeting with um, you know, that *other* guy?" From her intonation, I was pretty sure she meant Michael Adderly. Even though her supernatural contacts said vampires were dangerous, we'd agreed he was the likeliest source for more information about Christina.

"Another guy?" Nidhi's eyebrows raised.

I pursed my lips. "It's complicated . . ."

"Seems like that's your whole life," Nidhi said.

"So?" Zoe asked expectantly.

"I have his card."

"Call him!"

"Who is this guy?" Nidhi asked.

"He's someone I was supposed to meet up with before I got grabbed. Someone, well, dangerous," I said.

"Like a member of a gang or something?"

"Or something, yeah."

"Come on, you can't hold back on me now."

Should I tell her about Michael Adderly and how he'd made Billy a vampire? I wondered.

No. Too dangerous.

Why?

Why? Oh, I don't know. Because you don't really know what you're dealing with?

"I can't," I said. "Let's just say it's safer for you that way."

"Okay, okay. This is all so insane to begin with. I can't even imagine what you aren't telling me."

"Nothing you'd really want to know."

Nidhi glanced at her phone. "Responsibility calls. I've got to get to Chris Street for my shift. Where's the closest subway to here?" she asked.

"Woodside. I'll drive you. It's like two miles," Zoe said. "Coming?" she asked me.

I hugged Nidhi goodbye outside the station. She'd promised she wouldn't tell anyone at Chris Street she'd seen or heard from me and would avoid anyone asking questions about me.

Nidhi began to walk away and then turned back. "You know, you might want to, I don't know, get a wig or a hat or something. You're tall and blond with a red coat. You stand out."

"Good call."

As she ascended the stairs, I saw the subway line was the 7 train, the same line I'd gotten busted trying to sneak onto. "Zoe, are we near . . . uh, Lincoln and 52nd?"

"Yeah, it's the next stop down."

"Is there a cemetery near here?"

"Oh my God, you mean . . . yeah. There is. Calvary. It's huge. You think—?"

"I think, yeah."

"I need to stop by and see my mom at work—we'll drive right by the cemetery."

"Let's do it."

Within minutes, we were driving along Queens Boulevard. We went several blocks and then Zoe directed me to look out the driver's side window. "Over there. Is that it?"

I could see a stone wall and chain link fence and a green lawn. In the distance, there were headstones and crosses. "Well, it's a cemetery. I don't know. They all look alike."

"That's racist," Zoe said.

I guffawed.

The car drove on for several blocks and then pulled over in front of a hardware store. "Score," she said. "There's never parking out front."

I got out and surveyed the area. Something seemed familiar. A hardware store, and next to it, a dentist's office. Then a bodega and a hotel. I remembered this. I had been there . . . God, how many days before had it been?

"You okay, Maddy?" Zoe asked while she fed the parking kiosk a few quarters.

"Yeah. Yeah. I think this is where I was. When I came out." I looked around uneasily and pulled my hood up, thinking of Nidhi's comment about how I stood out.

She put the parking receipt on her dashboard and locked the doors and we went into the store.

It smelled of dirt and metal, industrial grease and . . . "Do I smell pine?"

"Yeah, they work with a lumberyard—it's behind the store."

A woman wearing a red kerchief over her hair stood on a stepladder, organizing a shelf. "Hey Zoe, you lookin' for Brenda?" she asked in a thick Queens accent. "She's in the back."

"Thanks, Donna," Zoe said to the woman, then to me, "You want to just look around? I'll only be a minute or two."

"Uh, sure," I said.

The aisles were tall and stocked full of items, loosely organized by utility, plumbing, gardening, electric, building supplies, paints, tools, furniture. In the building supplies aisle, I picked through a box of nails marked .39¢/ea. *Maybe Zoe has some spare change I can borrow.*

I walked down the furniture aisle, finding stools, folding chairs, deck chairs. Then sets of patio furniture. I turned the corner and my breath caught in my throat as a stack of plastic folding tables caught my attention. Each table had been plastered with a white and blue sticker.

A sticker of a family having a picnic.

What were the chances that Ammit had bought his folding table here? It wasn't that crazy really. The cemetery was nearby. It had seemed newer than the rest of the things in the basement, and he had said that he wasn't used to kidnapping people, so maybe he'd had to rush out and stock up on supplies.

And now here was Zoe coming back down the aisle, followed by a woman in her forties wearing a plaid shirt with jeans. "You're Zoe's friend? Hi, I'm Brenda," she said, extending her hand.

"She wanted to make sure you were real," Zoe said, making a face.

"Hi. Madison," I said, shaking her hand. Zoe had her mother's bone structure. Though her nose and mouth were shaped differently, you could see the similarity in their cheekbones and chins. Zoe's hair was different, too, longer and darker than her mom's mousey brown-gray pixie cut.

"Nice to meet you," she said.

"You too. I have a random question: do you have a customer who is an elderly man—fair skin but with liver spots, white hair, blue eyes, maybe about this tall?" I held my hand up to about Ammit's height.

Donna joined the conversation from her stepladder. "Oh, you mean that nice man who takes all of our sawdust?"

I worked to keep my expression neutral. "Maybe. I saw him drop, uh, an envelope, but when I caught up with him, he was gone," I lied. *An envelope. Okay, why not? What would I say was in it? A piece of mail? No, she'd offer to mail it. How about pictures? Family pictures.*

Zoe looked at me suspiciously but said nothing.

"That's Mr. Todd. He's a taxidermist," Zoe's mom said. "You remember, he stuffed Mrs. Morales' parrot?" she said to Donna. "What was in the envelope?"

"Oh, uh, pictures. Mostly black and white ones."

"Oh, *no.* Those could be family heirlooms. I would hate to lose old photographs! And he has such a sad story too. You wouldn't remember, Zoe, it happened before you were born—poor Mr. Todd. His wife and daughter both died when he wasn't at home. A gas leak, I think. He used to teach biology at Bryant, but he retired after that. Mostly keeps to himself."

"Does he live around here?" I asked, biting my tongue.

"Zoe, you know that old Victorian house over in Sunnyside? The one on the corner of 50th and 47th? It's practically across the street. He lives over there. We make deliveries to him sometimes."

"The one that used to be a funeral home?" Zoe asked her mom.

"Sure, honey. That's the one."

My heart was beating fast and I felt sick to my stomach. "Great," I said, my voice sounding odd in my ears. "Maybe we can just drop them by for him."

"That would be a sweet thing to do. I'm sure he'd be very grateful."

"Thanks so much," I said, swallowing the spitty feeling in my mouth and trying to smile.

Chapter Nineteen

"We're just looking," I said, echoing Zoe. We'd pulled up across the street and a few houses down from the Victorian monstrosity, a cream-colored three-story house featuring several gables, a long porch, and a tower topped with a dome. "It used to be a funeral home?"

"It did. The reason I know that is because a ghost told me it was where she'd had her wake. She loved it. 'Proper style,' she said. This happened when I was little. So I told my mother and of course she didn't believe me because it wasn't a funeral home anymore, was it? But I think the guy who lives here, if he's your guy—er, the guy, who kidnapped you? I think he's been living there a while."

"What was that story your mom was saying about his wife and daughter dying?"

"I have no idea. My mom knows half of Queens, I think."

"Maybe we could check city records or something."

"What for?"

"I don't know, to see how long he's lived here? Details about his wife and daughter's deaths?" The house didn't seem to be abandoned or neglected in any way. The windows were clean and had gauzy curtains in them. The landscaping was neatly trimmed and the porch and front walk appeared recently swept, though there was a newspaper sitting there. I tried to picture Ammit—the same guy who kept creepy frankencorpses in his basement—sweeping a walk. It was just too odd. What the hell kind of guy was he anyway?

"The point of that being . . . what?" Zoe asked.

"I don't know. Just, more information. Who is this guy. How long has he lived here. What does he do. That kind of thing. Getting info on the enemy." Had he taken the house from someone else? Had he lived there since Christina's kidnapping or before?

I thought about the things that I did know. He was old. He was creepy. He didn't want me dead or starving. He could paralyze me or put me to sleep with a single word. He could shuffle through my memories like a collection of old postcards.

I imagined what would happen if he walked up to Zoe's window and said, "*Sleep*."

"You know what? Maybe this isn't such a good idea. Let's get out of here," I said.

"Amen to that."

Chapter Twenty

Back at Zoe's, I was trying on some clothes. Taking Nidhi's advice, we'd settled on a goth look to change my appearance, and I was modeling a crocheted long-sleeve black sweater over a black tank top. "That looks way better on you than it ever did on me. It's yours," Zoe said.

Zoe's bedroom was magically protected with signs and symbols painted along the ceiling just like the rest of her apartment, with more dangling charms and crystals. Her four-poster bed looked to be made of solid wood and her sun, moon, and stars bedding looked soft and cozy.

I turned to the side and surveyed the look in a long mirror: the crocheted sweater, an ankle-length black skirt, the white cap toe of my sneakers sticking out from beneath. "You think my Converse look okay with it?"

"Classic."

My phone buzzed and the name Lenny appeared on the screen.

I picked up. "Hey, Len—" I got out before he interrupted.

"Your scarab beetle is a *nasty* little piece of magic."

"What do you mean?"

"I can't tell if it's just supposed to hypnotize you into going somewhere, or actually transport you in a hypnotized state, but it's like a date-rape drug. One touch with this thing and you'll go wherever the person who made it wants you to go, without question, without resistance."

"Wait, you're saying it would teleport me? And control me?"

"I'm not so sure about the teleporting, honeybun. It's hard to tell. This is a complex piece of spellwork. Nasty, like I said. Honestly, it gives me the creeps. Come and get it out of here."

"Now?"

"Now, later, soon. What works for you?"

"Hang on a second—" I put my hand over the bottom of the phone. "Is Long Island City far from here?"

"Not too bad," said Zoe. "Maybe a ten-minute drive, without traffic. With? More like thirty."

"I can come by later to get it. Do you want me to call before I come over?"

"That's alright, sweets, I'll be here." With that, he hung up.

"Who was that?" Zoe asked.

"That was one of the guys who made my ID."

"What's the deal with them?"

"Zoe, I don't . . . I don't even know where to begin. My life is . . . it's well, you know. You see ghosts. No one believes you. I see a zombie minotaur or undead butterflies or some kind of zombie dog and I can't tell anyone because why would they believe me? I met someone who Kip told me is a satyr. I traveled to something called the Goblin Market! My life is insane. And don't even get me started on the vampires."

"Vampires? *Plural?*" she asked.

I shrugged helplessly.

"This is not good," Zoe said.

"I know."

"You haven't called him yet, have you?"

"No," I said with a pout.

Zoe put her hands on her hips and pursed her lips.

"Okay, okay." I retrieved the dark blue card from the back pocket of the jeans I'd been wearing when I saw Billy.

It was thicker and more textured than Lenny's card. All that was printed on it was a phone number in shiny embossed silver. No name, no other information.

Zoe took it from my hand and looked it over, then handed it back to me. "Nice," she said. "Good card stock. I bet that cost a pretty penny."

I sank onto the bed and stared at the card.

"What are you waiting for?"

"I don't know. I just . . . I wish I knew why all of this was happening to me."

"Don't you think one way to find out would be to ask someone who might know?" she asked gently, sitting next to me.

A dreamcatcher with a speckled feather spun in lazy circles over her bed, moving with the air currents stirred by our movements. "But he's a vampire," I said. "You told me you were warned not to mess around with them."

"Yes, but that's me. You—you have magic. You can protect yourself. All I have is Casper and friends."

"Do you really know a ghost named Casper?" I asked with a bit of a smile.

"No. Now call your vampire."

"He's not mine."

"Uh huh. Just don't make plans to meet him in a dark alley. Go somewhere public. Or where there are other people you can trust."

I sighed. "Okay. I can do this." My chest felt a little tight and my hands felt vaguely sweaty. What the hell was going on with me?

I dialed the number and listened as it rang. And rang. And rang. Finally, a robotic voice picked up and said the phone number and "Leave a message." I opened my mouth but nothing came out and I hurriedly hung up.

"What happened?"

"It was just a generic voicemail."

"You didn't leave a message!"

"I didn't know what to say!"

"Call back!"

I shook my head frantically.

"Why not?" she asked.

I stood up and began pacing. "I don't know. I don't understand what's happening to me. I feel really weird about making this call, Zoe. Like, nervous, but excited, but scared, too."

"Okay, okay. Here's what you'll say: *This is Madison. I would like to meet. No funny stuff. Please call me at* and you give your number. And then you hang up! Easy peasy."

"*No funny stuff?*"

"Somebody always says that when arranging a clandestine meeting."

"Oh. What's my number again?" I asked, my voice going squeaky.

"Good lord, girl, you have got it bad."

"Got what bad?"

"You remind me of when I had a crush my sophomore year."

"That's ridiculous. He's . . . he's—"

"Hot?"

"I was going to say an arrogant, amoral, dangerous . . . jerkface."

"Ooh, hitting hard with the schoolyard insults now."

I did not have a schoolgirl crush on Michael Adderly. I couldn't.

I had just slept with Kip, what, hours before? Didn't that mean *anything*? Or oh, *ugh*, had I *used* Kip?

Everything was so confusing.

I exhaled noisily. "Okay, okay. What's my number?"

She scrolled through her phone and brought the number up, turning the screen so I could see it. I opened the phone again and called Michael's number once more. This time when instructed I spat out the message that Zoe had dictated to me and then I hung up again.

"There. Happy?"

"There's no such thing as a happy medium," she quipped.

I smirked and rolled my eyes.

"Come on, let's see what we can do about your makeup."

Almost an hour later, my eyes were heavily outlined in a cat's eye shape and my lips were black and seemed much fuller than usual. Between online tutorials on how to do gothic makeup and a fake septum piercing, I'd been transformed. We'd tucked my hair into a stretchy hat with a brim that was a little itchy but also looked good on me, and darkened my eyebrows to go with the rest of the dark makeup on my face. I didn't recognize myself in the mirror.

"Mysterious Madison, goth extraordinaire," Zoe said, observing my reflection. "I kind of like this look on you."

"Seems like a lot of work."

"You picked it up like a pro, though."

Going through the motions of drawing the cat's eye makeup onto my upper lid had felt intuitive to me. So much so that after reading through the instructions, I just went ahead and did it without consulting them again.

"Okay, I think I'm ready," I said. "Are you sure you don't mind driving me?"

"Yeah, you know, gas is awfully expensive," she said sarcastically.

"I mean it. I don't know what I would have done without you, Zoe."

"You shush now. I'm here for you. We're going to figure this out."

It was early evening as we pulled up outside the Collective Collective building and Zoe shuddered. "Maddy, I don't think—"

"It's an aversion spell. It's okay. Here, touch this nail and look again." I had been gripping the nail I'd bought with Zoe's money as we pulled up and experienced none of the feeling of dread I had the first time I'd been there. The building seemed unremarkable and bland.

"Whoa," Zoe said. "That's . . . wow. Maybe I'd better start carrying a nail around in my pocket, too."

"I'll be as quick as I can," I said, getting out of the station wagon.

"Be quicker," Zoe said, rolling up her window and locking the doors.

I wasn't certain what my plan was, really, just getting the scarab from Lenny and concealing it somewhere no one would find it, then laying low at Zoe's for a couple of days until my IDs and things were ready and then . . . what? Could I hide out indefinitely in New York City from a bunch of magical dudes who were trying to capture me?

I stood in front of the door and read the sign above it once more.

Cross this threshold and give ye no lie.

I rang the buzzer and a few moments later the door was once again opened by the imposing gentleman in the fedora. I gripped the nail in my pocket and suppressed a gasp as his facial features dissolved into those of a feral beast with sharp teeth and horns. He smiled at me unpleasantly.

"I'm here to see Lenny."

The man (or troll?) snorted and moved aside to let me in. Walking through the lobby now while holding the nail was a completely different experience. Green growing things climbed the walls and curled around pillars. The tile floors were beautiful mosaic, not monochrome. Nothing was as it had seemed.

I got to door 1337 and knocked.

At the same time, my phone buzzed, signaling an incoming call. I glanced at the screen and saw that it was the number from the card.

My mouth went dry. I cleared my throat and picked up, trying to sound calm and collected.

"This is Madison."

"Hello, Madison," came the familiar sardonic voice of Michael Adderly.

The door opened and the scent of musky incense came wafting out. "Sorry, not taking any new orders today," Lenny said, looking me up and down with a bored expression.

"Lenny, it's me, Madison," I said, holding the phone away from my chin.

"Ohhhh! Come on in, sweetcheeks!" he sang. "Look at you all dressed up fancy! Very Morticia of you."

"Is this a bad time?" Michael asked. There was a tone in his voice. Was he laughing at me?

"No. No, this is—well, actually, yes, it *is* a bad time. Can I call you back?"

"No."

"Grea—wait, no?"

"No."

"Um, hold on."

I covered the lower part of the phone with my hand. "I'm sorry, Lenny, I need to take this."

"Sure, sure. Come on in, have a seat," he said, closing the door after me. "I'll be back in a bit." He disappeared down a hallway and I made my way over to the orange carpet and mismatched couches and sat down, then put the phone back to my ear. The atmosphere in the room was smoky and a tall water pipe that reminded me of a hamster habitat stood on the coffee table in front of me.

"Okay, I can talk now."

"You said you'd like to meet."

"Yes."

"Why?"

"Why what?"

"Why do you want to meet? Why now?" His voice took on an almost hissing quality.

"Because I think you have answers to some questions I have and I'm finally ready to ask them."

"I also have questions."

"Then I propose an exchange. I ask a question, you answer, then you ask me a question and I answer, and so on."

There was silence on the line for several seconds. "No good. I'd be a fool to trust you, and you would be a fool to trust me. We're not fools, are we, Madison? How would you know lie from truth? How would I?"

He had a point. If only there were some way to magically tell if someone was lying . . .

"Hold, please," I said into the phone, then covered the lower half once more. "Lenny? Do you do freelance work?"

Seconds later, his face appeared around the corner, followed by the rest of him. "What do you need, sugarcube?"

"A neutral third party who will tell if party A or B is lying to the other."

"Ooh, sounds like a good time! It's for you?"

I nodded.

"How long?"

"Uh, maybe an hour?"

"I could do an hour."

"What's your fee?"

A mischievous glint appeared in his eye and he smirked. "Tickets."

I waited a beat, but he didn't say anything else. "Tickets to what?"

"Surprise me. I'll give you two weeks."

I could come up with tickets to something in two weeks, couldn't I?

"Done."

"Indeed."

I gestured with the phone and Lenny disappeared around the corner again.

"Okay, here's how it's going to go," I said into the phone.

Chapter Twenty-one

Kitty Sing's karaoke bar was on the edge of Chinatown and fit the requirement of a public space with private areas as well.

Immediately inside the tinted doors was a bar area. The rest of the place was filled with tables and chairs and a small stage spread out across the back wall. The bartender was engaged in conversation with two young women enjoying colorful cocktails with skewers of fruit and umbrellas in them. A few other patrons were nursing drinks at various tables, but no one was singing. Behind a black reception area to the left of the stage sat a young man with a clipboard.

Not seeing Michael or Lenny, I sat down at a small table to wait. It had been a little over twenty-four hours since our conversation. I'd invited Michael to pick the place and this was what he'd chosen.

I sat facing the entrance, my attention split between waiting for Michael to darken the doorway and the Japanese anime playing on the screen behind the bar, in which giant robots piloted by teen girls fought monsters.

Then the screen changed to blue. On it appeared:

HELLO, I LOVE YOU
In the style of The Doors

The familiar opening bars of the song repeated themselves and I glanced at the stage and did a doubletake.

It was Michael Adderly.

He wore black jeans and a black button-up shirt with the sleeves pushed up to his elbows. The hair remained the same, longish and framing his face, seemingly in need of a cut. His eyes were closed as he nodded along with the music. He opened them as he began to sing.

His voice was like honey on a sore throat. It was like his voice echoed through my ears into my brain, then traveled into the rest of my body, lodging somewhere in my ribcage, where it perched like a bird, trembling with joy.

What was it about him that made me feel this way?

While his eyes roamed over the entire bar as he sang the other lyrics, each time he got to the refrain, his eyes locked on me.

So much for disguises.

Was he mocking me, the whole name thing? Was he suggesting that I was playing games with him?

Once again his eyes locked on me as he sang the refrain and I wondered when I had stopped breathing.

The song came to an end and Michael took a bow as the small audience clapped enthusiastically. The screen went back to cartoons, and he stepped down from the stage.

Several female eyes glared at me jealously as he sauntered up to my table.

"Is this seat taken?" he asked, with a lopsided, too-sure-of-himself smile.

I waved a hand toward the seat. I didn't trust my voice.

He pulled out the wooden chair and sat down.

A female server seemingly materialized at my elbow to take our drink orders.

Michael waved a hand toward me, inviting me to go first, and maybe making fun of my obvious discomfort.

"Water," I said, clearing my throat.

Michael grimaced. "You don't have to be a cheap date with me. Get whatever you like."

"A Coke?" I asked. Michael's lips pursed a moment but he said nothing. The server nodded and jotted something on her notepad.

Michael ordered a gin and tonic, and the server went to the bar.

"A Coke? If you're going to dress like your old self, I don't know why you wouldn't drink like her too."

"What's that supposed to mean?"

"You know what it means."

"What? I don't drink."

"Whatever you say."

The door to the bar opened and in walked Lenny. He still wore his multicolor pantaloons, but instead of the tie-dyed t-shirt, he now wore a fuzzy burgundy sweater. His hair had been gathered in a low ponytail and his goatee, while still several inches long, was neatly trimmed. His cheeks had been freshly shaved as well.

He scanned the room and said, "Ah," when his eyes lit on me.

"And here is our mediator," I said.

"Please," Michael said, gesturing to an empty chair at our table.

Lenny sat. "Madison. And this handsome dish of a man must be Michael?"

Michael nodded at him.

"I'm Lenobios," he said to Michael, handing him a business card. "I'll be your truthsayer today."

Michael raised an eyebrow as he looked over the card. "Alright. Tell me how this works."

"You'd like a demonstration first?"

"Yes," Michael said, putting the card away.

Lenny rubbed his hands together and then held one out to each of us, palm up. "Place your hand in mine."

We both did so.

"Now, Michael, I am going to ask you three questions. You are going to answer truthfully to two of them and lie for one and you will not tell me which is the lie, but nonetheless I will know. Then Madison, we'll do the same with you. Yes? Good? Here we go. Michael, here are your three questions. Don't answer immediately. First, I will tell you the questions, and then I will ask each of them separately."

While Lenny explained, I studied Michael's face. I remembered the *Look!* magazine cover that had been my first impression of him. It had been colorized and they'd gotten the eyes wrong. In the magazine, they were a vivid aqua blue, but in person, Michael's eyes were a clear light blue. His cheek bones were prominent and he had a strong chin. His nose seemed to have been broken at some point. I wondered how it had happened.

Lenny continued. "I will ask you about your favorite season, what year you were born, and, just for my own amusement, what color underwear you're wearing. Ready?"

Michael nodded.

"What's your favorite season?"

"Winter."

"And what year were you born?"

"1976."

"And what color underwear are you wearing?"

"Blue."

I knew that 1976 was the lie, but would Lenny? While I'd warned him that we were dealing with a vampire, I hadn't given him any details about Michael's background.

"Now, Michael, I said two truths and one lie, but you told me two lies. Would you like me to tell you which ones?" Lenny asked.

"Please."

The server arrived with a tray and put my Coke and Michael's cocktail on the table.

"Can I get you something?" she asked Lenny.

"What's your wine like? Tell me you have a list and not just house wines."

"House wines," she said.

He made a face.

"We have a sake list," she said quickly.

"I suppose it's worth a look," he sighed.

Michael handed her some money and she departed.

" '1976' and 'blue' were lies," Lenny said.

Michael nodded.

The server returned with the sake menu and Lenny ordered something. "You want that hot or cold?" the server asked.

Lenny made another face and said, "Cold. You don't drink Nigori *hot*, are you mad?"

The server rolled her eyes and took the menu, departing once more.

"Now Madison, I'm going to ask you the same questions. Are you ready?" Lenny asked.

"Yeah."

My answers were: *spring, I'm not sure,* and *black*. Michael squinted at me for all three answers, as if he was trying to divine my lie by my face. I kept a carefully neutral expression.

"The lie was black."

"Correct."

"Prove it," Michael said.

"Excuse me?"

"I said prove it. Prove that's the lie."

"What do you mean?"

"Show us your underwear."

The server arrived with Lenny's sake.

"Are you okay with these guys?" she asked me, placing a blue bottle and a glass in front of Lenny, while glowering at Michael.

"I'm fine," I said.

She cast a suspicious glance at both men and said to me, "You let me know if you need *anything.*"

"I will. Thank you."

After she'd moved away, Michael said, "Underwear."

"Geez, no foreplay or anything," Lenny said.

"Fine," I said. I stood and pulled the elastic waistband of the black skirt down to my hip, exposing the purple polka dot waistband of my cotton undies. Then I pulled the skirt back up and sat down again.

"Let's see yours," I said.

"Turnabout is fair play," Michael said.

He stood and undid a button of his black jeans, exposing a silver waistband that read Calvin Klein in black letters.

I was unprepared for the tingle of desire that accompanied his actions and found myself blushing as I averted my eyes.

"Really, I don't know what you need me for," Lenny said.

"It could still be a setup," Michael said. "You two could have planned this whole thing."

"Ask her a question that you both know the answer to. Then you will both answer the question. and I will tell you which of you lied."

Michael thought a moment. "What color is the couch in my safe room?"

He meant the couch in the bunker, I thought, the one where I'd found him. It was white.

"Black," I said.

"Red," Michael said.

"Liar liar," Lenny said, raising both of our hands.

"Fascinating," Michael said.

"*Au contraire, mon capitaine,*" Lenny said. "It's a walk in the park. Buckle up, honey dumplings. Shall we?" He picked up his sake bottle and glass and walked toward the black podium next to the stage.

Room 2 had red walls and black floors. Two built-in upholstered benches as well as a couple of chairs offered seating. A big screen flanked by large speakers took up most of one wall. It was showing the same anime as the bar. Two round coffee tables held a couple of thick three-ring binders, as well as a remote control and two microphones.

Michael and I sat across the room from each other on opposing bench seats and Lenny sat in a chair between us. He spent a moment shaking the blue bottle, then poured a cloudy white liquid into the glass. He raised the glass and spoke in a formal manner. "As truthsayer, here is my troth: I will speak if lies are spoken or forsake all favors for a year and a day." There was a subtle quality to the air as he spoke—a thickening almost—and a high-pitched hum. It seemed magic was at work.

He took a drink and put down the glass. "Start whenever you're ready, muffin."

"Okay. So how do you know me, Michael? When did we meet?"

"Seriously? Okay, if that's how you want to play it. I met you in 1987. You were a waitress at a café I liked."

I nodded. "Your turn."

"What vampire has you in thrall? Who do you work for?" he asked.

"What? I'm not a thrall. I don't even know how to thrall. I work at a comic book store."

Michael pointedly stared at Lenny, who had his legs crossed. He was viewing the two of us with obvious amusement. "No lie," Lenny said.

Michael shook his head. He seemed disturbed.

"Why didn't you bite me when you woke up? You went after Billy instead."

"You asked me once, years ago, if you were food. You knew what I was. You wanted to know if I planned to drink from you. I didn't. I won't." He took a sip of his cocktail, and his face took on a look of resolve. "Are you associated with any supernatural creature that is using you to get to me?"

"No. How conceited are you? Why do you think this is all about you? I have met some supernatural creatures—obviously," I said, with a head tilt toward Lenny, "but not one of them is interested in you. Why have you been stalking me?"

"I wanted to know what your angle was. I thought you were working against me. How do you look so young without vampire blood?"

"Apparently . . . I time-traveled. Magically. I skipped ahead twenty-nine years."

Once again Michael looked to Lenny, who seemed both surprised and impressed by this information. "It's the truth, toots," said Lenny.

"What was I to you in 1987?" I asked.

Michael paused before answering, and then in a voice that caught in his throat, said, "The girl I loved."

Everything stopped. Or it didn't stop, but somehow came into focus, sharply, at that moment.

My chest felt full, yet empty.

Our eyes met for an instant but neither of us could bear it.

His declaration hung in the air like the last notes of a song.

He cleared his throat before continuing. "Did you know I was in the safe room? Did you come looking for me?"

"That's two questions," I said, "but I'll let it slide. No and no."

"Then how did you—?"

"It's my turn."

"Sorry."

"Do you know anything . . ." I stopped myself before I asked a *yes* or *no* question. "What do you know about my parents?" I held my breath, waiting for the answer.

"Your dad was a law professor. Your mom was a Hollywood stuntwoman."

"A stuntwoman?"

"It's my turn," Michael said. "How did you find me if you didn't come looking for me?"

"It was a coincidence, if you believe in coincidences, which I'm not so sure I do anymore. When I woke up standing on a sidewalk in 2016, I was wearing jeans, a V-neck sweater, these sneakers, and a weird key that only said *Fichet* on it. Six months later, I was in a garage at a haunted house with a lock labeled *Fichet.* We tried the key, and that was how I found you."

"I gave you that key. The last night I saw you. The rest seems incredibly unlikely," Michael observed.

"*That's* no lie," Lenny deadpanned.

"Tell me about it," I said. "That's the story of my life as I know it. Why were you down there?"

"I tried to kill someone and we fought. She threw me through a wall, and some wood pierced my heart, forcing me into dormancy—a kind of stasis. I lay there twenty-five years, give or take. Did you not bring Billy to . . . feed him to me?"

"No. Billy came of his own accord. I had no idea you were down there. What did you do to Billy?"

"I saved his life. When I had to choose between letting him die or turning him, I chose unlife. Do you have romantic feelings for him?"

"How is that any business of yours?"

"A question's a question."

"No, he's just a friend. Someone I care about. Why did you make him into your thrall or whatever?"

"I had just been awakened by the girl I loved who I thought had *died.* I'd been in torment for twenty-five years and needed someone to help me navigate the world. I would never have drained him under normal circumstances—but my need was too great." He paused and his eyes searched my face. "Do you truly have no memory of me?"

"Not from before I found you in that basement, no. Who is Irina Van Horn to you?"

"She made me a vampire, against my will, and likely killed my wives. She's the one who impaled me in my safe room after I tried to kill her. Why do you ask?"

"The ghost in my apartment, Tamara Meadows, showed me that Irina Van Horn killed her."

Michael took a deep breath, glanced at Lenny, and frowned. "She was so strong willed," he said quietly.

"Did you love her?" I asked.

"I felt affection for her and did what I could to help her. Why are you asking?"

"It seemed like Tamara was in love with you. I wanted to know if you felt the same. Did you care at all? Or were you just using her?"

"Of course I cared. I wasn't using her—"

Lenny, who'd been quietly enjoying his drink, said, "Lie."

"I wasn't finished. I was using her to some extent, but she was also using me. There was an exchange. A transaction. She gave me blood, I paid her rent and loaned her a piano."

Lenny nodded.

"Have I satisfied your curiosity?" Michael asked.

"Yes." For now, anyway. So he hadn't loved Tamara, but he had loved Christina. How had *she* felt? "So, was your love requited by Christina?"

He was quiet a moment. "I thought so."

His eyes caught mine and it seemed that some wall between us came down. This was the sincere man I'd caught glimpses of in our past interactions.

Whatever he was about to ask, he really wanted to know. "Does that mean you don't . . . love me?"

His expression seemed to hold both pain and yearning.

My heart hurt to see that expression on his face. A tangible tightness caught my breath.

I wanted to—some part of me wanted to—ease his pain.

Why did I feel this connection to him?

I didn't even *know* him.

I was suddenly reminded of Hank, the policeman who Ammit had transformed. Hank had had feelings for his wife, Hannah, though he had no memory of her.

What had Ammit said? *Like you, I took name and—with it—memory. But the heart was left behind.* Was this what he'd meant? My identity and all the memories associated with it were gone, but the feelings they inspired still existed, like emotional residue. Christina's heart still felt love for Michael even though I had no memory of him. It made sense.

"I have feelings for you, but I have no memory attached to them."

"It's your turn," Michael said. The wall was back up.

I couldn't think of what else I wanted to ask him. I took a long drink of my Coke and put it back down on the cocktail napkin where it had sweated a ring of moisture. That gave me an idea. "Why did you think it was weird that I was having a Coke?"

"Because Chris's favorite drink was an amaretto sour, followed by rum and Coke, followed by any variation of schnapps she could get her hands on." He smirked, seemingly amused by some private joke.

"I don't drink."

"I noticed. Here's something I want to know: How can you do magic?"

"I have no idea. I'm still trying to get a handle on that whole thing. What did you mean earlier when you mentioned my outfit? Is this how Christina dressed?"

"A lot of the time, yes. Black clothing, dark makeup, red or black lipstick. Your . . . *her* father hated it. I didn't mind but sometimes she went fresh-faced. I liked both. Why didn't you meet me two weeks ago?"

"I was kidnapped by an old wizard who calls himself Ammit."

"*Ammit*? Ammit *kidnapped* you?" Michael shouted. "That sonofabitch!"

"Friend of yours?"

"Hardly." He shook his head. "You're still in danger. Why didn't you say anything?" He pulled out a smart phone. His fingers blurred over the screen, then he stood. "I've got to go," he declared.

"Wait, did Ammit kidnap me because of *you*?"

"I don't think so. He doesn't know that I'm back. I have to leave."

"But you said we'd have an hour!"

"I'm sorry. Truly." His blue eyes met mine and seemed to be imploring me to understand. "I've paid for the room. You'll hear from me soon."

And just like that, he was gone.

Before the door shut behind him, a chorus of voices singing "New York, New York" came faintly through.

I frowned.

"I'm sorry, honeybunch," said Lenny. "That wasn't exactly what you were hoping for, was it?" He took a sip of his sake and added, "Men. Am I right?"

Chapter Twenty-two

I SAT THERE IN THE MUFFLED SILENCE OF THE soundproofed room for a moment before coming to a decision.

"You know what? That's bullshit," I said. I stormed out the door after Michael, but he was nowhere in sight. More patrons had come into the main bar and there were only a few empty tables left. On stage, three girls clustered around the microphone, singing Frank Sinatra's signature song.

"Did you see a guy dressed all in black a minute ago?" I asked the guy with the clipboard next to the stage.

"Huh?" he said, gesturing to his ear.

The girls on the stage had their arms around one another and were drunkenly attempting to perform high kicks like the Rockettes.

Michael wasn't in the audience or bar area, so I went out the front door.

"Dammit!" I yelled on the sidewalk. I looked in both directions but he wasn't out there either. Taxis and other cars flew by on the street, going one way. But wait, was that him, walking about a block away? I took one half of a step in that direction and was immediately grabbed from behind. The arms that held me felt like iron bands.

"Easy, Mads," came Billy's voice in my ear. "Easy now."

"Billy, you put me the fuck down right now or so help me—"

"So help you what?" he said. He let me go, but kept his hands where I could see them, perhaps so he could grab me again if I went after Michael.

"What the fuck are you doing here?"

"What do you think? Following the orders of my lord and master, of course."

"You mean Michael?"

"I didn't say that."

"Well, you just missed him."

"Yeah, I know. I was waiting for you. Nice look, by the way. I almost didn't recognize you."

"Why were you waiting for me?"

"I'm supposed to protect you from some evil wizard."

"But where did Michael go?"

"Don't know, and even if I did, I couldn't say."

"Did he fly away? What the fuck?"

Lenny exited the bar at that moment. "Goodness, sweetcheeks, you do keep interesting company," he said, seeing me with Billy.

Billy wrinkled his nose. "Jesus, Mads. Don't you know any humans anymore?"

"Charming," Lenny said. "Darling, do you see a black Escalade with a license plate that starts with FBY?"

I looked into the street and a black SUV with an FBY license plate put on its hazards as it pulled up to the curb. "That's it," I said.

"That's my ride, kids. See you later," he said, hopping into the backseat.

The SUV pulled away and I watched its bright red taillights turn the next corner.

"Well, shit," I said.

"What?" Billy asked.

"I was hoping to get a ride with him back to Queens tonight. Now it's going to take me forever to get out there."

"Well, he stinks, so you're probably better off."

"What do you mean? He doesn't smell."

"Sure he does. Like an animal of some kind. I thought it was his ratty old sweater at first, but I think it was actually him, whatever he is."

Could Billy smell that Lenny was a satyr? It suddenly occurred to me that I hadn't tried looking at Lenny while holding the nail to break his glamour. Maybe I hadn't wanted to.

"Besides," Billy said, "I would really rather not go to Queens."

"Who invited you? I'm staying at Zoe's tonight."

"You don't have to go all the way out there. You can stay with me."

"In the Bronx?"

"Nah, I've got a new place. It's in Soho. It's ten blocks or so from here."

"Long blocks or short blocks?" Long blocks are the blocks between avenues. Short blocks are the blocks between streets. Ten long blocks is practically the width of Manhattan.

"A little bit of both."

"I don't have any of my stuff," I said. "It's nice of you to offer, but I'd rather be on my own."

"It's not optional, Mads."

"Why are you calling me *Mads* all of a sudden?"

"What, you don't like it?"

"I don't know. Maybe I don't. Maybe I do. This is all crazy and weird and here you are, trying to tell me what to do. It's just . . . *grrrr*!"

"Look, this wasn't my idea. No matter where you go, I must follow, so I guess if you want to go to Queens, I'll be right behind you."

"What do you mean you *must follow*?"

"Orders. No choice."

"He just bosses you around and you do whatever he says?"

"Like I said, I have no choice."

"Sure you do. Just don't do it."

"Like it's that easy."

A group of twenty-somethings passed us to enter Kitty Sing's and we both grew uncomfortably silent for a moment until they were inside.

"Look, why don't you come hang out at my place for a little while and we can talk or whatever there?" he asked.

I had to admit that I was curious about what had happened to him and what he was talking about with this lord and master stuff.

"You aren't going to disappear on me again?"

"I'm stuck to you like glue, sister."

Billy's new place was on Prince Street between Thompson and Sullivan. We went through a nondescript door, down a long hallway, and then outside facing a concrete courtyard. From there, we went down steel stairs and walked along a passageway to a basement apartment with burgundy walls and gray-painted concrete floors.

I'd tried asking him questions on the way from Chinatown, but between a firetruck passing by that left his sensitive vampire ears ringing, followed by an ambulance that did the same, I'd decided to hold off until we got to our destination.

The small living room area contained a futon and coffee table with some folding chairs. A small kitchenette took up one wall. A fluorescent light on the ceiling cast an artificial glow over the whole area. The ceilings were a bit low, as well. Less than seven feet.

"Have a seat," Billy said. "You want a water or something? I might have some iced tea in the fridge."

I sat on the futon while Billy looked inside the small refrigerator.

There were no windows in the living room. There was a hall beyond it with a couple of doors. Did any of those rooms have windows? Or was this whole place vampire-safe?

"Can you not go out in the sun?"

"Correct."

"But you can go out during the day?"

"Cloudy days. With an umbrella." He handed me a bottle of iced tea and sat in a folding chair.

I sighed and opened the bottle.

He didn't seem deathly pale beneath the fluorescent lights. Pale, yes, but he'd always been pale. There was something else about him, though. Some difference that I was having a hard time putting a finger on. He seemed more confident somehow, and his facial features more pleasing to look at. He'd always had a large nose—beak-like, even—but now it seemed attractive on him. Vampire mojo, I supposed.

He wore all black, as always, though his t-shirt was plain, rather than featuring comic book characters, and black military-style pants, and black combat boots. His beloved black leather Wolverine jacket with the orange stripes around the biceps completed the ensemble.

"What happened to you, Billy?" I shrugged my red coat off and folded it in half on the futon next to me.

"Oh. You care all of a sudden?"

"Of course, I care."

"Yeah, well, I wish I could satisfy your curiosity, but I can't."

"You don't know?"

"Oh, I know. I just can't say. Literally. The words won't come out of my mouth. Just like I can't disobey an order. I've tried. It doesn't work. I end up doing what You Know Who wants anyway."

"What kind of stuff does he make you do?"

"Can't say."

"Well, this is fun. Do you have some checkers for us to play or something?"

"I'm really more of an online poker guy."

"Chess? Monopoly?"

"Why do you want to play board games?"

"I don't know, because I thought you were going to tell me what happened to you and now you're saying you can't so what the hell else are we going to do?"

"I might have *Tetris* on my phone. We could take turns."

"Wait, can you write about what happened?" I remembered how Hank had been able to write even though he hadn't been able to talk.

"No."

"But you can answer yes or no questions?"

"Sort of? It depends on what you ask."

"Are you a vampire?"

His mouth closed to a tight pucker and his eyes bulged.

"Okay, bad question."

"Ya think?" he asked.

"So there are certain things you aren't allowed to say or comment on, is that right?"

"Yes."

"Can you . . . I don't know, pantomime?"

"No."

"Are you sure?"

"I'm not playing charades with you, Mads."

"Do you remember everything that happened to you?"

"Mostly."

"But you can't say anything about your current state of being."

"Correct."

"Do you . . . uh, drink red stuff?"

He smirked, glad I thought, that I hadn't said *blood.* It might be just the loophole needed to get around his mental block.

"Sometimes."

"But you don't, like, thirst for it constantly?"

"No."

"Do you sleep in a . . . box?"

"No. This shithole," he said, gesturing around him, "is all the box I need."

"You're super strong, right?"

"Yeah."

"And fast?"

He shrugged. "A little."

"Your nose and ears are more sensitive now."

"It appears that way."

"Can you see in the dark?"

"Sure. Not pitch blackness, but low light conditions."

Hm. That could be useful. "And you work for . . . my ex-boyfriend from 1987?"

"Yes."

"And he made you what you are."

"No."

My eyes widened in surprise. "Is he the one who orders you?"

"It's complicated."

"Is the one who made you the one who orders you?"

"More or less."

"Orders you to follow orders from the other guy?"

Billy nodded, seeming impressed with my deductive reasoning. "You got it. Not bad."

"So you were ordered to protect me."

"Yup."

"So if I went into a situation where I was in danger, you would defend me?"

"I wouldn't have a choice."

"Then how about you help me get proof that Ammit exists?"

"I can't do that, Mads. That would put you in danger, and that's against the rules."

"But if I just went there, you'd have to follow me, right?"

"I would try to stop you."

"I would set you on fire."

"That escalated quickly."

"I'm just . . . you know, sometimes it feels like my co-worker Erica said. All of these dudes trying to protect me—whether from this wizard or *supposedly* myself—are just holding me back. I'm sick of it. I'm tired of running. Of not knowing where I'm going to sleep the next night, of waking up on couches and in strange beds. I want to go home. But the only way I can do that is if I can prove to this cop wizard that this kidnapping wizard exists. And I can't do it by myself because the kidnapping wizard can make me go to sleep or freeze with a single word! But with you there, I'd have a chance. You'd be fast. And strong, like you were with that zombie. We could take him out together."

"Ripping a head off a zombie is much easier than ripping one off a living person, I'd wager."

"So you haven't been ripping heads off all over Manhattan? I'm disappointed."

"I'll bet." He rolled his eyes. "Now I see what you want from me. You need some hired muscle. So what's in it for me?"

"What do you mean?"

"If I do this for you, what do I get out of it?"

"The satisfaction of helping a friend?"

He chortled. "Oh, we're *friends*? Isn't that swell?"

"Billy, what are you talking about? Of course we're friends."

"Right, because friends feed their friends to . . ." His mouth puckered a moment and he sighed angrily. "You know what I mean. That's what *friends* do?"

I shook my head. "No, no. I didn't feed you to Michael. Why would you think that? Did he tell you that?"

He shrugged. "Oh, I don't know. You bring your mysterious key to the basement where your monster ex is sleeping and free him and leave me there for him to devour. I was like a fly a mama spider leaves for her babies. And you looked so hard for me afterward, didn't you? All you cared about was *him*."

"I did look for you! I followed you from Chris Street to the Empire State Building and you were drinking blood—from him! And then you jumped! I looked on the street. You weren't there."

"No, I landed on the 80th floor ledge, I guess. I wasn't in any shape to know. My brain was kinda, you know. Splattered. I wasn't going to survive, so . . . yeah. This is how I got 'saved.' Now I get to live in a basement and be a flunky. Forget any dreams I had. Forget my old friends, my bandmates, my job. No, I can't be trusted. Gotta follow orders." He reached into the mini fridge and took out a bottle of iced tea. He held it aloft in a mock toast and took a swig. "I don't even get why. What's so special about you, Mads? Why am I supposed to protect you when it's your fault I'm like this?"

"Me? You *asked* to come to the ghost hunt! Don't put this on me."

"Save your Miss Innocent routine for Mr. Wonderful. I see through you. You're some kind of psycho manipulator. I should have known all along. You just use people. That guy Kip in the subway tunnel, me, Zoe, Derek, all of the other people at the ghost hunt, Mac . . . Everyone you come in contact with is just a means to an end. *Pretending* you have amnesia. What a crock. Oh, so *fragile*, poor little *Madison* . . ."

Why was he being like this? "Pretending? How could you even suggest that? You've got to believe me!"

"I don't *have* to believe anything. All I *have* to do is protect you. But I don't have to like it."

I stared at him for a good while. Maybe a minute. Maybe more. We'd gone from a Q&A session to complete hostility.

"I don't have to stay here and take this abuse," I said. I stood and picked up my coat.

In the blink of an eye, Billy was in front of the door to the apartment and his eyes had gone black: no white, no color. All black.

He said, "You're not going anywhere."

"No? What are you going to do? Yell at me to death? You have to protect me, so you can't hurt me, can you?" I pulled the coat on.

"Don't push me, Mads."

"Or what?"

Small fangs were just visible at the edge of his upper lip. "I'll push back."

Chapter Twenty-three

I was done. Done waiting, done running, done hiding, and done letting men tell me what I was or wasn't going to do.

Anger flared through me, from the set of my jaw down into my chest and expanded out through my arms to my hands. I balled my fists and walked toward Billy. I could feel the heat contained and waiting, like I was holding a handful of burning coals.

"Move," I said. I unfurled my right fist and my entire hand lit with orange and yellow flames. My hand itself was living fire.

"What happened to being *friends*?" he asked in a simpering tone. It made him look ugly. But there was some doubt there in his face too, and his posture leaned a little bit away from me and my burning hand.

I tilted my head and moved my hand closer to him.

"Don't," he said in a slightly panicked voice.

"Then move. Unless you don't value your . . . unlife."

He snarled. Actually snarled at me, and then he was across the room, again in the blink of an eye.

I turned back to him for a moment. "You know, I did think we were friends. But I don't know what the hell we are now." Then I walked out the door, balled my fist once more to put out the flames, and ran.

We'd passed the Prince Street subway station on our way in and it seemed the fastest way out of the neighborhood. I watched the entrance stairs from the platform but didn't see Billy come down. Once I was on the train, I checked my phone and saw that I had several texts from Zoe and one from Nidhi, both asking me to check in and let them know I was okay.

I told Zoe I was on my way to Woodside from Prince Street and told Nidhi I was fine.

I wasn't fine.

I was mad.

How could Billy think that horrible stuff about me? That wasn't like him. Was it? Had he always been so cynical and nasty and I hadn't realized it? Or had becoming a vampire changed him? At first, I'd thought he was the same old Billy, but now . . . no. Now he was just a dick.

And what was up with Michael Adderly ordering Billy to protect me? I could take care of myself.

Can you though?

Shut up.

No, seriously, I want to know. Can you take care of yourself? Can you protect yourself from the zombie-making, mind-controlling wizard?

I don't know. Maybe I can.

Maybe you need more information.

Zoe said she'd check city records and see what she discovered.

Do you remember seeing those notebooks in his lab?

I thought back to the horrifying lab and everything in it, from the steel tables and surgical instruments to the pillars and the fish tank with the monkeyfish and the creepy skinned body that blinked at me. And yes, there had been a desk, and the desk had handwritten notebooks on it.

I was so deep in thought that I nearly missed my transfer at 42nd Street/Times Square. I dashed out just as the doors were closing.

For some reason known only to the MTA, the 7 train platforms were closed, so I had to take the S train—the shuttle—to Grand Central to catch the Queens-bound 7 there.

A busker was playing a pan flute into a microphone in the station as I hurried down the long tunnel to the Grand Central shuttle. I looked over my shoulder several times but didn't see Billy anywhere. The shuttle was waiting. Several people were running to catch it, so I ran too, getting on seconds before the doors closed. There were only three cars to the shuttle. Billy didn't appear to be in any of them. I stood, holding onto the railing above my head, swaying with the motion of the train until we reached Grand Central.

Then it was up a flight of stairs, down a long hallway, and down a couple more flights of stairs until I was finally on the platform for the 7. I kept my eyes on the stairs but didn't see Billy come down them. When the Queens-bound train blew into the station, I got on it and found a seat and breathed a sigh of relief.

I wasn't sure what my next step was going to be. Should Zoe and I stake out the old funeral home? What would I do if we saw Ammit? What would he do if he saw us? More than likely, he'd put us both to sleep and turn us into zombies or something. Except, of course, that he seemed to want me alive. Not like Hank. Hank had already been dead when Ammit had taken his name and memory like mine, yet he didn't want to kill me. Why?

But was it *me* he wanted, or was it Christina? And why her? What kind of person was she?

Christina's dad was a law professor. That sounded like someone who was smart. And probably either rich or in massive debt. My former roommate Kara's boyfriend was a professor at Hunter College and said he'd probably never be able to pay off his student loans. And law professors, that meant they had to go to law school, didn't it? That couldn't be cheap.

What had Michael said about Christina's mom? She was a Hollywood stuntwoman? Was there footage I could watch of her? I wondered where Christina's parents were, if they'd divorced or something else had happened. Losing a child is hard on a couple.

What kind of teenager dresses in all black with heavy makeup, drinks several kinds of alcohol, and dates a vampire? It sounded like someone with, well, issues. Come to think of it, it sounded like Billy. When I met him at Chris Street, he spent a lot of time talking about getting hammered at bars all over the city. I often wondered if he had a drinking problem.

After two stops, the train emerged from the underground tunnel onto elevated tracks and I longed for my smartphone for research purposes. Instead, I took out the flip phone I'd gotten from Lenny and texted Zoe like she'd asked me to, letting her know I was getting close.

I sighed. I was distracted by questions about my past when I should be focusing on my future. Hell, I wanted my phone back, and my backpack, too. Should I try going through the cemetery and see if I sensed anything magical? I recalled an unsettled feeling I'd had in my hands while I was around both Michael and Billy—almost a tingle, a vibration. Was I able to detect their vampiric presence because there was some kind of death magic involved?

Or maybe I just have bad circulation, I thought, as the pins and needle feeling was starting again in my right hand. *Maybe I need gloves?*

"Surprised to see me?" Billy murmured to my right.

It was as if my spirit was momentarily jerked out of my body and slammed back into it. It's what I imagine it feels like to be falling and suddenly stopped in mid-air by a parachute.

"JESUS!" I exclaimed, my hands flying up in a defensive posture.

"Whoa, relax there, Firestarter. Take it easy now. I apologize. Just having a little fun." He took a swig from a silver flask, screwed the cap back on, and smirked at me.

I looked around the subway car, but of the twelve or so other riders spread out across the car, none seemed to pay any mind to my little freak-out. Granted, this is New York. I probably could have transformed into a six-headed lizard monster and nobody would have looked up from their phones.

"Where the hell did you come from?" I hissed angrily.

"Oh, I've been here all along, pretty much."

"That's not—"

"Possible? Yeah, I'd have said that, too, except I watched your hand erupt in fire earlier, so."

"So . . . you can make yourself invisible?"

"Not exactly. Physically, I'm still visible, but I can cloud a human's perception of me. I can obscure myself, causing others to overlook me, to avoid where I'm standing."

"That's a neat trick."

"The last Eagle Scout didn't clue you in on that one?"

"Eagle Scout?"

"You know, the guy whose orders I follow?"

"He's an Eagle Scout?"

"He *was*, apparently. A long time ago. You know what we bonded over?"

"No. Why are you telling me this?"

"Just listen. Captain America. Can you believe it? Totally makes sense now that I know the guy, but wow. He was in World War II. An entertainer for the troops—just like Cap."

"I must have missed the part of the movie where Cap starts draining the soldiers dry behind the mess hall."

"He's . . . you don't understand. I've been working for the guy for six months now, and I don't think it's an act. I think he's actually . . . nice." Billy grimaced.

"Nice. You think he's *nice*?" My voice got a little louder and I quieted myself. "I think he's imperious."

"Ooh, good word. What's it mean?"

"Look it up if you want. You have the internet in your pocket."

"I don't."

"Did you lose your phone?"

"Can't carry it with me."

"Why not? Does Mr. Nice Guy not trust you?"

"It's not his choice. It's the situation he finds himself in. It's part of why I can't talk about it."

"What are you talking about?"

"No one can know he, uh, woke up?" he said, choosing his words carefully. "It's too easy to let something slip. Phones are too easily hacked. And we're dealing with magic here. Psychics. Mind readers. The whole circus sideshow. That's why my brain's been pre-hacked to prevent future hacking."

As the train went around a corner, a high-pitched squealing sound caused Billy to cover his ears.

"Why don't you get yourself noise-cancelling headphones or something?" I asked.

"Because I have to *learn to control my hearing and reactions,*" he said, sounding like he was quoting someone.

"You can do that?"

"Supposedly. I'm not having much luck. The learning curve is a bitch."

The train screeched to a stop in a station and some passengers got out and others entered. The doors closed and the train started up again.

"Why are you here?" I asked.

"Just following orders," he said quietly.

"Considering what you think of me, I don't want your help, and I don't care about your orders."

"I don't care about them either, but it's either that or I—" His mouth became an angry pucker for a moment, then he continued, "or something bad happens to me, okay? So just accept it. If you want me to make myself obscure again, I can."

"No, that's worse. I'll think you're, like, watching me in the bathroom and stuff."

"Sorry, babe. Not into watersports."

"Ugh. Just stop. If you need to follow me, fine. Just keep your distance, I guess. Try to stay out of my way."

"Just tell me this: Can you light your whole body on fire like Liz Sherman?"

"Like who?"

"The pyrokinetic chick in *Hellboy*. She's . . . hot. Literally."

I shrugged. "I don't know. I haven't tried. It sounds dangerous, don't you think?"

"Yeah, kinda Human Torch, I guess. Or Nova. Or even Dark Phoenix."

"What—why—argh. I don't get it. You think I set you up to get eaten, but here you are making conversation with me like it's no big deal."

"It is what it is."

"You can't accuse me of *murder* and then pretend like everything's okay."

"I can't?" Billy said.

The train stopped again and people got off and on.

"What do you want me to tell Zoe?" I asked. "About you."

"Oh, right. Zoe. You're staying with her. I'll need a place to hide from the sun. Does she have a walk-in closet?"

"Uh, I doubt it. Her place is kinda small."

"I'll figure something out."

"Are you going to obscure yourself?"

"Nah. I don't care what you tell her. I can't tell her anything. Tell her whatever you want."

"I'll just tell her the truth, then."

"Good luck with that," he said. We both sat in silence for a short time and the train stopped at another station. "What's our stop?"

"Woodside," I said. My temples felt like they had a vise gripping them, and I rubbed them in small circles.

Billy stood and peered at the subway map across the aisle. "Three more stops."

I yawned. "I'm just going to think—with my eyes closed."

"I'll let you know when we get there."

"'kay," I said, yawning again.

I must have fallen asleep because it seemed like only seconds later when Billy said, "Mads, this is us."

We exited the station, and I spotted Zoe's yellow station wagon parked across the street. I kept glancing at Billy out of the corner of my eye to make sure he didn't disappear again as we approached.

The driver's side door opened and Zoe got out, visibly flustered,, her mouth open and working to say something. "You're a . . . a . . ."

"Handsome bastard? Why, thank you for noticing, Zoe," Billy said cheerfully, giving her a tip of an imaginary hat.

"I'm sorry, Zoe. He followed me."

"So, you're . . . I mean . . . is he . . . uh, safe? To be around?"

I shrugged. "I'm not really sure, to be honest."

"What's the matter, ghost girl? Afraid?" Billy asked with a smirk.

"I've heard that . . . your kind . . . isn't to be messed around with."

"So don't mess around with me."

"Give it a rest, Billy. We've all had a long day," I said and shook my right hand at him.

He rolled his eyes. "Can I get in the car, or do you want me to ride on the roof?"

Zoe looked at me, uneasy with the developing situation.

"I already tried losing him," I said.

"It didn't take," Billy said with a wink.

CHAPTER TWENTY-FOUR

"I REALLY DON'T FEEL COMFORTABLE WITH THIS," Zoe said on the way to her place.

"This . . . what?" Billy asked.

"Um, *you*," she said. "Coming to my home. Do you have to be invited in? 'Cause I'm *not* inviting you in. You can sleep on the stoop for all I care."

"Depends on the building."

"How so?" I asked.

"Public buildings are no big deal. Private residences get tricky, especially ones that are owned by a single individual. Apartment buildings are hit and miss."

"Okay, so that part of vampire lore is true. I can see you in my rearview mirror, so that's a myth. What about garlic?" Zoe asked.

"There's nothing special about garlic. Anything with a very strong scent revolts me. Most kinds of perfume. Raw onions, garlic, curry, most cleaning products with bleach or ammonia. But you know, I'm new at this. So there's a lot I'm not used to."

"Do you eat?" Zoe asked. "Like, people food?"

"A little. It's . . . unpleasant."

"Crosses?" I asked.

"No effect as far as I can tell."

"Sunlight?" Zoe asked.

"Not a fan. Though, I never was."

"I assume you drink blood?"

Billy made a face and his lips pressed together.

"He can't talk about that," I said.

We stopped at a traffic light and Zoe turned around to look at Billy. "Why not?" she asked.

Billy shook his head.

"Some kind of mind whammy. Same reason he has to follow me, apparently."

The light turned green and the car was in motion once more.

"But he does drink blood, right? Human blood? Like, how much danger are we in right now?"

"It seems like it's not a big deal unless he goes without a while," I said.

"Or if I overexert myself," Billy added.

"So you're not going to go all rabid dog on us?" Zoe asked.

"Have I yet?" he asked.

Zoe exhaled a sigh of resignation. "Do you want to talk about what you found out when you met Michael?" she asked me.

"Sure," I said, and began filling her in.

Between five and ten minutes later, we pulled onto Zoe's block and she parked the station wagon several buildings away from her own. "How do you remember everything so precisely?" she asked, as we got out of the car.

"I remember everything, pretty much."

"Wait, you remember from before, too, now?"

"Oh, no, no. Not from before. Just . . . the past few days, actually."

"How?"

"Huh?"

"How do you remember? Is there some trick to it?"

"I'm not sure. It's weird?" I asked as we crossed the street. Billy followed nearby like the Secret Service.

"Kind of. You seem like you remember every single word."

"I do."

"That's kind of amazing. Is it like, a photographic memory?"

"Not exactly. I guess I hadn't realized until now."

"Maybe it's magical. You should ask that Rowan guy if you ever see him again."

Maybe it *was* magical. Maybe it had something to do with Ammit looking through my memories. I had been able to go back to my research and remember everything perfectly. And ever since, I'd been able to recall every minute detail.

Billy was being uncharacteristically quiet and I wondered if he was hoping we'd forget he was there.

We got to her building, and he stood on the stoop while Zoe unlocked the front door. Billy seemed to have no problem crossing the threshold.

It was a different story at her apartment, though. From the inside of the entryway, I saw the mystical symbols painted above her door glow white very briefly. Billy bounced backward and hit the wall as if struck by an invisible fist.

"What the fuck?" he said.

"I wondered about that. You're not going to be able to come in. My apartment is warded against the dead."

"It's what?" he asked.

"It keeps the ghosts out," I said. "And you, I guess."

"Well, that's just fan-fucking-tastic. This place got a basement?"

Zoe raised her chin. "That door. Behind you."

"Is it dark?" he asked.

"It's a basement," Zoe deadpanned.

Billy regarded us both a moment and then shook his head. "You guys are assholes," he muttered on his way down to his own private crypt.

CHAPTER TWENTY-FIVE

THE FIRST THING I DID WAS GO TO THE BATHROOM and scrub all the makeup off my face. Then I put on a t-shirt and borrowed pajama bottoms and joined Zoe in her living room where she was looking at something on her laptop.

"Feel better?" she asked.

"Much." We were both quiet a moment. "I'm really sorry about Billy."

"Seems like you didn't have much choice in the matter."

"But now you have a vampire in your basement."

"Better than bats in the belfry, I suppose."

"Hey, did you ask him if he can turn into a bat?"

"Uh . . . no. What's a belfry?"

"Huh. I don't know. Let's see." Her fingers moved quickly across the keyboard and she said, "It's part of a bell tower, apparently."

"I guess that makes sense."

"Ya. But hey, while you were in the bathroom, I checked to see if your phone has been used in the past week. It hasn't."

"Well, that's good, I guess. At least Ammit isn't calling Egypt on my dime."

"And guess what else I found? Mr. Todd's wife and daughter's obituaries. Check it out."

Katherine Elizabeth Todd (née Bowen) was born May 19, 1946 in Butler, Pennsylvania, to Claire and Francis Bowen. She grew up in Evan's City, Pennsylvania, where she met her husband, Edward Todd. The two were married in 1965 and blessed with a daughter, Kristen Claire Todd, in 1966. The family relocated to New York City shortly after the birth of their daughter. Katherine found work as a secretary at Bryant High School in the borough of Queens, where she worked for thirteen years. She and her daughter tragically passed away of carbon monoxide poisoning at their home on April 23, 1984. The two will be interred together in Calvary Cemetery. She is survived by her husband.

Kristen Claire Todd was born January 14, 1966 in Butler, Pennsylvania, to Katherine and Edward Todd. She grew up in Queens, New York, and attended Bryant High School, where she was a cheerleader and honors student. Kristen had fought a courageous battle with leukemia but tragically passed away on April 23, 1984 of carbon monoxide poisoning, along with her mother. The two will be interred together in Calvary Cemetery. She is survived by her father.

She'd been so young. About my age, I realized.

"Wow, that's so sad," I said.

"Do you think that's how they really died?" she asked.

"What do you mean?"

"Well, do you think it could have been, like, a suicide thing? The mom, faced with her daughter dying, killed both her daughter and herself so they could be together forever?"

"That's dark."

"I've heard darker." Her lip curled up and she wrinkled her nose. "Anyway, I was thinking we should go to the cemetery tomorrow and visit their graves."

"That place is huge. I guess we can visit the office and ask where to find them."

"Or we can head over to FindAGrave.com and . . . Bingo. Plot, section, and grave numbers. I'll send myself the link to the page . . . aaand done. Map's online too."

"Impressive. Why do you want to visit the graves?"

"I want to ask them how they died."

"Wait, like, their ghosts?"

"Yes."

"So a proper burial doesn't stop someone from becoming a ghost?"

"Not as far as I can tell. I mean, it's not like there's a ghost for *every* grave, but there have been ghosts in every cemetery I've ever been in."

"So a place like Calvary must be chock full of them?"

She did some more typing. "Considering there have been . . . three million burials there?"

"Three *what*? Million? Can that be right?"

She typed several characters. "Calvary was founded in 1848. So that's . . . 170 years or so of burials for the most populated city in the United States."

"That's nuts."

"So, yes, there will be spirits there."

"And bats in the belfry?"

"Definitely."

As we drove into the cemetery, I asked Zoe if she saw any ghosts, and without even turning her head, she replied, "Yep."

"A lot?"

"Enough."

I stayed quiet until we parked.

We climbed the hillside of graves. The cemetery had a very different feel in the morning sunshine. It was less gloomy, and there were more trees and bushes in this part of the cemetery than the part I'd seen, though I wasn't entirely sure where that was. I wished I had looked for a family name on the mausoleum I'd come out of, but that's easy to say when you're not being chased by rat skeletons.

Zoe spent a moment looking at her phone. "Should be over this way," she said, cutting towards the right side of the hill.

I joined her, but my eyes kept roaming over various stones. Last names in all caps. Crosses. Statues of angels, Mary, Jesus. Dates and names. Repeated phrases: *In memory of. Our beloved mother. Died in infancy. Gone but not forgotten.* Then I saw it. TODD. Beneath it, the names with birth and death dates of the wife and daughter we'd read about.

"There." I pointed.

"Anybody home?" Zoe asked.

She wasn't talking to me.

I tried looking at the plot askance but didn't notice anything.

"Hey," Zoe said, looking off to her right. "Yes, you. Yes, I can see you."

"Is it one of them?" I asked.

"No. It's a guy," she said from the corner of her mouth. Then she turned her attention to her new invisible friend. "Hi, thanks for coming over. I'm Zoe. You are?" She paused, listening to a voice only she could hear. "How long have you been here? Have you ever noticed anyone here, at this grave? Yes, dead or alive. Okay, thanks. No, she can't see you."

I squinted from the corner of my eye in the direction Zoe was talking. "I can maaaaybe sort of seeeee . . . no, I don't know." It had been like the wavering of the air above a hot street in the summertime but disappeared when I looked head-on. "Zoe, do you think you could teach me to see ghosts the way you do?" I asked.

"I'm not sure. I've never *tried* to see them. It just happens." Then she spoke to the ghost, "No, she's not a medium. She's a magus, we think."

Whatever the ghost was saying, Zoe seemed surprised by it.

"Did you know a magus who called himself Orpheus?" she asked me. "Or hear about him?"

"No. Why?"

"Because he's in this cemetery somewhere. Salvatore here has met him."

"A person or a ghost?"

"Ghosts are people, too, you know."

"My bad. You know, I'm not really one of them. The maguses. Magi. I'm not trained or anything. Apparently that's not usual."

Zoe seemed to be listening to the ghost and repeating some of what he said to me. "No, you wouldn't have met this guy. He died in the mid-twentieth century. He was kind of famous for songwriting."

"What did he write?"

"Do you remember the dancing frog from the old Looney Tunes? With the top hat and the cane? *Hello, ma baby, hello, ma honey, hello, ma ragtime gal . . .*"

"It sounds kind of familiar," I said.

"This Orpheus guy wrote that song. And a bunch of others."

"And?"

"And apparently, when he was a magus, and alive, he used to come to this cemetery and talk with the spirits here. Maybe that means he could teach you how to do it. Salvatore is willing to make the introduction."

"So how do we find this guy?"

"No, he says you need to hold your hands like *this*," Zoe said. She placed her index and middle fingers on each hand together in a 90-degree angle and made her thumbs touch as the bottom part of the triangle.

"I *did* that," I said, holding my hands out at her.

"No, he says your triangle is wrong. Your hands need to be flat. Act like you're pressing them against a wall."

"But then my fingers overlap."

"It's okay if they overlap. They *should* overlap, he says. And the bottom of your triangle is wrong. Try moving your thumbs back a little, I guess? Towards you, towards you."

I flattened out my fingers and moved my thumbs slightly. Suddenly my hands aligned perfectly and I could see the triangle effect more clearly.

"Oh! Yay, you got it!"

"This feels very awkward."

"Okay, now hold your fingers up and look through the triangle to the east."

"Which way is east?"

"Uh . . ." Zoe looked around a moment. "That way," she said, pointing.

I held my fingers up and looked towards the east through the triangle shape they'd made. All I saw were rows upon rows upon rows of tombstones. No spirits.

"No magic words? Abracadabra?"

"No words. Just concentrate."

"On what?"

"I don't think she has one," Zoe said to the air.

"I don't have one what?"

"A magister?"

"My arms are tired. What's a magister?"

"A mentor magus. Somebody who teaches you how to do things like this."

"Not yet."

"What about that Rowan guy?"

My hands felt cold and my shoulders and elbows felt achy. "Ugh, this is not working. I don't know if Rowan will want to work with me after I ran away from Zero. Plus, he's *away*, whatever that means." I put my hands in my pockets.

"He says you need to stop talking and concentrate on your breathing."

I rolled my neck and shook my shoulders and tried again.

"He says now bring your hands together like this," Zoe demonstrated, her hands closing the triangle and leaving the index and middle fingers crossing one another in a V-shape. "Yeah, like that. He says now you hold them in front of your face, covering your eyes. You close your eyes for a moment and as you draw your hands apart into the triangle, your eyes open at the same time. But breathe and concentrate while you do it."

Breathe and concentrate. Put my hands up to my eyes. It all seemed so ridiculous. But that was probably part of the problem, wasn't it? For the magic to work, I needed to *believe* in the magic working. I exhaled slowly and held my hands up to my eyes. I closed my eyes and concentrated on my breathing.

"Elbows up more . . . that's good," Zoe said. "Whenever you're ready, start to pull your hands apart into the triangle and open your eyes."

Seeing. Breathing. Seeing.

I thought about those fluttery feelings, the jolts and tingles I'd felt in the presence of the dead or undead. I tried to concentrate on those feelings. What it was like to see a shadow or wispy, wavery air disturbance out of the corner of my eye.

Seeing.

I inhaled and exhaled slowly, and I felt a warmth in my hands, a feeling of power. As I slowly drew them apart into the triangle shape, I opened my eyes at the same speed.

A semi-transparent man stood before me. He existed inside the triangle, but not outside it. He had dark hair that was slicked down and parted on the side, and he wore an old-fashioned tuxedo with a stiff-collared white shirt and a bow tie.

He had a wide mouth, a large nose, and a prominent chin. He nodded in approval. "Adequate for a neophyte," he said. He spoke in a cultivated voice with long vowels.

Zoe clapped quietly, bouncing up and down like a little girl who'd just won a stuffed unicorn at a county fair.

"I thought the word was *novitiate*," I said.

"Not until you start your training with a magister. Rowan's a good man and teacher. You could do worse." His voice sounded a bit faint, as though it was coming from far away.

I supposed it was.

I introduced myself as Madison and he introduced himself as Orpheus.

"So do you know anything about Ammit?" I asked.

"No, that name is not familiar to me."

"What about . . . have you seen any, like, rat skeletons or skeletal hands running around? A zombie dog, maybe?"

"Foul necromancy," Orpheus said. "To speak with the dead, to help the unquiet ones find their rest, that is right and good. To animate their corpses to do one's bidding? Extremely rare and very wicked magic. From a practitioner of frightful power, too. You ought to wait for Rowan's return."

"Have you seen them?"

"I have heard rumors of such creatures. They offer no immediate threat to us. To you, on the other hand . . ."

"But do you know where they came from?"

"I do not know, but I may know someone who does. Salvatore, old fellow, where does young Miss Josephina bide her time?"

I shifted my perspective and another semi-transparent man with a handlebar mustache came into view, wearing suspenders over a white shirt. "Between the two overpasses. Western. North," he said.

"There you have it, my dear."

"Thank you for your help. And the instructions."

"Seek out Rowan. He will help you."

I pulled my hands apart. The edges of whatever window I'd been looking through seemed to dissolve and his voice faded away.

I wiped my hands on my jeans. I'd forgone the gothic outfit and makeup for our cemetery visit.

"Shall we?" Zoe asked.

"Oh, hell no. Not with you, and not without the uh . . . *bat* in your basement."

"You worried that those things will come after you again?"

"A little. And I don't want them coming after *you*."

Zoe nodded. "Alright. Let's go talk to the bat."

"Hello, Jane Doe," said a familiar voice. "Also known as Madison Roberts." It was Zero, accompanied by a guy whose unkempt red hair glinted in the afternoon sunshine. The two men emerged from behind a row of family mausoleums.

"Detective Wilson. Also known as Zero," I said. "Fuckety fucksticks. How'd you find me?"

"Quinn here suggested we follow up on your cemetery claim." Immaculately put together as always, Zero had a black trench coat folded over the arm of his gray suit, which he wore over a black shirt and tightly knotted tie.

Quinn wore a too-large tan trench coat over a wrinkled shirt and loosened tie. He was maybe in his mid-twenties or early thirties—at least a little younger than Zero.

"I didn't think you'd actually be here, though," Quinn said wearily. "But thanks for wearing red. That coat made you easy to spot."

The two came to a stop some twenty feet from us, barring our way.

"Maddy, how do you know these guys?" Zoe asked.

"One of them detained me."

"Hey, now, is that any way to thank a guy who made you breakfast?" said Zero.

Both Zoe and Quinn gave him a look.

"Not like *that*," he amended.

"Well, enjoy the cemetery," I said, taking Zoe's arm.

"Uh uh. No way," Zero said, his New York tough guy routine in full effect. "You gotta come with us."

"No, I don't." I looked at their feet, wondering if I could set their shoes on fire. Zero's were black and shiny. Quinn's brown and scuffed. Neither pair looked especially flammable.

Zero slipped a pad of paper out of his pocket and held a pen dramatically over it.

He and Quinn stood together against a background of headstones and crosses.

"Not this again," I said. "You know it didn't work out so well for you last time, right?"

"This time we're protected versus Fire," Zero said. He advanced on me.

The sun went behind a cloud.

Suddenly, Zero stumbled, as if he'd tripped over an invisible root. "What the—?"

"Hey, now!" said Quinn, holding his hands in the air as he was shoved by invisible hands.

"Quinn, take her," Zero said, his breath forming gray swirls in the air, air that had dropped in temperature several degrees.

"Me?" Quinn sputtered.

"Yes, you."

"By myself? Fuck that!"

"I'm not coming with you," I said, as my words smoked through the cold air. "Either of you." I felt cold. Very cold. Almost as if my body heat had drained out of me and I was standing inside a freezer instead of a cemetery hillside.

Zero's face went pale and Quinn, whose arms had begun to relax, put them back up high again. What were those looks of shock on their faces? What did they see that I didn't?

I looked to Zoe and realized it was no longer just the two of us amidst mausoleums. Standing all around us were ghosts. Visible, translucent ghosts, shimmering with a pale purple light. Orpheus, a commanding figure in his tuxedo. A young man in a Marine's dress uniform carried a sword. The man with the handlebar mustache and the suspenders held up his fists as if ready to fight. An older man wearing a suit and fedora pulled a revolver, and a woman with a beehive hairdo brandished a ghostly rolling pin. A glance over my shoulder revealed two boys with hollow cheeks in sailor costumes, a disapproving lady wearing a hooped skirt and bonnet, and a teen girl who appeared bedraggled and wet.

"Oh my God," murmured Zoe. "We have an army."

"Are you *commanding* the dead against us?" Zero asked, aghast as he stared at the assemblage of spirits.

I shivered slightly. "What if I am?"

Orpheus's voice echoed around us, a rich speaking voice full of rounded vowels. "You shall molest these young women no longer."

"The dead speak, boss," Quinn said, dropping his arms and putting his hands in his pockets. "That's like biblical end of days, isn't it? I think that's our cue."

"Let's head for the car, Zoe," I said.

The two men watched as Zoe and I gave them a wide berth.

Zero's disgust vied with anger and horror on his face.

"You can't run forever," he hollered as we walked away.

"Nope. But I can today," I said.

Still shivering, I looked back when we got to Zoe's car.

The ghosts remained on the hillside, forming a barrier between us.

Once we were inside the wood-paneled station wagon, the ghosts began to flicker out, one at a time.

"Can you believe that cop thought I was controlling the ghosts?" I said.

"It would come in handy if you could."

"Brrr. Turn on the heat!" I said as Zoe started up the car.

Quinn sat down on the hillside, shaking his head. Zero took out a phone, still looking very pale.

I almost felt sorry for them.

Chapter Twenty-six

Once we were out of the cemetery, I asked Zoe if I could borrow some money to run a few errands. "Not that I can pay you back for any of this right now, of course," I said.

Zoe laughed. It was a weird laugh. More the sort of chortle you might expect from a drunk person. "You have no idea what you've done, do you?"

"What I've done?" I got a slight panicky feeling. What had I done? My mind raced. Had I left the sheets on the couch in the living room? I knew I put the cap back on the toothpaste. As respcctful as I'd tried to be, I couldn't imagine what a burden I was.

"I'm sorry, Zoe. I've been so thoughtless. You're probably sick of me at this point. Driving me around. Feeding and clothing me. Talking to ghosts for me."

She giggled. "Sick of you? Are you *kidding* me? You *saw* them. Saw them! Just like me! And then! Then *they* saw them!"

"The ghosts?"

"Yeah. You saw ghosts. The same ghosts that I saw. You talked to them. They appeared to you. They appeared to those guys! That's *crazy*! Do you know how long it's been since I could share this part of my life with anyone? Since my Gram died. Everyone else I've tried talking to about it has run screaming. Oh, Maddy, will you be my bestie? I mean, you already are. So, no, I'm not sick of you. Don't worry about paying me back. These are the kinds of things friends do for each other."

My throat was incredibly tight and I felt tears forming at the corners of my eyes. I cleared my throat and wiped at the moisture with the side of my hand. "Hey, you better cut that out. I'll cry all over your car."

The front walk and porch of the Victorian (formerly funeral) home displayed more fallen leaves and two newspapers in their plastic cocoons, several feet from one another. Zoe refused to stop, not wanting to call attention to us in case Ammit happened to be peeking out the front windows.

"I think he's still out of town. Wherever he went, I don't think he's here," I said.

"Yeah, but you're not going to break in the back, right? We don't need you getting arrested again."

"I wasn't arrested. I was detained."

"Semantics. Did you hear back from the LIC dudes?"

I consulted my phone. Lenny's text said my "package" would be ready by 3PM. "So what do you want to do until then?" I asked.

"Lunch?" she said.

Zoe bought us gyros at a food cart and filled her gas tank. She drove me out to the Collective Collective a little after 3PM. Lenny was wearing a headset and holding a conversation when he greeted me and gestured toward the couches, holding up a finger to indicate I should wait a bit.

"That's not going to work for us, sleepyhead. We're going to need to restructure the entire payout schedule . . ."

I sat and he left the room, still talking.

The hamster tunnel waterpipe was gone from the coffee table, replaced by a bouquet of pink and purple flowers in a vase: lilies, carnations, roses, and others I didn't recognize. I leaned forward and smelled them. There was only a faint scent, but they were pretty to look at.

". . . have the paperwork drawn up. Uh huh." Lenny said, re-entering the room with a large manila envelope that he handed to me. "Done and done. Thursday at 5PM? Good. See you then." He tapped the wire around his neck and then removed the headset from his ear. "Sorry about that, peaches. Money never sleeps."

"It's okay," I said. "I was on a call the last time I was here. We're even." I smiled. The manila envelope was an inch thick, at least.

"Well, take a look at your package," Lenny said, sitting on the next closest couch, so that we were catty-corner from one another. "As long as Kipling keeps his half of the bargain, which he has already begun to fulfill, these will hold up under any sort of official inquiry or scrutiny."

I undid the metal clasp and slid the documents out, setting the envelope down. As promised, I found a Social Security card, a birth certificate, a passport, information for a bank account with a debit card, a YMCA photo ID, a Brooklyn Library card, and a letter from the State Education Department of the University of the State of New York. It appeared to be a group of test scores. Behind it was a certificate listing Madison Roberts as having achieved her High School Equivalency Diploma.

An incredible weight seemed to lift from my shoulders, or my chest, or brain. It was an evaporation of anxiety. I felt lighter. Less worried about . . . well, everything.

After a year of having no past, and no future, I now held the seeds of a real life. I could get a real job that didn't pay me cash under the table every two weeks. I could go to college. I could leave the country. I could even finally take a book out from the library.

I was a *citizen*.

"Wow." I didn't know what else to say.

"We also created a Facebook account with backdated info and some pictures, if you want it."

"What for?"

"Social media is part of twenty-first century culture, dearest. If you don't exist online, you don't exist."

"Uh, okay."

"There's something else inside the envelope," Lenny said.

A look into the envelope revealed a small velvet pouch, light gray in color and closed with a drawstring. I tipped the envelope into my hand and the pouch slid out.

"What's this?" I asked. There was something inside the pouch, which had a bit of weight to it.

"Kipling dropped it by for you. He asked me to make sure you got it."

I looked at Lenny and he looked at me.

"Aren't you going to open it?"

"I don't know. Things with Kip and I . . ."

"Are complicated? I know. I put that as your relationship status. Anywho, he told me to tell you it's a belated birthday present."

"Do you know what it is?"

"I don't. That's why I want you to open it!"

I sighed. I unknotted the drawstrings and opened the pouch, pouring out a silver chain with a multihued amulet. It was oval shaped, about two inches high and one wide, and polished smooth in a silver setting. The stone shimmered in the light, showing dark blue, gold, green, and violet with dark gray striations slanting among the colors. A small piece of parchment was attached to it, about the size of a business card.

"Oh, labradorite! That's a powerful stone," Lenny said. "What's on the tag?"

I turned the paper over and peered at the small calligraphy. Then I read aloud:

Shield from those who prod and pry
Lens for Spirit's inner eye

Ward against the Wyrd Ones' wrath
Opens magic's inner path
All these gifts herein will last
'Til autumn equinox is passed
'Ere the sun all thirteen sails
Then this magic fades and fails.

An M symbol appeared at the bottom, except it had an odd loop on the right side, like the M had grown a large ear.

"Ooh," Lenny breathed, seeming awed.

"What?"

He gave me an appraising look. "Do you not recognize the symbol?"

I shook my head.

"It's the symbol for Virgo, also known as The Maiden."

"Am I a Virgo? I thought October was Libra."

"That's according to the zodiac of twelve. In the zodiac of thirteen, you're a Virgo. Also, it's not strictly month to month—it changes partway through each month."

"I never heard of there being thirteen zodiac signs. *'Ere the sun all thirteen sails*?"

"Yes, its movement through all thirteen constellations. A year, basically."

"Until the autumn equinox?"

"Well, the equinox is in late September, lovey. So the magic will start to fade then, and go out by the end of the sun's journey through Virgo. You can have it recharged after that."

I shook my head in wonderment. "What's the rest of it mean?"

"Hmm. *Shield from those who prod and pry*—that's for protection of your aura. *Lens for Spirit's inner eye*—that should help you with seeing magic. *Ward against the Wyrd Ones' wrath*—that's versus the High Fey, to keep them from coming after you. And *Opens magic's inner path*—should help you along in becoming the magus you're meant to be. That's quite a gift, my lamb. Wear it well and blessed be and all that."

I unclasped the necklace and put it on, admiring the way the colors shifted in the light. It seemed to almost glow from within.

"Lenny, how can I thank you?"

"Don't thank me, sweetness. Don't thank the fey in general, actually. Trust me: You don't want to be beholden to them. Just let me know when you want to finish your truthsayer session so I can get my tickets, 'kay?"

"May I kiss your cheek?" I asked.

He smiled. "You may."

CHAPTER TWENTY-SEVEN

"I GUESS I KNOW WHERE TO GO IF I EVER NEED TO change my identity," Zoe said.

"Yeah, just save a faerie's life and you're all set."

She slid the pile of papers back into the envelope and handed it to me. "What are they like?"

"The fey?"

She nodded.

"Weird, I guess? They seem to have this bartering culture with favors and promises and no lying and . . . I don't know. Where do I even begin? I'm just crazy grateful to have this stuff, you know? Before I couldn't get a job, or go to school, or even get a freaking library card—a library card! Do you know how happy I am to have this thing?"

"You get a bank account and a passport and you're happy to have a library card?" She laughed.

"When I was at Spring House, the home for wayward mental patients trying to rejoin society, I couldn't watch TV because it gave me headaches. There were magazines, full of celebrities I'd never heard of and obsessions with clothes and makeup and who cares? I just wanted to read a book, but I could never take one out no matter how many times

I went to the library. The only books I ever got were ones that people left on the sidewalk in front of their buildings. Didn't have a job, didn't have money, so I couldn't even buy myself the most basic things I wanted. Speaking of which, is there a secondhand store nearby so I can get some clothes? And can we stop by the hardware store on the way back to your place? I want to pick up some supplies. Oh, and did I mention I may need to borrow some money?"

"*May*?"

"Okay, definitely."

"Do you think he's still in the basement?" Zoe asked me as she unlocked the front door to her building. It was just barely still light out, but the late afternoon rays of sun were reflecting off the windows of the building across the street and streaming through the glass door.

"Where else is he going to go?" I asked, following her into the building.

"Oh, maybe my cousin's place upstairs?"

"Your cousin lives upstairs?"

"Yeah, she's like, I don't know, my second cousin once removed or something like that. My mom's cousin, but a generation apart. She owns the building, so my rent is cheap." She unlocked her apartment door and we went in.

"That's a pretty good deal," I said.

"Oh, I'm lucky. No question there." She put down her purse and shrugged off her jacket. "You think he's in a trance down there or something?"

I dropped the rattling bag of supplies from the hardware store and took off the cropped motorcycle jacket I'd bought at Stray Vintage. "I have no idea. You want me to go check?"

"Would you?"

Billy had either found or created a little secluded corner for himself behind a couple of tall bookshelves and stacks of boxes that formed a wall and separated him from the rest of the basement. I could just see his combat boots hanging off the edge of a yellow couch.

The basement was unfinished, with concrete floors and walls and exposed beams on the ceiling. A washer and dryer stood against one wall, and more boxes and plastic tubs were stacked in various parts of the room, along with an old vacuum cleaner, dented luggage, and a lamp with a broken shade.

I came around the corner of the bookshelves and found Billy lying full-length upon the brassy yellow couch, his face obscured from view by the old *Reader's Digest* he held. He didn't look up.

"Enthralling article?"

"Eh, not really." But the book remained in front of his face.

"So I wanted to ask you about—"

He interrupted me. "Nope."

"Huh? You didn't even let me finish."

"Don't ask me anything. Just do whatever you're going to do. I have to go along either way. So don't ask. It's insulting."

"I was going to ask if you can turn into a bat." I wasn't going to ask that, but he didn't know that. I had planned to ask him if he wanted to come with me to the cemetery to look for the entrance to the mausoleum that would lead to Ammit's lair.

Now he put the digest down on his chest. He seemed amused. I was relieved to see that he still looked the same. I'm not sure what I thought, maybe that he'd look more vampiric after a day underground, but he was just Billy. Vampire Billy, I guess. But Billy.

"Just call me Batman."

"Seriously?"

"No."

"Can you fly?"

"No!"

After the sun went down, we did a bit of scouting, Billy and I climbed over a chain link fence into the cemetery. It was strange climbing into the oasis of dark, moving away from the neighborhood streetlights and creeping through paths between headstones. It was dark, but not pitch black due to the light pollution of the city, and it was quieter, insulated.

While we moved towards the portion of the cemetery we'd been directed to, the Manhattan skyline glittered in the distance.

Though Zoe had volunteered to join us, I'd dissuaded her. Instead, she would wait nearby in her station wagon for our call.

Billy and I were dressed in dark colors, my hair once again tucked in a hat. Calvary was closed after all, and it wouldn't do for us to be noticed by police, especially given my backpack of makeshift burglary tools, which would surely get us arrested as opposed to detained.

"Which way?" Billy asked.

"I'm not sure."

"What about your perfect memory?"

"I'm trying. I was only running for my life the last time I was here." I turned in a full circle, surveying the landscape, remembering what I had seen when I'd escaped the mausoleum. Everything was so different at night. Even when I flipped through the Rolodex of my memories, the images were blurred with frantic motion and panic. They were no help.

Maybe I should ask a ghost.

"Give me a minute," I said. I walked some distance from Billy so that his undead presence was no longer primary in my awareness. If I wanted to sense any ghosts, I needed a clearer head.

I closed my eyes and measured my breathing, then formed my hands and fingers into the triangle shapes that Zoe and Orpheus had directed. It was easier this time, and the feeling of warmth and the slight tingle came more quickly. When I felt an answering warmth at my throat—the amulet—I opened my eyes and hands.

The gasp that escaped me was involuntary.

They were everywhere.

Surrounding me.

Having conversations.

Walking by.

Here was a pale woman in a Victorian dress, lecturing a man in white t-shirt and blue jeans, the t-shirt covered in blood, his face half ruined.

There was an elderly man in slacks and a sweater with a knife sticking out of his chest. He smiled at me.

It was not reassuring.

A younger man in a blue Civil War uniform with a gunshot wound in his belly was making fun of Billy, miming his posture.

Two boys in short pants and newsy caps chased a hoop of some sort.

A woman in a pink dress and matching go-go boots had bulging eyes and a necklace of bruises around her throat. Swaying to music only she could hear, she opened her mouth as if to speak but all that came out were gagging noises.

I dropped my hands from the triangular viewing window, thinking it would break the spell like last time.

But it didn't.

I squeezed my eyes shut and took a deep breath, then opened them again. The ghosts were still there.

"Um . . . excuse me? Sorry to interrupt. Do any of you know Miss Josephina?" I asked, my voice going squeaky at the beginning but normalizing toward the end.

Miss Josephina, age twelve and wearing a long white nightgown, waved farewell to me from the hillside. She wouldn't come closer to the mausoleum. Her parents, buried right next to her many decades later, forbid it.

The wind whipped up, shaking the leaves in a nearby tree, and it was odd to see how it didn't affect her nightgown or hair at all.

I sighed and turned back to the business at hand. There was no name above the doors, just a small plaque on the right side of the doorway with a name, years of birth and death, and a motto: *She hath done what she could.*

Hathn't we all, I thought.

Billy approached the doors while I rummaged in my backpack, quickly finding the bolt cutters I'd purchased in case the chain and lock had been fastened, which—as evidenced by the quick yank Billy attempted—it had been.

"Here, use these," I said.

"I don't need those," he sneered.

"Don't use up your super strength. Save it in case we need it later."

He shrugged and took the bolt cutters. I pulled on the gardening gloves I'd bought and readied a flashlight.

After a loud *ka-chunk*, the chain clanked to the ground. Billy turned back to me just as I turned on the flashlight. The beam hit him in the face.

He hissed—actually hissed—at me.

"Jesus, Mads. Are you trying to blind me?" he said after I directed the beam downwards.

"Sorry! I didn't know you were going to turn around right then!"

He made a sound of disgust and held the bolt cutters out to me. I took them as he flung both doors open. The wind blew fiercely, creating an eerie moaning between cemetery monuments and sending a few leaves spinning across the mausoleum's threshold.

It seemed to be the right place. The stone sarcophagus and stone urns inside were as I remembered them. I looked for the stained-glass window. The ornate border around the three white lilies showed up red and blue beneath the flashlight's beam.

Yet one thing was missing: There was no secret door opening that I could see. Billy observed this by saying, "The fuck we're supposed to go now?"

"Shhh!" I looked around nervously, listening for skeletal critters. A sound near the doors made me jump, but the flashlight revealed only the dry leaves as they danced in a circular waltz on the marble floor.

"Relax. It's just leaves. Are you sure this is the right place?"

I exhaled. Wherever the rat skeletons and skeletal hands had gone, they didn't seem to be here. "Let me see. The first thing I saw was . . . the image of the stained glass. On that wall," I pointed. "It's the same window. But the image of it was on—" I moved so that the layout matched my memory of it "—this side of me. So the door must be . . ." I rotated, shining the flashlight on a stone urn standing inside a curved niche. "Here."

"Well, that's some Scooby-Doo shit. How's it open?"

"There was a lever inside the tunnel, but it's on the other side. I don't know about this side."

I shone the flashlight over the area for a closer look. The niche was hollow above the urn, which meant that the entire thing slid into it when the secret door was opened. I waved Billy over and showed him.

"Do you think it's one way? Exit-only like the subway?"

"You're asking me?" he said.

"Look, there's a seam where the slab meets the floor," I said, tucking the flashlight under one arm. The crowbar I'd purchased hadn't quite fit in the backpack, so it was easy to grab.

"There's nothing like a pretty girl who knows how to burgle," said Billy.

"Cram it, you."

I inserted the end of the crowbar into the seam, then applied pressure to wedge it open. At first, nothing happened. Then I applied more pressure, putting my whole weight into it. I was glad to have the gardening gloves on as I felt the rough metal tear at the fabric. Moments later, the secret door slab was lifted by about half an inch.

"Can you get your fingers in and lift?" I asked. "This is as far as I'm getting it."

Billy put the flashlight on the floor and awkwardly straddled the crowbar, then squatted and jammed his fingers into the space I'd created.

He made a sound of exertion and repositioned his arms. Another grunt of effort, then the grinding sound of stone on stone echoed in the tunnel and out into the mausoleum as Billy slowly stood upright, sliding the urn up into the hollow above the niche.

As he lifted, a whooshing sound passed into the space beyond, like some huge beast sucking in air.

"Holy shit. This really *is* a secret door."

"What do you think I brought you here for?"

I slipped around him and stepped into the dark recessed space with the flashlight and found the lever inside the tunnel. I slid it in the opposite direction in hopes that it would lock the door open.

There was a loud clicking noise and Billy said, "Huh."

"What?"

"It moved. What'd you do?"

"I flipped the lever. Do you think it will stay up if you let go?"

"Can you open it again if it doesn't?"

"Unless you broke it," I said.

"Very funny." He pulled one hand away slowly and then the other. The slab held and he joined me inside the narrow tunnel. "You first." He gestured with one hand, waving me ahead.

The flashlight played on the roughhewn walls of the tunnel. It was less creepy than I remembered . . . until I heard an odd sound.

"Shh! Did you hear that?" I asked. The sound had a ticking, skittering quality.

"Yeah, it's just the leaves, Mads. Relax," Billy said.

The wind once again groaned eerily into the tunnel.

We made our way up a few steps, through the rusted gate, then down several steps.

"Why are there stairs here? That doesn't seem practical."

"Yeah, I don't get it. What's that smell? It smells like . . . corn chips."

"That's what bone dust smells like."

"*Bone* dust? How do you know that?"

"I've spent time in a few crypts the past several months, alright?"

Another stealthy sound. A scratching maybe.

"Did you hear that?"

"Seriously? I don't know why you're so nervous," he said, as something white climbed over the shoulder of his leather jacket.

The object that crept into view was some bastardization of a rat's skull and ribcage that had had human finger bones attached to it so that it moved like a spider.

"I mean, what do you have to worry about—"

"Billy—"

"You can do magic—"

"—there's a—"

"—And I am what I am—"

"BILLY!" I said through clenched teeth.

"What?"

"There's. A. Thing. On your jacket."

"What like a spider or some—HOLY FUCK WHAT IS THAT?" he yelled.

Suddenly, there were four or five more of them in the tunnel with us, the rat skulls gnashing their yellow incisors, the sharp finger bones that made up their legs grasping and grabbing at our clothes and skin like horrid skeletal spiders.

I smacked one with the flashlight, whacking it against the wall. It came apart like a Lincoln Log cabin. Billy pulled the one on his jacket apart into pieces of bone and grabbed another, doing the same.

Something was crawling up my pant leg. I clobbered it with the flashlight and the creature fell to the ground. I dropped the flashlight as well, grabbing the crowbar sticking out of the backpack.

I tried stabbing at the thing but it evaded my thrusts.

It sprang onto the wall and then onto my wrist, clinging to the sleeve of my new leather jacket and biting my hand.

"Gah!" I yelled, shaking it off.

It came running back at me again and I managed to step on two of its legs, pinning it in place. This time my stab with the end of the crowbar was successful, though it took a few thrusts to get the creature to stop moving.

"Any more? Come on. What you got? Huh?" Billy had just dropped the remains of another of the creatures he'd destroyed. "That's it? Lame." He seemed to be enjoying himself. Small bones and rat skulls were scattered at his feet.

"Is that it? Is it over?" I asked.

"There's one on your leg!"

I became aware of the pressure of the pokey finger bones on the back of my calf at the same time that I heard a familiar sound—an odd *kerflumphing*. Suddenly, the feeling of pressure was gone, and the tripod zombie dog came into view, loping along on the three skeletal hands it had for legs. It held the rat-spider thing in its jaws and shook it viciously from side to side, crunching and chomping on it until the thing stopped thrashing.

Then the little dog dropped the dead spider-thing at my feet. Like a gift for its master. Had it been a terrier? Or maybe a dachshund? The torso seemed a little long. Its fur appeared to have once been gray, now matted in mangy tufts.

Its tail was wagging and it stood on its back leg-hands, a gray tongue lolling from its open, smiling mouth. It seemed . . . happy?

"GARF!" it barked, rotating its front hand into handshake position.

"Mads, what the fuck is that thing?"

I stared at the creature with my mouth open and nothing came out at first. "A dog? I think?"

"GARF!"

The zombie dog hopped around in a circle and offered me its front paw-hand again.

It was kind of cute.

"I think it wants to shake," Billy said.

"Yeah. I see that." I leaned forward and grasped the hand for the briefest of shakes. "Good dog?"

"GARF GARF!" it yapped again, the small tail frantically fanning the air.

I patted it gently on the head. "Good boy." It *was* cute. Dead, and weird, but cute.

The little dog hopped back down to all-threes, trotted in a circle for a moment, then headed back down the passage toward the mausoleum.

This was insane.

This was my life.

I resisted the urge to slide down the wall and sit on the floor. Not only would going to pieces not do me any good, but there were pieces there already, of skeletal rats and hands, and I wasn't ready to join them.

I took a shaky breath and laughed weakly. "So now you know what I was nervous about."

Billy was unscrewing the top of his silver flask. "You didn't tell me they were frankenskeleton rat-spiders!"

"They weren't! They were just rat skeletons last time! And hands, too, but they were separate. He must have done something. Changed them."

He took a swig from the flask then spoke. "This Ammit guy needs a new hobby. What about that dog?"

"To be honest? I had kind of forgotten about it."

"You forgot about a zombie dog?" He took another swig, evidently emptying the flask.

"There's kind of been a lot." I stowed the crowbar and picked up the flashlight. The lens was cracked, and it flickered when I picked it up, but it still worked. I bounced the beam over to Billy, making sure to avoid his eyes. "You okay?"

"You kidding? This is the most fun I've had since I died. C'mon."

"You need to get out more."

"Tell me about it."

It was dark except for the bouncing beam of the flashlight and quiet except for the sound of my movements. We'd been walking in the roughhewn tunnel for several minutes and my own breath and footsteps seemed excessively loud. Billy, on the other hand, hardly made noise at all.

"Can't you at least pretend to breathe?" I asked.

His inhale was loud. "Sure." The exhale was less so.

The flashlight flickered off and on. It was my own fault, I supposed. Dropping it, using it as a weapon. Probably damaged the wiring. Or maybe it needed new batteries. I had spares. But what good would they do if the flashlight was broken? *I should have brought a spare flashlight.*

It flickered again and went out just as we reached the next set of stairs. Maybe the batteries were just loose, I thought. I stopped and unscrewed the bottom then rescrewed it.

"What are you doing?" Billy asked.

"Stupid flashlight died."

"Well, turning it on and off over and over again isn't going to make it work."

"What are you talking about? I'm not doing that."

"Then what's that clicking noise?"

I listened to see if I could hear what he was talking about. *Click clack. Click clack*, I heard.

It was coming from above.

I really, really wished that the flashlight was working again. I shook it vertically and miraculously, it came back on. The white beam shot out of it towards the ceiling, revealing a nightmare-horror.

Suspending itself on the ceiling with its spider-arms splayed to the walls was another hybrid creature—this one combining the gray-skinned head and torso of a small child, another larger lump of flesh below that, and once again, eight legs arranged like a spider's, but made of human arms, some skeletal, others gray but fleshier.

"What in the fucking fuck?" said Billy. "What the actual fuck is *that*?"

The creature—its head slightly larger in scale than the torso—opened its mouth and clacked its teeth. As it plunged from the ceiling onto the two of us, I screamed.

I dropped the flashlight and it went out.

Hands scrambled over my shoulders and upper body, clutching at my clothes, trying to gain purchase. "Get off me, you hand-footed freak!" I yelled.

"Guh-guh!" screeched the horrible clacking-toothed thing.

"Aw hell no!" Billy shouted.

A hand grabbed my throat, painfully squeezing my windpipe. The hand felt sharp and cold and bony and I felt a surge of panic because I couldn't breathe.

Oh. Hell. NO.

My reaction was instantaneous. The heat came at once, five gouts of fire roaring from my fingertips and illuminating the darkness, engulfing the creature and setting it aflame.

Billy had torn a skeletal arm off and was holding it aloft like a weapon. A different zombie hand—this one on fire—scrabbled at his chest and gripped his collar.

He cried out in fear as his t-shirt caught fire and his eyes shifted to black.

One second, he was there. Then there was a blur of movement and he was gone.

It was just me and the creature.

The bony hand and arm that had held my throat wouldn't catch fire. It didn't seem to affect the creature at all. It didn't scream or panic or even try to put my flames out. It just kept squeezing.

Fuck!

I couldn't breathe.

Finger flames out, I concentrated on prying the grasping icy digits off my throat with both hands, my throat aching, my lungs burning, my heart beating frantically.

In the darkness, the zombie tot's additional hands were all over me, pinching, grabbing, and clawing. *CLACK CLACK* I heard in my left ear. The teeth sounded much too close.

"Guh!" it rasped.

Hands were pulling my face closer to the sound. Jagged nails raked my cheek.

I stumbled, gasping for breath. Somehow I kicked the flashlight which turned on and spun, illuminating the tunnel with a strobe effect. One of the hands grabbed my hat and pulled it off while another tugged at my hair. I balled myself into a protective crouch, avoiding the chomping bite by covering my head with my arms.

The weight of the backpack shifted, and that was when I remembered the crowbar.

I yanked it out of the backpack.

A hand grasped it immediately.

I wrested it away and stabbed blindly upwards, still protecting my face and head with my other arm.

My thrust missed and the creature backed off for a moment before leaping onto me once more. I stabbed again, feeling a dull resistance as the blow connected. I grunted with effort and stabbed again, harder, the sharp end of the crowbar entering the beast's lower abdomen and shoving the horrid thing away. *Is that an adult human torso?* Couldn't look. Had to look. The arms still slapped and the hands grabbed at nothing. The mouth was still chomping away. It was back on the floor now and I stabbed at it, trying to keep distance between us.

The flashlight slowed its spinning and went out again, but not before I saw the creature readying itself to spring at me again.

I raised the crowbar to my shoulder and swung down where I'd remembered it being. The crowbar clanged as I hit the stone floor, sending vibrations through my hands and making me once again glad I'd put on the gardening gloves.

Now I swung wildly, trying to connect and succeeding. The arms flapped and flailed and I whaled on it, getting a few solid hits in. I could have been glad it was dark but the horrible image of the gray-skinned spider-child had been seared into my brain and I could picture everything it was doing.

Once again it sprung onto me and got an elbow around my throat. I began choking. Then another arm joined it, squeezing harder. Another hand grabbed a fistful of hair and yanked.

"Guh guh guh guh," it gulped.

"No, damn it! GET. OFF. OF. ME!"

I dropped the crowbar.

This time I managed to grab the thing's head and watched as the flames went up in its hair and then caught the rest of its torso and fleshy arms on fire. A horrid stench of burnt hair and meat and smoke hung in the air.

Now I had burning hands and arms all over me and *Ow, what the hell?* The flames were burning *me*. What a new and awful development.

The flames died and I was plunged back into darkness.

I couldn't seem to get away from it. Just as I'd get one hand pried off me another would take its place.

Where was Billy? Long gone, apparently.

I was alone. Alone with a horrifying monster that I'd set on fire briefly. And unless I did something soon—it would kill me. I was constantly fighting off hands that felt like they were coming from all sides and the chomping mouth kept getting closer.

I was already tired, but the thing showed no signs of fatigue. Tired of fighting this horrible jumble of parts. Tired and frustrated, scared and angry, too.

How could this be happening to me? *Why* was it happening? Tears of frustration leaked down my cheeks. "Noooooo!" I wailed.

I'd felt the same when I blew up Zero's car.

But I lost control.

That was then.

A pair of skeletal arms locked themselves around me.

"Enough!" I screamed, crossing my wrists to grip each arm.

Like an echo of the way the crowbar had shaken in my hands—tremors vibrated through each attacking arm and I felt and heard bones crack in my grasp.

Holy . . . yes!

Don't get cocky.

A hand grabbed ahold of my hood while the remaining hand-feet stomped and snatched at the rest of my clothes. "Break, you bastard! Break!" I yelled.

I did it . . . whatever it was . . . again. Once again the bones cracked in my hands. I wasn't even sure what I was doing. It seemed to be all instinct.

It felt as though I was channeling kinetic energy—a shockwave that emanated with a low hum from my voice and palms into whatever I touched.

I shattered another arm. It hung loose like a sock full of puzzle pieces. The others kept on coming.

The mouth came for my face again.

I tried not to think of what it looked like, that awful, evil child-face with its gnashing teeth and gross gurgles. I reached out blindly and grabbed it by the head.

"Die!" I shouted.

A hum from my palms. The skull crushed inward. A final thrash and then the monster stopped moving altogether.

I allowed myself to slide down the wall. Despite the arm parts that were everywhere and the bad barbecue and corn chips scent in the air, I rested my head against my knees and just breathed.

I wandered forward in the dark, softly calling out Billy's name every so often. I didn't want to raise my voice because I had this impression that a girl calling a name over and over again in the dark and getting louder and louder was the surest way for said girl to get herself killed in the horror movie that was becoming my life.

So tired. I had almost nodded off while sitting on the floor after the battle with the spidertot zombie. I'd had to force myself back to my feet.

I had to go forward. I needed proof. It was the only way I could get back to some semblance of my regular life.

Proof that Ammit existed. Proof that I wasn't the one making these crazy undead creatures. But if those creatures guarding the entrance to the mausoleum and his lair were just the first line of defense, what else could I expect? Had Billy basically flown into a trap?

I felt a strong breeze of air flow and a whistling sound once more. Was that the ventilation system? I tried to remember if I had seen any ventilation shafts or ducts in the basement.

I had. In the lab. The embalming room, or whatever it was. And the breeze was coming from . . . there. I opened my flip phone and examined the walls by its meager light, noticing a three-by-three grating below waist height that was acting like a mild vacuum. Why did he need an air duct so big? Maybe it had to do with all the chemicals used in embalming—not to mention his other hobbies.

The screws were Phillips head.

Screwdrivers were in the front pouch. I rummaged in the backpack and got to work.

I crawled on my hands and knees through inches of dust. The duct was filthy, and the black powder stuck to my jeans and the gardening gloves. I used the light from my phone to see if there were any junctions or grates I needed to be wary of. It was dark everywhere, except for a bit of light up ahead that I saw as I came around a corner.

I continued my slow crawl towards the light and found myself looking down through a vent grate into Ammit's lab. The lights were on, but no one was home. Well, no one except a creepy undead monkeyfish, a skinned human in a glass case, and some zombie butterflies.

And something under a sheet on the table. A body, clearly. But whose? Would it get up or was it really dead?

Ammit's desk was immediately below. I could see the compartmentalized plastic box of glass eyes as well as the notebooks. On the other side of the desk, next to a cardboard box of bones, was unbelievably, my backpack. Had it been there the whole time?

All I had to do was grab my backpack and a notebook and then I could get back to the surface and call Michael. He'd tell me how to find Billy, surely. And have words with his thrall for slacking on his bodyguard duties.

I got out the flathead screwdriver and pried up the grating, then carefully began to lower myself feet first into the room.

My feet had barely touched the top of the desk when I heard the familiar slam-screech of the door that announced Ammit's arrival.

CHAPTER TWENTY-EIGHT

SHIT! IN MY PANIC, I KICKED A NOTEBOOK AND knocked it to the floor. *Double shit!*

The sound of footsteps stomping down the stairs was different his time, louder, more jumbled, more steps, more feet.

I was trying to pull myself back up into the duct and failing. The metal was too smooth to get a grip on and I felt myself slipping. The footsteps were getting closer and now I could hear a woman's voice, accented queerly and angry-sounding, getting louder as they approached. There was some other sense, trying to warn me, but I was panicking.

"No, I do *not* believe you and I will *not* take your word for it. *Where* is this girl?"

"I told you, I've taken steps—"

"I know about the steps you took! How *could* you? You know the Viscount won't stand for such base disregard of the laws! And now the magi will be looking for you. You must give up this foolish hunt at once."

I quickly swiped away the dust that I'd tracked onto the desk and somehow managed to wiggle myself all the way back into the duct. I quietly placed the grate back where it belonged.

Dammit. The notebook was still on the floor. There was nothing for it now.

"I just need a few more hours," Ammit said—sounding and looking exhausted—as he came through the door, followed by an icy blonde in her early twenties. Her makeup was flawless, her clothes designer, her attitude all superiority.

Now I knew what the sense I'd felt was, what the warning was. I'd felt it before.

I'd felt the presence of a vampire.

It was Irina Van Horn. I recognized her from the painting in the Adderly House and from the vision I'd had of Tamara's death.

She looked pretty good for a woman who was over three hundred years old.

Holy shit. They were working together.

"Do not try me, Ammit! You *know* what I can do. Is that what you want? I thought you were still looking for a cure."

"Come now, Irina. Does our bargain mean so little to you?" he asked in a placating tone.

"If you expose yourself again looking for this girl, you expose *me*, and everything we've planned, and what else shall I—and what is *this*?" she asked, gesturing at the dead body on the table.

Ammit wore a sports coat over a turtleneck and slacks. He'd been about to switch on the radio, but dropped his hand and sighed loudly in response to Irina's question.

"Male. An experiment. It doesn't concern you," he sneered.

"*Everything* you do concerns me, starting *immediately*." She peeked under the sheet and let it fall again. "Ugh, this reek. Death, chemicals, spices. But there's something else . . ." She inhaled deeply, her eyes roaming the room.

I held my breath, hoping I hadn't been discovered, then panicking when I thought I had. Abruptly, Irina blurred across the room, moving faster than my eye could follow.

Seconds later, my heart jumped into my throat when she plucked a person from beneath the worktable he'd been hiding under.

It was Billy.

CHAPTER TWENTY-NINE

"HAVE YOU GONE *INSANE*?" IRINA YELLED. "IT was not bad enough that you magicked your own *daughter* into a vampire and now you have made another?"

"Spare me these theatrics," Ammit sniffed. "He's not mine. *Obviously,* he's your spy."

"Were he my spy, he would not have been caught so easily. Who are you?" Irina asked, shaking Billy.

Billy's eyes were completely black and his skin was ashen. "I'm . . ." he rasped, pausing as if the effort of speaking was too much for him. "I'm . . . Batman." He smiled defiantly.

Her backhand slap knocked him off his feet. "Insolent worm! Who made you?"

Billy opened his mouth and fangs popped out. He hissed, weakly.

Suddenly, he was several feet off the ground, Irina's hand suspending him by the throat. "Do not try my patience, *jongen.* I'll ask you again, who are you, and who made you?"

Ammit observed all of this with some curiosity. Billy shook his head. "Can't help you, babe," he rasped.

"I'll teach you to respect your elders," Irina said, letting Billy fall to the ground and giving him a kick in the ribs.

A loud crack was accompanied by a groan of pain. I flinched and covered my mouth to keep from crying out.

My eyes popped wide as I got a mouthful of black dust from the glove. I gagged on the foul-tasting powder and I had to fight myself not to cough and spit. My eyes watered and my nose ran.

Ugh! Gross! Double triple disgusting gross!

I pulled my shirt collar up to my face, frantically trying to rid my mouth of the acrid substance and smearing more of it on myself. Tears poured down my cheeks as I silently grimaced in a series of more and more ludicrous expressions of disgust. After I managed to pull the filthy gloves off my hands without making additional noise, I didn't know what to do with them. They remained clenched in my fist as I watched events unfold below.

"Get up!" Irina yelled.

Billy reluctantly got to his feet, holding his side. There was blood at the corner of his mouth, which he licked away.

I wanted to act. To do something. Anything.

But I knew, I knew if I tried to confront the two of them together, I'd be dead, and so would Billy.

"Do you want me to take a look in his head?" Ammit murmured.

"Suit yourself," Irina said, rolling her eyes.

Ammit moved to Billy's side. Billy jerked away and Ammit did something with his fingers, then said, "*Stop.*" Billy froze. Ammit put a hand on the top of Billy's head and stood before him for several seconds, his eyebrows drawing together. Finally, he shook his head.

"No, it's no use. His memory, his knowledge, it's all been locked. You won't get anything out of him." Ammit then checked Billy's pockets. He removed the silver flask, checking it and tossing it to the floor with a clang. "Looks like he ran low on juice. No phone, no wallet either."

"Is that so?" Irina came close to Billy and pressed her body against his, stage-whispering in his ear. "I have ways of making you talk, ways of teaching you your place, giving you the subservience you crave. You want to serve me, no? To love me, to worship me. You *want* this, do you not?" she purred, rubbing her cheek against his.

Billy did nothing. Just stood there.

Irina's body went stiff with outrage and she stomped a dainty high-heeled foot. Apparently, she was used to more of a reaction from her prey. She whirled to face Ammit. "Release him. Right now!"

He shrugged. "As you wish." To Billy he said, "You can move now."

Billy's posture sagged with exhaustion, but his eyes followed Irina's every move.

"Oh, poor *slachtoffer.* You're so weak, so hungry," Irina said to him. "Come. I have just the place for you, somewhere quiet you can think about telling me what I want to know. What do you say to that? You say, *thank you, mistress.*"

"Thank you, mistress," Billy echoed dully.

I closed my eyes tight. Why was this happening? Why wasn't he fighting against her?

"Come along, *idioot*," she said, grabbing his shoulder and pushing him ahead of her.

Rather than resisting at all, Billy allowed himself to be pushed forward.

Was he out of vampire powers? Hypnotized? Both?

Irina paused in the doorway. "You swear on the life of the girl you hold dear—you didn't make him?"

"I swear," Ammit said wearily.

"Very well. Watch yourself, Ammit. Do *not* allow yourself to be discovered. If you do, it will be the end of all that we've worked for." With that, pushing Billy ahead, she exited the room.

What should I do?

Nothing. There's nothing you can do. Just wait it out. She wants information from him. Information she won't get.

I needed to get to Michael.

Echoing steps went upwards, then the screech-slam of the door.

"*Watch yourself, Ammit,*" Ammit sneered, imitating Irina's accent and delivery so perfectly I thought she'd re-entered the room, even though I was watching his mouth move while he said the words. Taking items from cabinets, he placed them on the counter. He shook his head, and with some amount of disgust, muttered, "Vampires," before switching on the radio.

The notes of a melodic piano piece rose and fell, backed by a symphony orchestra, and Ammit walked around a corner, disappearing from view.

I finally dropped the disgusting gardening gloves and made another effort at wiping my face with the inside of my shirt.

The song drew to a close. "This is New York's Classical Station," said the announcer. "You just listened to Rachmaninov's Concerto No. 2 played by Tetyana Borova with the Boston Symphony. Our next piece we'll hear is Suite No. 1 of Ravel's Daphnis et Chloé, performed by the Berlin Philharmonic Orchestra." The new song started. A high flute accompanied by slow strings, plaintive, contemplative.

When Ammit reappeared, he wore a white linen tunic and a blue beaded necklace-collar in the style of the ancient Egyptians. A substantial square of spotted fur hung from his shoulder. Was that cheetah fur?

Had this asshole killed a cheetah?

An ornate dagger with a crystal pommel hung at the sash on his waist.

Ammit pulled the white sheet off the body on the table.

The handsome man lying upon it was strapped down. He wore a white coat over a shirt and tie, like a doctor. An ID tag with a photo hung from a breast pocket. I couldn't make out the words from where I was.

Ammit viewed the man briefly and turned back to the counter and cabinets above it, removing various implements and objects, pouring materials from one container into another, and placing everything on a shiny chrome tray.

The man was probably in his late twenties or early thirties. Dark brown hair, high cheekbones, a cleft chin. Wait, he looked . . . healthy. Tan, not pale. Was his chest moving ever so slightly?

My God. He was *alive.*

Woodwind instruments joined the strings briefly, like a chorus of women singers.

Ammit leaned towards the man and said, "Wake."

The man's eyes fluttered open and he gasped, "Where am I? Who are you?" He struggled against the straps.

"All answers will come in time," Ammit said. Hadn't he said that to me? *Get a new evil villain line, buddy.* I wondered how many times he'd said it, to how many people.

Ammit moved to the chrome tray and removed a small dark jar.

"Hey, man, just let me go. Just let me go, okay? I've got a wife, a family, you know?"

Ammit uncorked the dark jar and stirred its contents with a thin metal rod.

My eyes darted around the room, frantically searching for something other than the notebooks to set on fire. The sheet on the floor, maybe? Or could I go to the cops at this point?

No, it was no good. Even if I could get out without Ammit hearing me, the man would be dead or otherwise changed before I got back. Maybe I could send a text to Zoe? I carefully opened the flip phone and found that the battery, which had been low to start with, had finally died. *It doesn't matter anyway. There was no way I could get a signal down here.*

"Please. My wife. I have a family," the man repeated.

The woodwinds and strings got louder.

Ammit sat at the desk, and looked into a handheld mirror, using it to apply black makeup around his eyes. "Oh, yes. Your wife. Heather, isn't it?" he said, outlining his upper lid. "I just love the new Egyptian exhibit she curated at the Brooklyn Museum. And you have . . . two children, correct? Adopted, if I'm not mistaken. So generous." One eye finished, he began work on the other. "Akeem is in the second grade now, isn't he? And how is Nadia adjusting to kindergarten? It would be a shame if anything happened to them."

The doctor's eyes widened as he listened to Ammit's casual commentary on his family.

"Please, don't hurt them. I'll give you whatever you want. You want bank accounts, credit cards? Ransom money?"

With his makeup completed, Ammit left the stylus-like object on the desk and went back to the work area beneath the cabinets. "It's not money that interests me," he said. He wheeled the tray over, folding back the piece of cloth he'd draped over the objects, revealing several bowls with various salves and oils, a small box of grayish-white powder, and a clear jar with a crumbled amber material in it. He combined several oils with the powder and the crumbled amber stuff in a stone bowl, using a pestle to mash them together. An incense-like odor with notes of pine and sweet citrus wafted up into the ventilation system.

"Please. I'll do anything," the man on the table said.

"Yes. Yes, you will," Ammit said, and dipping a finger into the combined ointment, smeared a shining line of paste vertically across the man's lips. "Shhh. Your family will come to no harm. I have plans for you, you see."

A horn of warning played beneath the trilling of a harp.

Ammit pulled the cloth from the tray completely, revealing a fluffy white ostrich feather.

Oh, no. I had to do something to help this guy.

Ammit crossed the room and opened the heavy door that I hadn't gotten to in my previous exploration. The room beyond was cloaked in darkness, and he disappeared inside.

His prisoner made a whimpering noise and I could see the shining track of a tear rolling down his temple.

It was now or never.

I removed the grate of the vent and the movement caught the attention of the man on the table. He thrashed in his straps and his eyes bulged, but he didn't speak.

His actions spoke volumes, though. They said: *Get me the fuck out of here!* A desperate trumpet of noise came from his throat but his mouth didn't open.

The dark room had taken on a flickering quality as one lit by candlelight and Ammit's footsteps announced that he was on his way back.

I nodded frantically at the man and held my finger to my lips.

The strings came in once again, stirring, longing.

Ammit emerged from the doorway and began to cross the room, stopping when he noticed the notebook on the floor. He bent and picked it up, his eyes searching the room suspiciously. For a moment I thought he was going to look up and discover me, but the doctor on the table trumpeted another sound of frustration and Ammit's eyes jerked back to him.

"Ah, what strength of personality you possess! What delicious heart and spirit!" Ammit joyfully proclaimed.

This praise seemed to be wasted on his victim.

He did seem to forget about the notebook, however. He stood it next to the others and went to the table. Flipping a small extension tray from beneath it, he placed the stone bowl and the feather in the dark jar onto it and wheeled the man into the flame-lit room, closing the door behind them.

Grab the notebooks and go.

I can't leave that man here with Ammit!

It's too late for him. Save yourself.

I can't. I can't do that. I can't let him steal this man's memory and ruin his life. I can't, and I won't. I can do this. I can take him.

I lowered myself feet-first toward the desk and let myself drop the last few inches. I landed without a sound but so close to the plastic box of glass eyes that it shifted towards the edge of the desk. I quickly put a foot on it, stopping it from falling, and silently exhaled. *That was close.*

Clumps and smears of black dust clung to my sneakers and jeans. I probably looked like a coal miner.

The music seemed to have a purpose now. Violins and flutes were rising. The music bounced along, intensifying to a march.

I slid the box away from the desk edge and was just about to climb down to the floor and formulate a plan when the heavy door opened again and Ammit came back into the room.

The horns triumphed as they joined in and marched alongside singing strings and a crash of cymbals.

The look of surprise on Ammit's face was comical, but I wasn't laughing.

Neither was he.

"You!" he shouted.

I couldn't tell if he was upset or happy to see me. Possibly both.

His mouth opened again and I kicked the box of glass eyes at him. They went bouncing and breaking and rolling all over the lab. The box shattered on the concrete. I jumped to the floor, pitching notebooks, the hand mirror, the lamp—anything and everything at him—before I took cover behind the desk.

The drums in the song thumped along, accompanied by the rest of the orchestra in a parade of sound that suddenly quieted to a woodwind then rose again.

Ammit had one arm raised to fend off the flying objects and keep his head safe, but pointed at me. "St—" he began, then cursed as I disappeared behind the desk. "Enough! You will answer for all of this and more!" he yelled and moved towards the desk.

Did he need to see me to control me?

Distraction! I need distraction!

On one side of the desk on the floor was the open cardboard box of bones and the backpack I'd had when Ammit had taken me. On the other side was the tank with its creepy occupant. I pushed it over. Gallons of greenish liquid spilled across the floor as the creature came sliding out, its little paws scrabbling at the floor, its tail flapping uselessly. Then the tank crashed to the concrete becoming a jigsaw puzzle of glass.

Ammit let out a cry of anger and dismay.

I looked in the box and grabbed the first thing I saw.

Ammit made it around the corner of the desk and pointed at me.

I leapt forward, wielding an arm bone like a mace, the rounded knob of a socket joint connecting with his head.

He reeled, then sprang toward me, taking me down to the floor. I dropped the bone to try to catch myself.

"Sleep, damn you! *Sleep*!" he yelled.

I braced myself for the expected turn to unconsciousness.

But nothing happened.

Nothing except a slight warmth at my throat where I wore the labradorite amulet. *Holy crap. It works.*

He scrambled to his feet. His mouth jabbered but nothing came out at first. "That's not possible," he finally said. He managed to compose himself and said, "*Stop. You can't move.*" Some hand gesture accompanied this statement but I didn't see it, too busy enjoying the incredulous look on his face when I didn't freeze up like he commanded.

His eyes grew wide and he scowled at me, then disappeared through the door of the room where he'd taken his prisoner.

I felt a moment of fatigue but shook it off and followed him through the door. It was darker inside, lit by oil lamps but still dimmer than the lab room. As my eyes adjusted, I realized the room was covered in Egyptian murals, painted on the walls and pillars with bright colors and hieroglyphics from floor to ceiling. Beetles, hawks, and feathers amid shapes like bowls and snakes and squiggles.

Gods and goddesses with animal heads and darkly lined eyes stared from the walls. I recognized them from the research I'd done on Egyptian afterlife belief. The jackal-headed god Anubis kneeling with a heart on a scale. Osiris, the green-skinned god with his sister-consort, Isis, holding an ankh. A boat with a red sun behind it, the journey of the sun god, Ra.

The bottom half of the sarcophagus I'd seen before stood against the wall, its stone lid standing next to it, and next to that, a vertical linen pennant patterned with hieroglyphics. The doctor lay on a slab.

Somewhere in the shadows, I heard guttural chanting from Ammit.

A glowing orb of purple light came at me from the darkness.

I ducked and the orb hit the linen pennant, which turned black and crumbled away into nothing. *Jesus, is he slinging Death orbs at me?*

"Stupid girl!" he yelled angrily, like it was my fault he'd ruined his dumb pennant.

In the room next to us, the music soared as the voices rose, chanting rhythmically.

Where was he?

There!

He held his hands in front of him in a triangular shape, at 90-degree angles, as though they were flat against a wall. I recognized the gesture at once—it was the same one I'd been taught by Orpheus.

Ammit continued chanting and slowly pulled his fingers apart, a purple glow licking from his fingers, which he shaped into another glowing orb.

Oh no you don't!

I felt the flash of fear and anger as a heat that I sent to my hands, imagining the feel of Ammit's linen tunic beneath them as I snapped my fingers. Flames licked at the hem just as he let the orb fly.

He screamed and the orb went wide, hitting the corner of the sarcophagus lid, which blackened as it was knocked to the floor.

Ammit beat at his burning tunic frantically.

I'd hoped to see a bigger flash of flame, but producing even that much had felt draining.

His hands returned to the triangular formation.

If he could do it, so could I. I mimicked the gesture, moving my hands apart and feeling the tingle of death magic in them, seeing sparks of purple emerge flickering from my fingertips. I expected to feel fatigue, but instead I felt somehow invigorated.

Ammit's brows drew together and he snarled as he threw the next orb at me.

Instead of creating my own orb, I caught his. One moment I had it, and in the next it imploded, disappearing into my hands, which now glowed more brightly. The jolt of energy refreshed me like a nap and a cup of tea.

Ammit looked at me as if he had just swallowed a bug. He made a gesture and the lamp closest to him went out, plunging him into darkness.

"My, my, my. Such a good keeper of secrets," came his voice from the shadows, mocking me.

"What secrets?" I asked, hoping to keep him talking so I could figure out where he was.

"Absorption! Come now, no neophyte could conjure so well. I am impressed you hid those memories from me. Who *is* your magister?" The voice came from the darkness and echoed off the stone walls and pillars around me.

"He's pretty obscure. You probably don't know him." I pushed myself against a pillar, listening. There was no immediate reply. "So, uh . . . what's up with your costume?"

"This is no costume. It is the ceremonial garb of a priest." His voice somehow managed to convey both outrage and pride.

I moved to the doorway and said, "I hate to tell you this, but I think someone lied to you. That's not how priests dress."

"What do you know of such things? Nothing!" came his sneering voice.

He seemed farther away now.

I peeked into the brightly lit lab room but didn't see him. At some point the music had changed to Beethoven's Ninth Symphony. The classical disc jockey was apparently feeling epic this evening.

On the floor a few feet away, the monkeyfish crawled and flopped, gaining no purchase on the slimy floor. I grimaced. "Ugh. Why do you like playing with dead things so much, Ammit? It's pretty gross."

"I'll not be baited by your prattle," Ammit said.

"But it's such fun prattle."

"Ha! It will be a shame when I wipe your mind completely. I've so enjoyed our little chats." His voice seemed to come from everywhere in the dark.

"What do you want with me anyway? Why me?" I spoke at the ceiling and stood in a shadow, my back against one of the pillars.

"And ruin the surprise?" he asked. The source of his voice was moving.

"You plan on turning me into one of your pets?"

"No, no. Nothing so crude as that." A lamp went out.

"What then?"

"All answers—"

"—will come in time? Bullshit. I've heard that before." There was something I hadn't heard before, though. "What did Irina say? That you turned your daughter into a vampire? Is that what you're going to do with me?"

He extinguished another lamp and the darkness grew. Now there were just two lamps left. He seemed to be moving towards the brightly lit lab room.

"Hardly. If you must know—" he sighed heavily. "All those years ago, I had prepared you to be my daughter's new vessel." His voice moved into the other room.

"Vessel? Like a ship? I'm going to carry your daughter around with me and sail the seven seas?" I got to the doorway of the lab and peeked in again.

"You're being facetious, but yes, something like that."

I couldn't see Ammit, but his voice seemed to be coming from the back, near the broom and arm closet.

"You took my memories so that you could . . . give me hers?" I entered the room as stealthily as I could, tiptoeing toward the back of the lab.

"Essentially."

I was getting closer.

"That's pretty fucked up." I tried to throw my voice back towards the Egyptian room.

"Your vulgar language only demonstrates your lack of sophistication and ladylike graces." Closer. I silently lifted another arm bone club from the box at my feet.

The music playfully piped along.

"Your sexist comment only demonstrates that you're *old*," I said, hoping that it sounded like my voice was coming from farther away than I was.

"How dare you!" He had to be around the corner of this pillar.

I hefted the bone and sprang around the side of the pillar to confront him, only to find myself lifted off my feet, my arms pinned to my side. The bone fell from my hand.

Ammit smiled. "Foolish child." He'd been baiting *me.*

He waved his hand and my feet touched the ground in tandem with his movement, but I was still held fast.

The arms that held me were red corded muscle, dry, like leather, without skin. I was being held by the skinless zombie. I remembered it blinking at me. I strove to escape its grasp but it held me firm.

Ammit drew the ornate dagger from the scabbard at his waist. The blade was gold.

"I'll carve the runes into you if I have to," he growled as he approached me.

Something was happening. I could feel a hum in the air that raised the hairs on my arms.

The alarmed look on Ammit's face told me that he could feel it, too. And whatever it was, he wasn't the one doing it.

The hum was louder now, intensifying a feeling of pressure in my temples and a feeling of static in the atmosphere. A rectangular portal of blue light opened in the air and two men stepped out of it. They were guarded in their posture, defensive, ready, and absolutely astonished to see an old man in an Egyptian priest costume holding me at dagger-point while I struggled in a skinless zombie's arms.

It was Zero and Quinn.

"Sleep!" Ammit shouted. Quinn slumped as if he'd had his strings cut while a blue globe briefly flashed around Zero's body.

Ammit took another step toward me with the dagger and Zero made a complex motion in the air and a yellow bolt shot out from him, striking Ammit's hand. The dagger clattered to the floor, spinning within feet of me.

Dammit. I struggled in the zombie's grasp, battling to break free.

Ammit cried out in a guttural language I didn't understand, then said, *"Stop, you can't move!"* Another flash of blue appeared around Zero while Beethoven cascaded and surged.

Zero shot another bolt at Ammit, but a flash of purple around Ammit's body protected him.

Ammit formed a purple orb and launched it at Zero, who threw himself flat to the ground to avoid it. The orb hit one of the wall cabinets, which turned black and crumbled. The glassware and other objects inside the cabinet spilled out, knocking the radio over and switching the station to a fast-paced pop song. The look of fury on Ammit's face was a joy to behold. I probably had my own look of fury as I grappled with the skinless corpse, trying to escape its kung fu grip.

My arms were locked against my body. I kicked my legs and twisted my shoulders, trying to break the zombie's hold.

Ammit chanted urgently in the same guttural language and made arcane gestures. He seemed to be creating his own portal of some kind. A different doorway-sized rectangle of light was forming in the air by his side. I thought I could see pillars or columns on the other side.

No! I can't let him get away!

But I couldn't get free. The more I struggled, the tighter the zombie held me.

So what if I stopped fighting?

The result was instantaneous. My dead weight was too much for it and I slipped from its grasp.

The dagger!

I fell into a forward somersault like I'd done it a million times, grabbing the dagger as I came up, hurling it at Ammit with all the force I could muster.

I hoped I'd be lucky enough to hit him in the leg, but the dagger buried itself up to the hilt in his chest. My eyes bulged. *How the hell did I do that?*

Ammit staggered back, taking a partial step into the portal of light that had begun to open next to him. His eyes were wide with shock as he looked at the dagger. Then they went blank. In the same moment, the portal suddenly collapsed like the blade of a guillotine falling, shearing the back half of his body clean off.

As I watched in horror, his front half continued the backwards momentum, falling to the floor, sheared-side-down. It made a loud splat like a wet towel.

All that was left of him looked like a very realistic sarcophagus lid.

The back half never fell. It was nowhere in sight.

I couldn't seem to take my eyes off the awfulness of his half body.

A groan came from across the room as Quinn shook himself awake, running one hand through his tousled red hair. "Oh, man, I miss everything," he said. He stood, dusting off his trench coat. "We good?"

Zero eyed the half-Ammit with distaste. "I'm good," he said, picking himself up off the floor. The pop singer hit a high note and Zero sent a bolt of magic at the radio, silencing it. "You okay, Madison? You look like you crawled out of a grave."

I exhaled noisily. "Yeah. Yeah, I'm okay." I put my hands on my knees and let my head hang a minute, just breathing. "How did you know where to find me?"

"We divined activity from the magical signature that created the minotaur and traced it here."

"Ugh, look at that thing!" Quinn said, pointing. "Why doesn't it just fall down?"

The skinned zombie slouched, staring at nothing, unmoving. It looked even more like a museum exhibit.

The monkeyfish scrabbled out from under the desk and Quinn flapped his hands in alarm. Zero shot it with an energy bolt and the creature stopped moving.

"No way. Is that a Fiji mermaid?" Quinn asked, crouching to get a better look.

"No idea. We're going to have to call this in."

"There's a guy," I said. "A prisoner. In there." I pointed at the doorway.

They immediately went to each side of the doorway. Quinn took point and Zero followed him. I followed Zero.

The man was prostrate on the slab. The white ostrich feather sat upon his forehead, glowing hieroglyphs shifting on its shaft. The man was still.

"He's unresponsive," Zero said.

Was I too late?

No, I had been able to give Hank his memories back. I could do it for this man too.

"I've seen this once before," I said. "I think I know what to do."

Zero gave me a skeptical glance before stepping aside, watching me closely. Quinn seemed more curious than anything.

There was no eye-like sigil on the man's forehead, like Hank had had. Holding the feather like a quill, I traced an invisible eye between the doctor's eyebrows, then added an eyebrow and the alchemical symbol for lead. Nothing happened for a second, but then the feather pulsed with power and the skeptical look on Zero's face transformed to surprise—only to be replaced by suspicion.

The glowing hieroglyphics traveled down the feather's shaft in a tightening spiral until the last one was gone. The feather crumbled to dust which fell upon the man's forehead. Nothing happened at first, but then his eyes fluttered and opened. "What? You . . . where . . . is he?"

"He's gone," I said. *Speaking of which* . . . "And I need to get going too."

"Whoa, whoa, whoa," Zero said.

"I've got to get to my family," the man said, attempting to rise from the slab.

"Look, Dr . . ." Zero peered at the ID badge the man wore. NYC OCME it read, with his photo. "Dr.

Alejandro. Easy." Zero helped him sit up. "The danger is over. The man who held you is dead. Your family is safe. Let's get you out of this room, okay?"

Dr. Alejandro nodded. "Okay."

Zero put one arm around the man and the redhaired man took the other side. They helped him off the slab, half-carrying him to the brightly lit lab room where they put the man in the desk chair. Zero pulled out his badge wallet and showed it to Dr. Alejandro. "NYPD. My associate needs to ask you some questions, okay?"

"Yes. Of course. Whatever you say."

"Quinn?" Zero said.

Quinn was poking the monkeyfish with a pen. He seemed both horrified and fascinated. "Yo!"

"Get his statement, will you?"

"Right, yes. Absolutely." He left the little creature and came to Dr. Alejandro's side, pulling a small notepad and pencil from his pocket. "Can you tell me how you came to be here, sir?"

"Well, I . . ." the man began as Zero walked with me toward the room's exit. Dr. Alejandro continued speaking quietly as we moved away.

"You can't—" Zero launched into lecturing tone immediately.

I interrupted him. "*Ugh*! I'm sick of you telling me what to do! Can't you just trust me for once? Please? My friend is in danger and it's because of me, okay? I need to go help him and I need to make a phone call. In fact, I need a phone. Can I borrow yours? Mine is dead."

He gave me a long look with squinted eyes and then turned to Quinn. "Phone!" Zero yelled.

Quinn pulled a phone from a pocket. He pressed a button and tossed it to Zero, who caught it neatly. "Don't make me regret this," he said, holding the phone out of reach.

"I won't." I hoped I wouldn't anyway.

"We're going to need your testimony."

"I'll give it," I said, holding out my hand.

I took the phone and, after gathering my things, I used its light to navigate my way back to the world above.

CHAPTER THIRTY

I STOOD ON THE SIDEWALK IN FRONT OF THE Victorian house, gulping in the cool night air. The flip phone with all of my numbers in it was dead, but by concentrating, I could see in my mind's eye the expensive dark blue card with Michael's number on it.

I also gave myself a stabbing headache between my eyes.

I pressed the buttons, imagining what I'd say when the machine told me to leave my message. I let the image of the card go and the stabbing pain receded to a poking one.

The line rang once. Then just silence. Dead air.

I was so surprised I didn't say anything at first. Then, "Hello?"

"Hello, Madison," Michael said.

"I didn't expect you to answer," I said. "Wait, how did you know it was me?"

"No one else has this number. Where are you?"

I leaned against a streetlight next to a parked car. "In Queens. Listen, Michael, Irina took Billy."

"She *what*? Are *you* all right?"

"I am. Ammit's dead."

"Meet me."

"Where?"

"The speakeasy. You were there before. You know where I mean?"

It took me a second and then I said, "In King Kong's basement?"

"Two hours," he said, and ended the call.

He hadn't even waited for me to say okay.

We were going to have to work on his phone manners.

I needed to make another call, so I spent a few moments combing through my memory to find the number. The pain between my eyes intensified briefly, then faded again to a dull throb. I pinched the bridge of my nose, listening to the ringing on the other end.

"Hello?" came Zoe's voice.

"Hey, it's me," I said.

"Madison, thank God," Zoe said. "Are you okay? I texted you—"

"Yeah, I'm fine. The phone I had died."

"Where are you? I'll come get you."

Sirens were approaching from the distance.

"Don't. There's too much going on here."

"Where's *here*? What happened? Do I hear sirens?"

"The funeral home. Yes, those are sirens. The short version? Ammit's dead and Billy's missing."

"What? *How?*" her voice was shrill over the line.

"I'm going to go meet Michael now."

Two police cars pulled up to the house, followed by an ambulance. Zero and Quinn came out the front door onto the porch, Dr. Alejandro between them.

"Don't you need a ride?" Zoe asked.

Paramedics offered Dr. Alejandro support. They walked him to the back of the ambulance and sat him down.

I was going to tell her no when I caught my reflection in a car window. I looked like I'd smoked an exploding cigar. "Yes. And a shower. Meet at your mom's store in fifteen?"

"You bet."

"I gotta go," I said as Zero approached me. Quinn was talking to a couple of the cops in uniform as two others went into the house.

"Be careful," Zoe said.

"You too," I said, and pressed the End Call button.

My finger lingered on the screen a moment and several options popped up: Add to Contacts, History, Delete. I selected *Delete* for Zoe's number and then did it again for Michael's.

"Here," I said, offering the phone to Zero.

"Keep it, for now," he said.

"But Quinn—"

"It's one of his backup phones. They die on him all the time. He keeps losing his charger."

The paramedics had put an oxygen mask on Dr. Alejandro and a blanket around his shoulders.

"It looks like he's going to be okay," I said.

"Yeah, thanks to you," Zero said, taking a deep breath and sighing heavily. "I owe you an apology."

"I owe you one too," I said. "Sorry about blowing up your car and setting your notepad on fire."

He shrugged. "And I'm sorry for doubting you."

I checked the time on the phone. "I need to go." I picked up my breaking-and-entering backpack from the ground, the crowbar still jutting from the zipper.

"Maybe you should leave that behind?" Zero said quietly, indicating the uniformed cops with a jerk of his head.

"Oh, right. They're not with you?"

"Not exactly. Different precinct."

I put the B&E backpack down and transferred what I needed from it to the backpack I'd reclaimed.

"So what now? What happens next?" I asked, slinging the other backpack over my shoulder once again.

"Lieutenant?" one of the uniformed cops called to Zero, walking towards us.

"Keep the phone. I'll call you tomorrow," he said quietly, then, more loudly, "There's nothing to see here, miss. Please go back to your home." He turned to the cop approaching him. "Yes, Officer . . . St. John?"

I walked away, overhearing Zero saying, ". . . a neighborhood kid," in response to something Officer St. John asked him. A small group of neighborhood people in various states of night dress were gathering on the sidewalk, and one of the other uniformed policemen approached them.

I checked the time again and quickened my step.

Chapter Thirty-one

I ENTERED THE REVOLVING DOOR TO THE BROWN marble lobby of the Empire State Building and signed in at the security desk. *Here goes nothing.*

"ID please?"

I dug through the envelope of documents and pulled out the driver's license.

The guard stared at me a moment, then looked over the ID, glancing from it to me and back again.

Would it work? I bit my lip.

"Miss Roberts," the guard said.

"Yes?" I asked anxiously.

"Congrats on getting your license," he said, handing it back to me. "Do you know where you're going?"

"Oh! Thank you," I said. I told him I did know where I was going and wished him a goodnight.

Down the hall and around a corner, then down another hall, listening to the echo of my bootheels on the tile floor as the long skirt swished around my legs. I spotted the potted plant I was looking for and pulled the brown marble-printed curtain behind it aside, revealing the cage doors of an old-fashioned elevator. I got inside, hitting the button for sub-basement two.

The long, tiled hallway was exactly as it had been. I made my way to the door marked KRIS KONG, ESQ. then turned, opening the door across from it marked JANITOR.

Kris Kong, King Kong . . . I wondered what the connection was.

Mops, brooms, and buckets leaned against shelves of cleaning products, brushes, and boxes on the right wall. The left wall was bare, except for barely noticeable rectangle, about the size of a credit card, at waist height. Then I saw it: a small rectangle, hardly visible, at waist height. It was the same hidden panel I'd found the first time I'd been there. The metal compartment flipped open, exposing a small metal lever. I slid the lever to the right, and the wall slid as well, revealing a dark passage.

The dark passage opened into a much wider room, dimly lit. Some work had been done since the last time I'd been there. The fabric had been replaced on the walls and covered pillars, and there was a fresh coat of paint over half of the tarnished tin ceiling. Other signs of incomplete renovation included partially sanded floors, stacked tables and stools. One wall of booth seats had been replaced, while others remained threadbare and faded.

The crystal chandelier had been cleaned, and little bulbs shone gently from it, giving the room a warm illumination.

Michael sat at the bar on a stool, scrolling through his phone. He seemed to have adjusted to the 21st century a lot faster than I did. He glanced up and stood when he saw me.

"I'm so sorry," I said, moving quickly toward him.

He blurred to my side. "You're okay? She didn't hurt you?" His eyes combed my face and shoulders down to my feet and back. "And why—hang on, is your hair *wet*?"

"I desperately needed a shower. But no, she didn't see me."

"How? Come, sit. Over here."

I hung my coat on a hook and we sat at one of the refinished booths. "It was my fault. I had to prove that Ammit existed or the magi were going to blame me for everything he was doing. I scoped out his house, and it really seemed like he was out of town. I couldn't tell for how long, but I figured that was my chance. And Billy went with me. He said he had no choice. But then we were attacked by these zombie things and I set one of them on fire and Billy's t-shirt caught fire too. After that, he just vanished. The next time I saw him, when Irina discovered him, he was pale and listless and his eyes were all black."

Michael's face went through multiple emotions as I recounted the details and he shook his head when I mentioned the fire. "He couldn't handle the flames. Young vampires simply can't control their reactions to some stimuli. He went into panic mode, and it drained him."

"Well, we've got to go and get him back, don't we?"

"Tell me what happened next."

I told him about how I'd crawled into the ventilation system and about the conversation I overheard between Irina and Ammit, and what she'd said about "the Viscount" and laws and Ammit making his daughter a vampire.

Michael raised an eyebrow at that and looked over towards the bar.

I looked where he was looking and was startled to notice there was a person standing behind the bar that I hadn't noticed was there previously. There'd been no movement, no sound, no anything. The figure stood there as if he'd been there the whole time.

He was pale, and bald, with heavy eyebrows over sunken eyes and hallow cheeks. A prominent nose hung over a wide mouth etched in a feral grin, with two larger front teeth taking up more than their fair share of lip estate. He wore all black and held his fingers interlaced at his chest.

"How delightful!" he exclaimed in a high voice, and I stood without meaning to, ready to run.

"Stop it, Kris," Michael said. "You're scaring her."

"Am I? My deepest apologies," he said, making a sweeping bow at the waist. When he turned his head, I saw that his ears were pointed.

I just stood there, hesitant, looking from Michael to the other vampire and back. The bald man in black spoke. "Fascinating that she doesn't remember," he said. "Allow me to introduce myself. I am Kris Kong, the anonymous proprietor of this establishment and a long-time associate of young Michael here." He came around the bar to our table.

He didn't blur the way that Michael did, but his movement was creepy, a sort of glide like he was on tracks. He extended a long-nailed hand.

I glanced at Michael and seeing no warning or concern, shook the hand he offered. It was dry and cool to the touch. "Kris Kong, Esquire?" I asked, thinking of the plaque in the hallway.

He continued shaking my hand. "Yes! I am a lawyer, in the common parlance, as well as a real estate magnate, holder of properties and stocks and other investments. I am quite pleased to make your acquaintance. I understand you prefer the name Madison?" Throughout the speech he continued shaking my hand until Michael cleared his throat and glared at him, at which point Kris patted my hand politely before setting it down like a delicate teacup.

My hand felt slightly tingly from the contact. I could feel that he was a vampire when I touched him, just as I could feel that he was a vampire from across the room. But why was he surprised that his appearance alarmed me?

"What did you mean it's fascinating that I don't remember? Don't remember what? You?"

"Oh, yes. We were great friends before," he said, nodding avidly. "May I join you?"

"Um, sure. Sit down?"

"I'd love to. Thank you, my dear. I am most interested in your story."

"I knew you would be," Michael said.

"And what happened to young William is of interest to me of course as well."

Suddenly, I got it. "You made him," I said. "Billy. He couldn't tell me anything but I guessed that Michael didn't have anything to do with it. I was right."

"Oh, don't go polishing our Mikey's halo just yet, sweet girl. I think of us as William's two fathers, both equally responsible for his existence and education. Aren't we, Michael?"

"Yeah, we're proud papas," Michael said, shaking his head slightly. I couldn't tell if he was just tired or exasperated with Kris.

"I never would have dreamed of making another one of us but Michael came to me with the broken boy and told me you'd never forgive him if William died. Was he right?"

My eyes flicked over the two of them, Michael's light blue eyes watching me, Kris's brown ones darting here and there as if watching imaginary butterflies pollinating an invisible floating garden.

"Yes."

"Well, then. Seems like you do still know her well," Kris said, "despite her memory loss. Now, tell me more about Van Horn and what she said."

When I finished explaining, Kris clapped his hands and bounced up and down in his seat. "Finally! We have her. The *magical* creation of a vampire? How long has she kept this secret hidden from the *Sangreal*? Such a transgression will be punished most severely. Her pet magician obviously had more than tarot cards up those sleeves. But Michael said you killed him, is that right?"

I thought maybe I should feel a little more guilty about it than I did, but I when thought about how gross the half-body was, I shuddered.

"I didn't really *kill him* kill him. Like a sort of happenstance," I said.

"Feel no guilt, my dear. The man was a pestilence. Tell us how it happened, won't you?"

"But what about Billy? We've got to find him," I said.

Michael and Kris glanced at one another uneasily. Michael looked as if he was about to speak but then shook his head dejectedly and sighed.

"Is it too late? Will she have killed him already?" I asked anxiously.

"No, no. Katharina Van Horn is far too sadistic a cat to kill a mouse immediately. She likes to *play*," Kris said.

"What does that mean?" I asked. "And is her name Katharina or Irina? I'm confused."

"She changed her name to Irina in the 1800s. I use *Katharina* because it annoys her. She will likely store and starve him, just as she did me, and as she did to Michael many times over, isn't that right, old friend?"

Michael sighed again and shook his head angrily.

"Then we have to help him," I said.

"It isn't that easy," Michael said.

"Sure, it is! You just said you were both responsible for him. Well, do something!" I raised my voice and it took on a hysterical edge.

"We will, we will. Calm yourself, Miss Madison," Kris said. "You wish to act, to save your friend, to rush to his aid, no matter that he's vampire? I commend you."

I looked at him suspiciously to see if he was making fun of me, but he seemed sincere.

"But where will you go? Where is young William? Where is the nasty little trollop hiding him? We do not know. Presumably, the daughter she spoke of is hidden in a similar, secret location. She has many such hideaways. Too many to search for in a single night. Furthermore, as demonstrated when the magician tried to read his memories, William cannot divulge certain details. He cannot speak of me, his maker, nor his own name, or anything about Michael. He is and will remain a complete mystery to her. As such, she will secret him away, hoping to use him as leverage when she learns who turned him. For now, he is completely safe."

"For how long?"

"What was the longest time she left you staked, *mon ami*?" Kris asked Michael.

"From '45 to '69. Twenty-four years."

"And the shortest?"

"A little over two years. From late '87 to early '90."

"What do you mean, *staked*?" I asked.

"Shall I?" Kris asked, and Michael shrugged. "In for a penny, as they say. It is a kind of sleep, a hibernation if you will—a living death that leaves our kind in a semi-conscious state, unable to move. Wood enters the heart, and the vampire succumbs. Remove the wood, and the vampire wakes."

"But that's . . . that's horrible! So that's what happened to you in the safe room?" I asked Michael. "But I dislodged the wood and that's what woke you up, right? I thought it was an accident. But you're saying she does it on purpose?"

He nodded, eyes closed, lips pressed together.

"So that's what will happen to Billy? She'll just . . . stake him, and . . . store him? Like a can of creamed corn in a pantry?"

"Until she decides what to do with him? Yes. So, while we do desire to free him as quickly as possible, there is little to do right this minute. You see?" Kris said.

I nodded, taking a deep breath. "Okay. I see. He's not in immediate danger. And you're sure, because you have both known her . . . how long?"

"Too long," they both said at once, then chuckled ruefully.

"Do you feel able to tell us the rest of your tale—how you came to kill the magician?" Kris asked.

"I do. I don't suppose you have any water or anything . . ."

"My apologies. I see so few of your kind. I forget my manners!" He glided behind the bar and came back with a bottled water, which he placed in front of me.

After quenching my thirst, I launched into the other part of the story, leaving nothing out. As I got to the end, I found myself blinking a lot. Both Kris and Michael had been attentive and astonished and dismayed by all that had occurred.

I yawned. "Is it past your bedtime, poor child? You can rest here if you like."

"Thank you, but I have to say, I am really looking forward to my own bed, you know?"

Michael nodded. "Of course. You must be exhausted. Let me drive you home."

I nodded off in the black BMW as it sped from Manhattan to Brooklyn, waking once as we crossed over the Brooklyn Bridge and falling asleep again just as quickly.

"Hey," the gentle voice woke me. We were parked outside my apartment building, the engine off. "You're home."

I rubbed my eyes and yawned. "I can't believe I slept the whole way here."

"I can. After what you've been through. Chris—" he broke off suddenly, realizing he was using the wrong name. He swallowed hard. "Madison. I . . . will you . . . let me call you?"

I gazed into his blue eyes and saw only earnestness and vulnerability.

"Can I . . . try something?" I asked.

"What?"

"I want you to think back to a memory, a good memory you have, of you and Christina. Concentrate on it. Okay?"

"Okaaay," Michael said, mystified.

"And close your eyes."

He closed them.

I reached forward and ran my fingers through his hair. It was soft and clean. My hand moved from his forehead to the crown, and I rested my palm there. It was different than trying to read my own memories, but after several seconds I felt the answering warmth in my hand as the images began to flit across the screen of my mind's eye.

The edges of the scene are dark, the center washed out but still vibrant in color. The two sit before a mirror, Michael and Christina, him looking much the same, and she like a slightly younger version of me. They can't take their eyes off one another. She wears dark makeup around her eyes and red lipstick. Her body easily leans against him, her shoulder just below his chin. One hand is across her body, palm resting against her chest, feeling her heartbeat. Both wear black sweaters. His other hand entwines with hers on her jeans, on his hip.

I realized I wasn't just seeing the images of what had taken place. I was falling into the emotion of it as well, feeling his feelings.

Undeniable, unadulterated love suffuses Michael's thoughts. Longing is there as well, and as Christina tucks her chin into her shoulder, her blond hair brushes across his chin. He quickly kisses her cheek.

"No fair!" she cries, trying to seize his face in her hands and failing as he catches them by the wrists.

"No fair? No fair, tra-la-la?" Michael says, quoting . . . David Bowie, from some movie she likes.

"If I'm not allowed to kiss you, you shouldn't be allowed to kiss me!" she says, laughing and pouting.

He's captured her hands. She's helpless. He could bite her, force her. Instead the feeling of love that wells from him deepens and swells with that feeling of longing. He brings her hands to his lips and kisses them oh-so-gently. "Alas. I am a tyrant," he says softly, teasing her.

"I love you," she says, her pupils dark and wide.

His emotions soar. They sing with jubilation and wonder. All is light, rainbow, music. The feeling of joy, of hope, is overwhelming.

It was the first time she'd said it, I realized. I abruptly released my hold on his head, my hand still tingling.

Like a lighthouse beacon, a passing car's headlights illuminated Michael's blue eyes.

They held an ocean of loss.

I stared into the depths of those eyes for a time that contracted and stretched impossibly between a second and a minute.

I couldn't tell which of us was drowning.

CHAPTER THIRTY-TWO

"MADDY! OH MY GOD, ARE YOU OKAY? YOU LOOK okay, are you okay?" Julie stammered as I lurched from my bedroom the next morning.

She and her boyfriend Tad lounged in the living room, both wearing pajamas and drinking coffee. They looked so comfy . . . so *normal*, I wanted to cry.

"Yeah. Yeah, I'm okay," I said. And I was. Once again, my life had been thrown into complete supernatural chaos, and once again, I had somehow come out the other side with my sanity intact. Well, as intact as anyone could expect it to be.

"You want a cup of tea?" Julie asked. "I'll put the kettle on for you."

"That'd be great," I said before disappearing into the bathroom.

When I came out, the two were cozied up on the couch, holding hands, his tall, lanky form spread out across the couch with her petite one against his, much like I'd seen in the memory that Michael had shared of him and Christina.

"So I see you two got back together," I said.

Tad squeezed Julie's hand and she squeezed back. "That was kind of a foregone conclusion," she said.

He smiled and kissed her cheek. It was almost too much, too sweet. "But no more binge-drinking with former co-workers, correct?" he said.

"Correct," she said. "Unless you're with me." She smiled an impish smile.

Tad rolled his eyes but a smile twitched at the corner of his mouth. "Mm hmm."

"But enough about us!" Julie said. "Tell us what happened to you! I was so worried!"

I told them a variation on the story I'd told the detective in Queens, about fighting with Kip and losing my backpack and jumping the turnstile which led to my arrest—or detainment—in Queens.

"But that other guy—Wilson? He said it was an ongoing investigation."

"Yeah, *that* was a case of mistaken identity. Can you believe it?"

"Well, yeah, I mean, kind of. It's not like you . . . well, you know. I mean, you're sure it really was mistaken?"

"Babe," Tad said, squeezing her hand again.

"I'm sorry. Of course you're sure," she said with a smile. "So it's all over now? You can go back to your regularly scheduled programming?"

"Uh, I think I have to . . . um . . . testify or something. I'm supposed to hear from someone today about that. But then, yeah, that should be the last of it!"

"Well, that's good news, isn't it?"

The kettle began singing in the kitchen. "Yep! Now, if you'll excuse me . . ." I said, headed for the loud whistle.

The call came in the late afternoon, an invitation to an address at a specific time on a specific day. All that Zero would say was this: "You may be asked questions about Ammit. You will *definitely* be asked questions about your magical abilities. They may not be particularly nice questions. Get plenty of sleep and make sure you eat something before you come. It will be . . . a long day."

The appointed day and time arrived and so did I, fifteen minutes early, at the Flatiron Building's 19th floor. I entered the reception area of the Rhodium Foundation. A young man with a bowtie and a headset directed me to a pair of leather couches next to an impressive indoor waterfall. A sheet of water hung translucent over stone blocks from floor to ceiling, with a calming sound like rain.

I sat, nervously wondering if I should have dressed up more. My black pants and light blue sweater had both been bought at a thrift store, but they fit me well enough and didn't have any holes. That's practically wedding attire for me.

One of a set of double doors opened and a tall man approached me. He wore a stylish striped shirt with a vest and green tie, with gray tinged dreadlocks gathered at the nape of his neck. "You are Madison," he said in a deep voice. "I am Anubis.

Pleased to make your acquaintance." He offered his hand and I noticed a beaded bracelet on a leather cord around his wrist. His hand was warm and dry and his grasp firm.

"Zero mentioned you," I said.

"You as well," he said with just a hint of a smile. "This way." He waved a hand at a scanner, and when the door beeped, he held it open.

We entered into a large room of cubicles with shelves and cabinets and desks and chairs and people sitting in them, talking on headsets, typing on keyboards, or deep in conversation with colleagues, pointing at images on tablets or the screens at their desks. Anubis led me down a center aisle that ended in a door, which he opened with a wave of his hand. Beyond was a well-lit stairwell, the railings ornate and painted white. I followed him upwards to a landing, where another hand wave secured us entry to the 20th floor. This room was much smaller, with a few cubicles and several doors with panes of glass alongside them so that you could see into the private offices. One door did not have the pane of glass, and it was this one that Anubis opened.

Inside was a conference room, with a long table and ten chairs, three of which were empty. Tall windows illuminated the room with daylight. A pitcher of water sat in the center of the table and glasses had been distributed for every chair. The occupied chairs held both men and women, ranging in age from thirty-something to golden years. All wore business clothes but with odd accessories like medallions and beads. Some had clipboards or pads and seemed ready to take notes, while others had phones or tablets they were consulting.

Anubis took one of the chairs on the long side. At the head of the table, an attractive gray-haired man gestured at the empty seat at the opposite end, closest to the door. His vivid blue shirt was immaculately pressed.

Zero was there, but not Quinn, and not Rowan. A stately woman with white hair nodded pleasantly at me, and another woman with dark blond hair smiled at me in an encouraging way, her eyes crinkling at the corners. The blonde had a beauty mark on her upper lip and a golden treble clef pin attached to her lapel.

I sat.

The man in the vivid blue shirt spoke. "Thank you for coming today, Madison. I am Janus, the head of the New York magisterium, such as it is, and founder of the Rhodium Foundation. To my right is Halia." He nodded toward the stately white-haired woman. "You've met Anubis, and Zero, of course. This is Melodia." The smiling blonde nodded. "And Shakti." She was a woman with chin-length dark hair wearing a fuchsia scarf, sitting between Anubis and Zero. Melodia and Shakti seemed about the same age, around forty.

"To your left is Nicomachus," he said, referring to an older man in a gray suit with watery blue eyes and thinning white hair. "And next to him, last, but not least," Janus said, gesturing to an imposing man with a dark beard and long dark hair, "is Montferrand."

Montferrand had wide shoulders and thick arms and wore a dark brown suit. His huge hands held so many gold rings it looked like he wore brass knuckles. He grunted an unintelligible greeting.

"You have been asked to come here today so that we can determine your affinities and aptitudes, to expose your magical signature before witnesses, and to end the rumors regarding your background and abilities via expert testimony."

"Wait, so am I . . . in trouble?" I asked. "Is this a trial?"

They pointedly did not answer my question.

Janus took a sip of water and his shiny silver wristwatch caught the light. "It is not uncommon for neophytes to occasionally lose control of their power in the early stages of discovery, before they learn control. That is what we wish for you to show us today. Your power *and* your control." His teeth were very white and straight. He seemed to have a good humor about him, though it was almost a little too rehearsed. Polished.

"You are here so we can determine whether to offer you admission to the New York magisterium," Halia said.

"You want me to join you? But why would I want to do that?"

"Why?! *Why*, she asks! You might as well ask the president of Harvard why one would want to go there," Nicomachus said.

"She means no offense," said Melodia. "This is all new to her."

"You'd get the training you need," explained Zero, "To help you control your magic."

"To prevent you from blowing up cars every time you get upset," Janus said. "Shall we continue?"

I nodded.

"Let us start with the rumors. I have been told that you are unaware of your birth name. Is that true?"

"Well, it seems like my name used to be Chr—"

"Stop!" Janus interrupted, holding up a hand. "Answer the question. Is it true that you do not *know* your birth name?"

"No. It *was* true before, but is no longer true. I know who I . . . er, was."

Zero's eyebrows went up.

"And you have amnesia?"

"Yes, but—"

Janus held up a hand again. "You are time-lost, correct?"

Halia's eyebrows drew together as she regarded me. Her hand briefly touched an amethyst amulet at her throat and she swallowed.

"I'm sorry. I don't know what that means."

"You are come from another time. This is not your native time stream?"

"That's what I've been told. But I don't remember." There were some murmurs and a grunt from Montferrand.

Janus didn't seem to be affected by my answer at all and continued smoothly asking questions. "Among your elemental affinities you include Fire and Sound, is that right?"

"I guess?"

"How have these powers manifested?"

"I have produced fire from my hands and maybe some minor, um, explosions."

I heard, "So young," among other murmurs, but couldn't tell who'd said it. A few heads turned toward Zero. He nodded and said, "She has also used concussive force versus an opponent." How did he know that? They must have found the spidertot in the tunnels.

Janus continued. "And you have an aptitude with Death magic?"

"Yes."

"How has that manifested?"

"I can see and talk to ghosts, and sense . . . well, dead things, I guess. Zombies and vampires and whatnots."

Heads nodded around the table and copious notes were taken.

"Anything else?" Janus asked.

Should I tell them about absorbing the Death ball?

No.

Why not?

Don't.

"Madison?" Janus's voice saying my name interrupted my thoughts.

"Yes?"

"Have you demonstrated any other powers?"

"I can sift through a pile of grains with my mind."

Some looks of surprise and more notetaking.

"And I produced a bright white light from my hand when a black portal opened."

Mistake.

What?

Montferrand looked up from his phone and made a grumpy face. "Preposterous."

Shakti frowned. The others looked at me more closely.

"Is that all?" Halia asked. She seemed to be perched on the edge of her chair.

"She was aware of Mind magic when it was used on her," Zero said.

"Mind too?" Montferrand muttered. "That's impossible."

You need to be more careful.

What? Why?

I was disconcerted by the inner voice's warning.

It didn't respond.

"Madison? What other aspects of Mind have you demonstrated?" Janus asked.

"Oh, right. Yeah. Memory stuff. If I concentrate, I can remember anything that happened to me in the past year or so. But it gives me a headache."

"That is not Mind magic. It is a combination of Time and Mind." Shakti spoke with an accent that made her sound like Nidhi's imitation of her mother's lectures. I wondered if she was from India.

Nicomachus's eyes seemed to bulge slightly. "She can't be human," he rasped.

More murmurs filled the room as everyone began talking all at once.

"Order. Come to order," Janus said, raising his voice. The murmuring stopped. Janus continued speaking. "The neophyte has claimed Fire, Sound, and Death. Other *possibilities* include Mind and Time."

"Don't forget Light," Montferrand said, curling his lip. "A neophyte with *six* possible spheres. Ridiculous. I agree with Nicomachus. She must not be human. Amnesia? Loss of identity? Time travel? These are Everworlder traits. Changelings and other fey. All of her so-called affinities and aptitudes could be mere glamours."

Nicomachus nodded, his eyes still wide.

Halia's knuckles whitened as she gripped her necklace.

"I can assure you she is absolutely human," came a familiar voice.

CHAPTER THIRTY-THREE

THE DOOR TO THE ROOM HADN'T OPENED OR closed but the empty chair now had an occupant. It was Rowan.

"Perfect timing as always, Rowan," Janus said.

Shakti, noticing Rowan, sat up straighter in her chair.

"What say *you* to these accusations?" Janus asked him.

"I have tracked Madison's emergence from her time stream into our own and back. Furthermore, I have discovered the origin of that disruption as well as the reason for her amnesia. Not to mention the curious existence of the minotaur revenant."

The water pitcher was being passed down the table for refills and had run out at Melodia. Halia reached across the table and touched the rounded side, silently invoking magic, and her hand glimmered for a moment as the pitcher refilled itself. Melodia whispered her gratitude as she filled her glass.

Rowan put his hands on the table. "All of these disparate events have been enacted upon this girl by a single rogue sorcerer—a necromancer, in fact."

The pitcher had made its way to me but ran out a quarter of the way through my glass. Nicomachus, who was sitting to my left, seemed to be watching me closely. I set the pitcher down and looked at Halia, hoping I could get her attention. Her wide eyes were on Rowan.

Nicomachus scowled, muttering what sounded like "*Mayim*." He touched the side of the pitcher with a glowing finger and magically refilled it once more.

I whispered, "Thank you." He ignored me.

"That signature is seen here," Rowan said, gesturing at an easel that somehow wasn't there a minute ago. A white board showed a loopy symbol that looked as much like a doctor's signature as it did artwork scribbled by a two-year-old. "Anubis and Shakti, is this the signature you saw used in the animation of the minotaur?"

"Aye," they both said.

Rowan flipped the page, revealing another symbol.

"No," Melodia said. "It can't be."

"And Janus, would you please?"

Janus drew the two symbols in the air with light.

"Janus, please rotate the second sigil by 180 degrees on both the horizontal and vertical planes."

Janus made two gestures: the first like he was flicking a cigarette butt and the second like flipping a light switch. The glowing symbol rotated as directed.

"Now overlay the alchemical symbol for lead in roughly the same scale."

Janus drew in the air once more and the glowing symbol transformed.

As he completed the movement, gasps came from everyone in the room except Rowan, me, and Janus, who merely raised his eyebrows.

The symbols were the same.

Melodia put down the glass she'd just sipped from, nearly choking on the water. She gasped for air and coughed several times before finally speaking. "You actually mean it. The Mage Killer? *He* did all of this to her?"

"Indeed. The mage who murdered so many of your peers your novitiate year, Melodia, whose Death magic signature has not been seen since the mid-to-late 1980s—Madison's native time stream."

"How could we not know? Has he been underground this entire time?" Her face had paled and she seemed shaken.

"That does appear to be the case. Anubis analyzed the signature on the minotaur himself, verified by Shakti. We now have reason to believe that a mass rising of the dead in rural Pennsylvania in 1966 can also be traced to this same man."

Many eyes widened.

Nicomachus angrily muttered, "Impossible. All that time-jumping has finally scrambled your brain, Rowan. The mage from the Penn Woods Rising is dead. I read that report. I knew magi who were there."

"There is evidence to the contrary, Nicomachus, which we can discuss at another time. Regarding today's proceedings, however, it is clear that in late 1987, the rogue magus Ammit kidnapped the girl who you see now standing before you—an innocent neophyte, unaware of her true potential—then erased her memory and forced her forward in time by use of an ancient artifact—whereupon she exited the time stream in our present just over a year ago with no knowledge of her past or identity."

Halia spoke quickly. "I move that now that the neophyte knows who she is, she be remanded to her native stream." She stroked the amethyst she wore with thumb and forefinger.

The room suddenly erupted into chaos.

"That would be sentencing her to death—

"Don't you know how many—"

"We don't even know why—"

"But we can't—"

"Order!" Janus shouted and his voice echoed in the room. "Is the move seconded?"

"I second," Nicomachus said, his lips pressed into a grim line.

I looked at the faces of the magi. Zero was watching me carefully. Melodia had tears in her eyes. Anubis made a "tsk" noise under his breath.

Janus said, "Third?"

Montferrand seemed as if he were about to speak when Rowan said, "Halia, forgive me, but you don't have any aptitude with Time, do you?"

Halia inclined her white-haired head graciously. "I do not."

"Janus, Shakti, will you describe to the council members and adjuncts what you see when you examine her through Time's lens?"

Shakti stood and bowed, holding her palms together beneath her chin. When she looked up at me, I saw a faint glow in her eyes. "Nothing. I cannot even see her aura."

A few murmurs.

"Madison, your amulet. Please remove it?" Rowan said.

I unclasped the labradorite necklace and pulling it from beneath my sweater, placed it on the table. How did he know about my amulet?

Shakti repeated the motion and the glow returned as pinpricks of light. "I see . . . a repair. As if it has been rewoven into the current stream," she said with a tone of wonder.

More murmurs.

Janus made a gesture in the air, then drew his hand across his eyes. That same faint pinprick glow appeared in them. His brows drew together and he cocked his head, peering at me or my time aura-stream-whatever. He gave a laugh of surprise. "Indeed. I must admit I've never seen a thing like it."

"If you had to interpret that repair, how would you say it represents her current place in our stream, Shakti?" asked Rowan.

"She is fully present here. She has a much stronger connection to this time—almost as if she has reincarnated. Her former life is ghost-like. *Now* is when she belongs. Not *then*."

"Do you concur with that assessment, Janus?"

"I do. There will be no more talk of remand."

"But what of these claims of *six* spheres? It's simply not possible at her age," Montferrand intoned. He had a slight drawl to his speech that seemed to peer around the edges of his longer sentences.

"It *is* possible, Montferrand. How quickly you forget our histories," Rowan said.

He gave a sardonic laugh. "Oh, is she to be the next Merlin perhaps?" He stood, addressing Rowan. "Maybe a Circe or Medea? Or Pythagoras himself? I suppose she also has your so-called thirteenth sphere?"

"Order!" Janus said loudly.

Montferrand ignored him and continued his mocking speech. "Christopher Columbus, man! Is she to be the next *Christ*? Now that's something I'd like to *see*!"

Gasps and voices arguing, complaining, sounding shocked, angry.

"ORDER!" came Janus's echoing voice, and the room silenced at once. He looked angrily around the room. "There can be no consensus without the examination of two council members who come to the same conclusion *as you all know*. As such, this neophyte must be treated as any other would be—"

"But she's not—" Montferrand interrupted.

"YOU ARE OUT OF ORDER, SIR," Janus said and the effect was odd, as if the shout came from inside a tunnel that was just around the bearded man. Montferrand's chair moved forward, and the man sat at once, hard, as it bumped the back of his legs.

Janus continued, his white teeth flashing as he resumed his cordial manner. "As I was saying, she must be treated as any other would be, *regardless* of whatever beliefs you *may* or *may not* hold. What say you about her character, Rowan?"

"Under the most trying of circumstances, Madison has shown extraordinary courage, fortitude, honesty, and integrity," Rowan said.

"Seconded," Zero said, much to my astonishment.

"There is, however," Rowan said, "one more thing."

The room fell quiet.

Everyone was staring at Rowan, but Rowan was staring at me.

Oh. He wants me to talk.

Don't.

Don't what?

"Madison?" Rowan asked.

"Yeah?"

"Tell them about the Death orbs."

"We have heard already about those orbs from Zero!" Nicomachus sneered.

"You mean what happened when I . . ."

Rowan nodded encouragingly.

Don't.

I bit my lip.

Don't say it.

The silence was making my eardrums hurt.

"I can't believe this," Montferrand grumbled.

"I, um, well, I guess I sort of absorbed it," I ventured.

Gasps.

"And Vita believes she may have the Life sphere as well," Rowan said.

Halia's face drained completely of color and she stood and pointed at me. "Then it's true. She *is* a necromancer, just as I feared!"

A babble of arguing voices broke out, with faces locked in expressions of anger or self-righteousness.

"—malarkey and horsefeathers—"

"—too powerful—"

"—isolation isn't—"

"—must keep her close!"

"—cannot be true! Just—"

"—but that's a myth—"

Melodia stood, her hands raised, palms out.

Suddenly, the room went silent.

The faces were still angry and the mouths were still working, but nothing was coming out. I tried clearing my throat.

Nothing.

The mouths stopped moving. Lips were pursed and jaws set indignantly. Nicomachus crossed his arms like a grounded teenager.

Melodia's eyes were on Janus.

He nodded, and sound came back into the room. The ventilation system seemed especially loud as did the ticking of the three clocks over the room's door. I hadn't even noticed them before. Each had a placard beneath it. PARIS. NEW YORK. HONG KONG.

"Madison, will you excuse us?" Janus said smoothly. "This council needs to confer after a short break."

Melodia offered me a hot chocolate and showed me a sitting area where I could wait.

Left alone with my thoughts, they began their own argument.

You shouldn't have told them about the absorption.

What else was I going to do? Rowan already knew!

Knowledge is power. Now that they know, they have power over you.

They had power already.

Now they have more.

How do you know? Stop arguing with me!

As you wish.

The inner voice sounded cross. And not really like me.

Is that you again, Zero?

No.

A demon?

You're crazy.

Says the voice in my head.

It didn't respond.

I guessed it was pretty crazy to sit there arguing with myself.

I sipped the hot chocolate and waited.

Halia invited me back to the room. I sat in the same seat. The NEW YORK clock showed it had been thirty-eight minutes since I'd left.

Once she'd seated herself, Halia smiled cordially and spoke. "We've decided it would be in your best interest to join the New York magisterium."

"Oh," I said. "Really?"

The Harvard of magi wants me?

"Are you sure?" I asked.

Janus chuckled. "Yes. We're sure. Now say you accept."

"I accept?"

There was a general feeling of relief suddenly, a release of tension in the small room.

Everyone stood and applauded.

Am I supposed to applaud too? Or bow or something?

I stuck my hands in my pockets and tried not to feel embarrassed.

Halia, Nicomachus, and Montferrand clapped politely, but the others all seemed pleased and welcoming. Even Zero.

"I move to examine the neophyte's abilities," Melodia said once the applause had petered out.

"I second," Anubis said.

"I third," said Shakti.

"So be it," Janus said.

"Is this some kind of test?" I asked.

Rowan came to kneel beside me and put a hand on my shoulder. "You'll do just fine, Madison. No need to worry."

"Who's worried?" I asked, my voice betraying me with a squeak.

Rowan whispered, "I've just returned from three days in the future. Spoiler alert: You do fine."

"Zero? The field will do, I think," Janus said.

Zero stood and walked over to Janus. The two of them stood side-by-side, next to the tall windows at the end of the room. Janus, mouthing silent words, kept one hand on Zero's shoulder while

Zero sketched in his notepad. Several seconds later, a light blue portal opened.

A fresh breeze of cooler air entered the room, and I could see blue sky and yellow-green grass beyond.

Janus released Zero's shoulder and made several complex gestures involving both of his hands. There was a sense of rushing air and movement and suddenly the table and chairs, the water pitcher and glasses, and all ten of us were in the field, blue sky above us. The light blue portal was behind us, showing the conference room.

In the field ahead, several wooden structures of different shapes and sizes stood. Near them, a pile of tires. A pool. Some kind of rope swing. It looked like an obstacle course of some kind.

Janus smiled. "Now how about you show us what you can do."

THE END

Madison will return

in

ASHES AND FLAMES
Book 4 of the *Madison Roberts* Series

APRIL 2021

Thanks for reading and supporting an independent author as her publishing dreams become reality.

If you're enjoying Madison's paranormal adventures, please post a review!

ACKNOWLEDGEMENTS

SELF-PUBLICATION OF THREE BOOKS WITHIN A year has felt like an insane journey, especially considering this year's pandemic and its associated challenges. I have had a lot of help from a lot of people.

As ever I thank my sagacious, discerning, and reassuring editor, Marcel Leroux, who seems to have an endless tolerance for anxious ramblings about mutant zombies, hegemonical magi, and heartbroken vampires. I thank him also for his kind handling of the reappearance of my go-to Madison sentence ("I realized I'd been holding my breath and let it out.") and the dreaded return of the needless hyphen I sometimes insert in "shut-up" (I really do NOT know why I do this). I thank him lastly for his mercilessness in the x-ing out of those unnecessary side quests that slowed the plot, among all of the other suggestions, corrections, and notes he gave me. Marcel, you are a true wizard of wording.

Thank you to Steven Novak, for taking my suggestions and sketchy ideas and transforming them into yet another amazing cover illustration. You are a genius at what you do.

I once again thank my beta readers, Diana Ballard, Evette Alvarado, and Amy Marcoux, for their encouragement and feedback. I also thank beta reader Staci McG, not just because she runs our neighborhood book club (whom I also thank for their interest and support), but Staci needs special recognition for constructing wonderful-horrible toys of the spidertot and the tripod dog for my birthday. Staci, your buoying enthusiasm gives me life (and I really am sorry about the nightmares that my writing has inflicted on you). A separate thank you goes to Darnel Omelchuck for selflessly agreeing to read a proof copy of this book; I'm sure it had nothing to do with the cliffhanger that ended the previous one.

I am grateful for Nanea Hoffman of *Sweatpants & Coffee* for her uplifting posts that prompt us all to be kinder to ourselves and others. I thank author and teacher Jordan Rosenfeld for accountability-buddying and keeping the writer's life real with commiseration over setbacks and celebration of finish lines—it's so good having you in my corner. And speaking of corners, I thank Amy Goudy (owner of Charlotte's The Corner) for running to meet me when I was passing through her local airport for a hug and book signature and making me feel like a real author.

I must of course thank my spouse, partner-in-all-things, and muse, Sam Garrett. For spoiling me with Earl Grey tea and Earl Grey martinis, fresh-made guac, and fresh-baked chocolate chip cookies.

For the marathon gaming and plotting sessions and for reading the pages when they've just-been-written and saying, "More." Thank you also for encouraging my Halloween decor addiction, my odd sleep patterns, and my fuzzy sock obsession. Lastly, you must be given credit for effortlessly crafting the amulet poem: please don't hex me with your mad fey poetry.

I also thank Pflugerville Library and Austin Public Library for their promoting and publicizing of my books, as well as providing virtual meeting opportunities that allow me to connect with creative writers from ages 8 to 80.

Finally, I'd like to thank my sixth-grade teacher Mrs. Edison, who couldn't have known when she introduced me to Egyptian mythology and culture that I would form a lifelong fascination with its iconography that I also share with my spouse, but there it is: Thoth on the mantle, Bast on the bookshelf, Anubis on the refrigerator. Scarabs, ankhs, and papyri decorations. A tiny sarcophagus. A mug of the Rosetta Stone. And on and on. We likey the Egypts in our house.

In closing, I'd also like to acknowledge some of my research and influences in the creation of this book. It is true that songwriter and Vaudeville performer Joseph E. Howard co-wrote "Hello, My Baby" aka "The Michigan J. Frog Song" with his wife, composer and lyricist Ida Emerson. The real Howard is interred in Calvary Cemetery, just as our fictional one is. Readers interested in learning more about Calvary Cemetery in Queens need look no further than Kevin Walsh's excellent *Forgotten New York* blog on the topic, which is filled with history and images. Joan Aiken Hodge's *Watch the Wall, My Darling* influenced this novel and inspired certain aspects of Madison's character. Dan O'Bannon's movie *Return of the Living Dead* was most definitely an influence in some of the set dressing of the basement lair, and finally, I confess that the references to classical music are an homage to Richard Matheson's novel *I Am Legend*, which itself has inspired multiple films in the horror genre.

www.ingramcontent.com/pod-product-compliance
Lightning Source LLC
LaVergne TN
LVHW050927080826
845145LV00001B/239

9781733454551